AN ANL  ...

'*The author brings to life a pivotal moment in the history of Europe in an imaginative and exciting way ...*'

– Ahmad Thomson, Author of 'Making History' and 'Islam in Andalus'

'*Fantastic...heart-stopping adventure told by a writer who takes us back to the beginning to see the drama unfold. A terrific read.*'

– Dr. Osman Latiff, Islamic Historian, Author and Senior Researcher and Instructor, Sapience Institute, UK

S. N. JALALI

**BLACKSTONE
HOUSE**

First published in Great Britain in 2022
by Blackstone House Publications
PO Box 1091, Harrow, HA1 9HG
www.blackstonehouse.com

A CIP catalogue record of this book is available
from the British Library

ISBN 9780956900067

Printed and bound by CPI Group (UK) Ltd, Croydon, CR0 4YY

Typeset in Baskerville

Other titles available by S N Jalali

From The House of Ibn Kathir series :

**The House of Ibn Kathir –
The Competition Begins**

**The House of Ibn Kathir –
The Competition Begins
Teaching Resource**

The House of Ibn Kathir – Year Captain

**The House of Ibn Kathir – Year Captain
Teaching Resource**

All of the above titles are available to purchase
via the website www.ibnkathir.co.uk

Please visit www.blackstonehouse.com for
more information

A book for Jamil

PRINCIPAL CHARACTERS

THE UMAYYADS

Historical Figures

Caliph Al-Walid Ibn Abdal-Malik – *the Umayyad Caliph*
Musa Ibn Nusayr – *the Governor of Qayrawan*
Tariq Ibn Ziyad – *the Governor of Tangiers and an Umayyad General*
Tarif Ibn Malik Abu Zahrah – *an Umayyad General*

Fictional Characters

Humayun – *an Umayyad Lieutenant*
Hisham – *an Umayyad soldier*
Qasim – *an Umayyad soldier*
Ya'qub – *an Umayyad soldier*
Abdullah – *an Umayyad scout*
Mustafa – *an Umayyad scout*
Waseem – *an Umayyad Captain*
Abu Yasir – *father of Qasim*
Bilal – *Musa Ibn Nusayr's secretary*
Hani – *a Seafarer from Alexandria*
Nu'man *Ra'is* – *Boat Master of a* maraqib *(Umayyad ship)*
Umm Hamdi – *a baker*

THE VISIGOTHS

Historical Figures

King Roderick – *the Visigoth king*
Count Julian – *the Governor of Ceuta (known to the Umayyads as Count Ilyan)*
Lady Florinda – *the daughter of Count Julian*
Count Theodomir – *the Governor of Murcia (known to the Umayyads as Count Tudmir)*
King Wittiza – *the former Visigoth king (father of Princes Achila and Olmund, and father-in law to Count Julian)*
Prince Achila – *the eldest son of King Wittiza*
Prince Olmund – *the younger son of King Wittiza*
Oppas – *King Roderick's minister (and King Wittiza's brother)*
Count Sisibert – *a minister and a Governor*

Fictional Character

Father Martin – *a priest*

THE IBERIAN PEASANTS

Historical Figure

Old Mother Magda (*an old woman rumoured by historians to be a real figure*)

Fictional Characters

Ben / Benjamin
Bella / Bilha
Father of Ben and Bella
Mother of Ben and Bella
David
Jacob
Old Joshua
Leander

ANDALUSIANS OF MUSLIM SPAIN

Historical Figure

Abbas Ibn Firnas – *an Inventor*

Fictional Characters

Sumayya – *a Lady Physician*
Uwais – *an Apprentice*
Hiba – *a Neighbour*
Old Moshe – *a Jewish Neighbour*

IBERIAN, ARABIC AND MODERN-DAY PLACE NAMES

Iberian Name (Visigoth Rule) – Arabic Name (Umayyad Rule) – Modern-Day Name

Barbary – Al-Maghreb – the countries of Northwest Africa

Iberia – Andalus – the region of Spain and Portugal

Portucale – Andalus – Portugal

Mons Calpe, The Pillars of Hercules – Jabal Tariq – Rock of Gibraltar

(Gibraltar is said to be derived from the Arabic name *'Jabal Tariq'* meaning 'Mount of Tariq')

Isla de Las Palomas – Isla de Andalus / Tarifa – Punta de Tarifa

Julia Loza – Tarifa – Tarifa

(The name 'Tarifa' for both the island and the municipality originates from the name Tarif Ibn Malik)

White Port (derived from the name which had been given to it by the Romans, *Portus Albus*) – Algeciras – Algeciras

Cordova – Córdoba – Cordoba

Gades – Cadiz – Cadiz

Guadalete River – Not to be confused with the much larger Guadalquivir River which rises in the Sierra Grazelema and flows down to the Bay of Cadiz

(The name 'Guadalete' derives from the Arabic, meaning 'River of Forgetfulness'. After the decisive battle on its banks in 711 CE, it also became known as 'Rio de los Muertos' meaning 'River of the Dead')

OTHER HISTORICAL PEOPLE AND PLACES

Umar Ibn Al-Khattab – *the second Caliph of the Rashidun Caliphate*

Uthman Ibn Affan – *the third Caliph of the Rashidun Caliphate*

Khalid Ibn Al-Walid – *a Muslim General*

Uqbah Ibn Nafi al-Fihri – *a Muslim General*

Anas Ibn Malik – *a companion of the Prophet*
Aamir Abu Tufail – *a companion of the Prophet*
Nusayr – *father of Musa Ibn Nusayr*
Ceuta – modern-day it is a Spanish autonomous city on the north coast of Africa
Tlemcen – a village in present day Algeria
Qayrawan – modern-day Kairouan, a city in Tunisia
Constantinople – modern-day Istanbul, Turkey
The Roman Empire – known today as the Byzantine Empire (or Eastern Roman Empire) which was the continuation of the Roman Empire during the Middle Ages
Ayn At-Tamir – a city in modern day Iraq

AUTHOR'S NOTE

THIS book is a work of fiction inspired by real life historical events. With the exception of famous historical figures linked to the period, all the characters in this book are fictitious. However, the fictional characters have been inspired and imagined by reading accounts by historians such as Ahmed Ibn Mohammed Al-Makkari and many others, about the lives and conditions of the local people of the time who lived on both sides of the Straits.

This applies both during the period in which the encounter between the Umayyads and the Visigoths took place and also generations later, with regards to those who lived in Muslim Spain.

With respect to historical figures, creative license has been used in the storytelling when attributing actions or dialogue to the famous real life people, although at times historical records have been used, where their actual words have been preserved by historians.

The conquest of Spain (Iberia) in 711 CE ushered in a new era in world history. It was the first major interaction between the Islamic civilisation and the European West. The next 900 years saw the rise of the Islamic civilisation in Andalus and then its erosion and eventual decline. However, at its height this civilisation was a beacon of knowledge and a conduit of learning characterised by a culture of tolerance that saw it thrive at a time when elsewhere, the European continent remained shrouded in darkness and ignorance.

CONTENTS

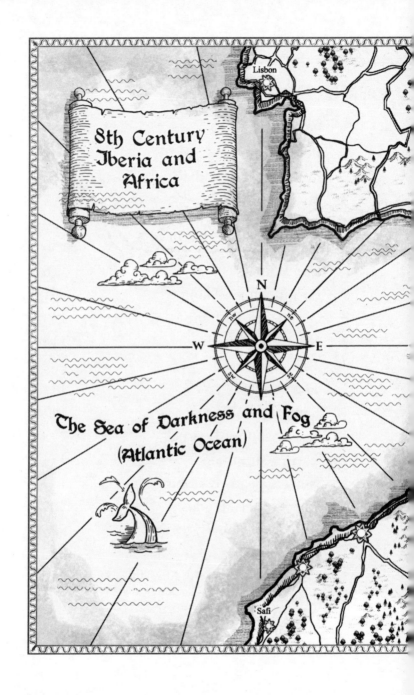

8th Century
Iberia and
Africa

Lisbon

The Sea of Darkness and Fog
(Atlantic Ocean)

Safi

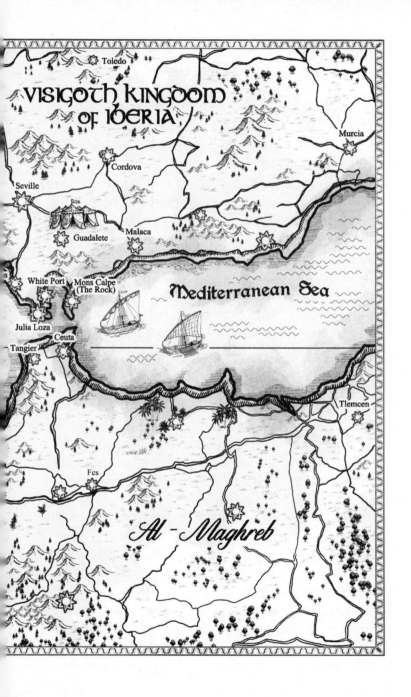

PROLOGUE

━━━━━━━━➤

THIS is the story of two civilisations: the Caliphate of the Umayyads and the Kingdom of the Visigoths.

The Umayyads sprang forth from the hot deserts of the Arabian Peninsula. Their lands stretched as far to the west as *Al–Maghreb* upon the most distant shores of Africa. The Kingdom of the Visigoths lay across the Iberian Peninsula, separated from Africa by a stretch of silvery water known as the Straits. Their frontiers almost touched each other, yet these two dominions of the earth could not have been more different.

The Umayyads thrived with prosperity. The inhabitants whether man, woman or child and regardless of colour or creed, were protected by law under the folds of the new religion of Islam. Their lives were not always easy, but from the richest to the poorest, their voices were heard. It was a young civilisation where honour, the rights of ownership and wellbeing of lives were cherished. It wasn't long before its lands began to blossom with a vibrant culture, rich in both enlightenment and innovation.

The other Kingdom, in contrast, ruled with an iron fist; the lands of Iberia were plunged into darkness, built upon the greed and tyranny of a Visigoth king. His reign did little other than to plunder his subjects, inflicting great pain and suffering across his domain. Could the plight of people have been more wretched than these? Perhaps, but such was the existence of those who dwelt in this corner of Europe, in the medieval age. It was a life of persecution for the poor and the weak, for man, woman and child, even more so for those who would not submit and follow the Catholic Church. It was a time of great fear, disappointment and shattered dreams.

Yet across the Straits, in the lands of *Al–Maghreb* a glimmer of hope began to burn. Medieval Europe was about to awaken and its shroud of darkness lift.

The year is 711 CE, ninety-two years after the *Hijra* of the Prophet Muhammad, blessings and peace be upon him, and seventy-nine years since his death. The capital of the Umayyads lies in the city of Damascus and its leader is the Caliph Al-Walid Ibn Abdal-Malik.

On the misty banks of the river Guadalete in the Iberian Peninsula, two armies are about to converge. Roderick, the Visigoth king, and his formidable army of one hundred thousand men gather, positioned face to face against a determined contingent of the Umayyads, twelve thousand in number. They stand under the command of one man, a Muslim freedman – his name is Tariq Ibn Ziyad…

BEN AND BELLA

Summer of 711 CE, 92 AH
At the Pillars of Hercules, Mons Calpe, Iberia

A BOY sat at the mouth of the cave, beneath a bright moon and stars. He drew his cloak close about him as he watched the ebb and flow of the waves along the shore below. Their soothing sound lapped gently and reassuringly in his ears. His eyes had already accustomed themselves to the darkness of the night, with the heavenly lanterns above as his sole source of light.

For some time now, he had followed a shadowy shape sailing silently over the sea on a steady course, with the bright, brilliant moonlight glistening over the waters, illuminating its way. Then, as the first fine thread of golden light split the horizon, dawn approached. The sky, yet to surrender to the light, turned a cobalt blue.

The curious shadow he followed now became a discernible shape. It was a tall mast with a sail that occasionally billowed out under the command of the levanter, making the most of every breath of wind. As his mind lingered over the approaching galley boat, sailing freely upon the tide towards their shores, there came a whisper at his side that intruded upon his thoughts.

"Can't you sleep again?" asked a familiar soft voice, as a warm figure slumped down gently beside him. Ben's eyes tore away from the galley to look at his older sister. Bella's face was veiled by the shadows, but he would know her voice anywhere. The land slept in a deep slumber, except for Ben and his sister. He could never steal away from his bed without her knowing.

"You'll look tired," she chided, "and you won't be able to concentrate – you're sure to get us into trouble then. It's enough that they suspect us already," said Bella. She shuddered inwardly, overcome by the vision of Father Martin. His cold, sallow face and hawkish eyes would fix upon them shrewdly as their lips moved over the prayers at mass. He always seemed to be suspicious, as though he wondered if they were making a show of reciting their prayers.

"Do we have to go?" asked Ben after a moment's silence. His eyes fastened longingly back upon the galley. Having reached close to the shores, it had dropped its anchor.

"You already know the answer to that," said Bella quietly, her voice hollow, emptied of any feeling or emotion. She turned her face away from her brother to stare out across the sea.

"It's either go to mass, face slavery or expulsion – so take your pick," said Bella simply. Ben ground his teeth in an effort to hold back the anger rising within, but in that moment something of a resolve seemed to break free from inside him.

"Then I choose expulsion – I hate this place!" said Ben through gritted teeth, his breaths now coming heavy.

"I want to leave – cross the Straits to that land out there where they say I won't have to hide my religion, pretending to be someone I'm not," spat Ben, his voice laden with raw emotion.

"*Bilha*, this is no way to live. Poor and always worrying, afraid of being caught and punished…"

"*Oh hush* – are you *mad*? Someone will hear you!" said Bella sharply, panic rising somewhere deep in the pit of her stomach, as she listened to her brother's anger and frustration. Worse still, was to hear him call her by her *real* name. Nobody *ever* called her Bilha beyond the confines of their home and even then seldomly. No, she was Bella now and she had been for a long time.

She looked nervously over her shoulder, more out of a fearful habit, as though someone lurked in the nearby cave behind them. Perhaps they were concealed by the bushes, or even between the limestone rocks that littered this great mono- lithic promontory they sat on. They could be ready and waiting to pounce and arrest them at a moment's notice. But the growing patches of crimson light in the sky overhead had now begun to illuminate their surroundings.

It was clear for anyone to see that there was no one else around. The mouth of the cave no longer looked like a dark abyss. It was a hollow of a rock, perhaps once the home of some wild creature. It now lay uninhabited, an empty shell, having long since been abandoned by its occupant. Only a sleepy silence lay over this rocky terrain that belied the threat that could consume them at any moment.

"I don't care!" snapped Ben defiantly as his voice continued to grow louder. "Besides, it's the early hours of the morning – everyone's asleep!" he continued to speak wryly. "There's no one out here but us on the bluff."

"*Please* Ben, *hush*! You know the king has his spies everywhere!" hissed Bella nervously, not wishing to take any chances. She stared up at Ben's profile, but he wasn't listening. His eyes were only fixed across the Straits, at a ghostly land mass which was by now visibly etched across the horizon with its rolling peaks that reached out for the heavenly skies above.

"You know, they say 'expulsion', but do you suppose they'll really let you leave? *Never* – they need us!" said Bella angrily cupping his face in her small hands, forcing him to look at her. In the growing light she could see her brother's young face and her heart suddenly softened out of pity.

Ben was a boy of sixteen summers, worn down by years of working hard with his family in fields and orchards that they would never come to own. Nor would they ever fully enjoy the fruits of their own labour. Instead, they lived on a diet of meagre food under the levy of heavy taxes imposed by their Visigoth king. To her, Ben looked like nothing more than a child, thin and wiry from poor nourishment. His cheeks were hollow and not full. At his young age his eyes ought to have been bright from contented smiles, free of all worries and care. Instead, they were like haunted pools, restless, always searching for something and never finding it.

"The Goths watch the shores," whispered Bella, now more kindly. "Are you willing to risk everything for a fanciful tale?"

"It's *not* fanciful I tell you – it's true!" retorted Ben stubbornly back at his sister, pulling his face free from her hold. "I *know* you've heard the stories whispered too and I heard it from Old Joshua himself – he knows people that have travelled to far off lands and seen the likes of those whom we can only dream of," said Ben.

In misery, he turned his head to look back at the anchored galley near the shore. But his gaze soon strayed past it to look longingly out again at the land of North Africa on the other side of the Straits. It was as if his eyes could glean a better life for himself if he could but go there.

"Old Joshua says they fare better across there than us," he said sullenly. "Their ruler rules over them in a way *we* can only imagine."

Ben remembered the hours he had tilled away on their land, listening to Old Joshua beside him. He would speak of people, in a distant world that stretched from as far as the Arabian Peninsula to the north-western shores of Africa. He described how their ruler governed his people according to the teachings of a new religion. Old Joshua had also said that their own people and even the Christians lived alongside them peacefully across the Straits and under their protection. They were treated well; each being permitted to practise their faith without fear of any persecution. They just

5

paid a tribute ("but 'tis nothing like the back-breaking taxes we pay out to this wretch Roderick the usurper, while living out our days in secret!" grumbled Old Joshua angrily as he spat to one side).

After listening to Old Joshua's stories, Ben had taken to visiting the cave in the early hours of the morning. The salty morning air did much to soothe his calluses and sores. He would perch on the rocky mountain they called Mons Calpe. Like a giant sentinel, it looked out over the Straits. From here, he too liked to sit and watch the mysterious land of the Umayyads on the other side of the Straits, especially as the sun rose over it. It was the only time he had to himself when he could imagine, dreaming up his escape from the clutches of the Goths.

"And what of me?" asked Bella sullenly, breaking in on his thoughts. In her heart she knew what he wanted. "If you run away what becomes of me – of Mother and Father – what becomes of us Ben?"

"If you go, it will raise suspicion. It might lead to our interrogation," continued Bella. "You know what happened in the year of the revolt. You know what became of our kin. They once dreamt help would come from across the Straits – from those among our people who had escaped to live there in exile. Do you want our fate to be same as theirs if we're discovered?" demanded Bella as slow tears began to fall unchecked.

Of course, Ben knew what Bella spoke of. Years ago, there had been a revolt in the kingdom, against a decree. Anyone who refused to be baptised by the church would be sold into slavery and their children taken away to be raised as Christians.

The decree had been the final straw, too much for an already beleaguered people. Unwilling to convert and unable to escape, a plan was hatched amongst them. It was formed between those who lived in the Kingdom and those exiles who had found refuge on the other side of the Straits. The exiles would return to attack the Iberian Penin-sula, with the help of those already living there. Together they would rise against the Visigoth – but their plan was doomed to fail.

The king's spies discovered the plot, which was quickly foiled by the then Visigoth king – Egica. He ruled over an indulgent feudal society, sup-ported by the official Catholic Church. Many lost their lives in the revolt, and those who survived, like Ben's uncle and aunt, were sold into slavery. The fate of their young cousins, David and Jacob had been far worse. At the tender ages of five and six they had been taken from their parents. They were to be raised as Christians, as was the decree for any child under the age of seven years.

What became of them after that, Ben's family knew not, but those fateful events forever silenced his parents to a life of secrecy. As far as the world knew, they were baptised. Although in secret, they continued to practise their Jewish faith, living ever fearful of discovery. For if found out, their fate would be sealed, just as those before them. They would surely be killed or sold into slavery. Ben and his sister would be expected to marry amongst Christian slaves and not from among their own people, which was forbidden by law.

This was Bella's biggest fear. So far, she had managed to evade matrimony, but as a slave it might be a different story. Though for Ben, being a serf was meaningless. There was little difference between being a serf or a slave in his mind. After all, in their own ways, both lived lives bound by shackles of oppression.

Ben hung his head in shame as he listened to his sister weeping beside him. The deep cowl of her woollen cloak drawn over her head masked the side of her face.

"No – I couldn't see you all harmed, any more than I could leave you!" comforted Ben, taking her now cold hand in his and pressing her fingers warm. He stared miserably back out to sea. The sun had slipped out of the horizon and begun to rise. In the daylight, Ben could now see the galley clearly. It had stopped close to three other anchored boats nearby. They pitched and heaved from time to time against the waves that rolled away towards the shore. Then, there was a sudden flurry of activity about the galley that Ben missed, just as he abruptly got to his feet.

"Looks as though Roderick's treasury won't be wanting for anything any time soon," he said bitterly, changing the subject as he got himself ready to leave. On the crest of the mountain high above his head, Ben could see the familiar thick white fleece of curious, cumulus clouds collecting. They gathered in a formidable formation, as the

The king's spies discovered the plot…

warm air blew in from across the Mediterranean. As he stood up, he suddenly became conscious of his clothes made damp from the morning dew.

"There've been merchant galleys ferrying to and fro so much of late," said Ben as he shook out the dirt from his clothes, collected from where he had been sitting. All the while, he was thinking about the precious cargo on board the galley, bearing the promise of a handsome profit.

Given another time or place, he would have liked to have been a sea merchant, sailing the high seas and exploring far off lands. He would cross beyond the Pillars of Hercules to see how far he could sail without tipping off over the edge of the world (if one even could) – but it was useless to ponder over such thoughts. Even that vocation was forbidden to his people, if the Goths ever came to know who he really was. Besides, he was bound by the harsh strictures of the feudal laws to sow the earth to the end of his days.

With one last fleeting look at the land of the Umayyads, Ben finally turned his back on the sea. He couldn't bear to look at that watery abyss of lost hopes any longer. Bella had stopped crying, but she had not spoken for some moments. Ben looked at her curiously under the sunlight as it dappled on her face. She sat rigid, her mouth slightly open, staring out to sea. Something was wrong.

"What is it – what's ailing you now, are you unwell?" asked Ben. They had stayed longer than he would normally have done had he been alone. He was anxious to be away, with plenty of chores waiting to be done back home.

But Bella's eyes were fixed upon the galleys.

"Benjamin," said Bella scarcely above a whisper, pointing a trembling finger suddenly straight ahead of her. "Those aren't merchants!"

"What d'you mean?" asked Ben. He swung round and moved to the edge of the rock ledge. It was his lookout, below where a steep drop lay, with waves crashing over a pebbly beach. What met his eyes took his breath away.

With the turn of the tide, wading powerfully out of the sea towards the sandy shore in knee deep frothing waters, were hundreds and hundreds of men. Strangers with white cloth twisted and bound tightly about their heads. On their chests glistened chainmail, caught up by the morning light, bedazzling the eye. Bows were slung across the arches of their backs and swords hung suspended from their girdles. They carried spears grasped tightly in their hands and were mounted on the most magnificent horses that Ben had ever laid eyes upon. He gasped. Below, the golden beach had become a gateway to a secret encampment and something much, much more.

COUNT JULIAN AND THE LADY FLORINDA

*One year earlier, in the City of Qayrawan
North Africa, 710 CE, 91 AH*

COUNT Julian, the governor of Ceuta paced restlessly up and down the hall. The sound of his footsteps echoed sharply in his ears as they bounced off the stone walls of the Government House, *Dar al-Imara*. That's what a young goat herder he had met outside the walls of the city of Qayrawan had called it.

Julian waited patiently in the hall for the polite Arab secretary to return. The great cavernous hall was pleasantly cool. After a time, he ventured to look out of a nearby window, drawn to it by the blinding sunlight streaming in from the outside. He felt a blanket of heat smother his face. But accustomed as he was to the arid heat of this clime, he didn't flinch a muscle. Instead, he stood looking out thoughtfully over the beautiful city of Qayrawan and admired its view.

It was incredible to think that the great forest of olive trees had been enough by itself to furnish this small city. It had provided all the wood needed without causing the least bit of harm to its population.

Close by, he could see a mosque built of warm earthen brick. It had a square enclosure containing a beautiful courtyard delicately cultivated with exotic shrubs and flowers. In the midst of this paradise stood a playful water fountain with its glistening argentic pool.

Surrounding the mosque was a maze of colourful streets, replete with homes, shops and lively stalls. Beaming children laughed and played, running wildly in and out between the noisy hawkers who stood expectantly beside their carts. Shouting aloud over their heads, they invited passers-by to look at all manner of goods and delights they had on offer. There was everything; from perfumes to spices to rich, colourful, exotic fabrics. Some stopped to mingle and browse while others carried on, going about their daily business and chores.

Then in a few moments the bustle came to a sudden halt. The melodious voice of the *muadhin's* call to prayer (a far cry from the ringing of bells to which he was accustomed) captivated his attention as it lifted through the air around the mosque. The *adhan* was quickly picked up and echoed by yet more harmonious voices elsewhere in the city, calling the faithful to prayer. Vendors shut shop and hawkers covered their carts before moving sedately with other worshippers in the direction of the mosque. It seemed that all around, whether between friends or strangers, sunny smiles and greetings were exchanged, with even the odd warm embrace thrown in.

It struck Julian rather forcefully that this was a

happy place. There was an air of peace and contentment about Qayrawan, with not a hint of fear or restlessness amongst its people, as he had witnessed in other places that he could think of.

At this thought, the cogs of his mind began to turn. Returning to his purpose, Julian meditated over the urgent mission that had brought him so far out from his home to Qayrawan. He recalled the rich, changing landscapes of North Africa as he travelled by sea from Ceuta, his home, in the north-west tip of Africa, following the coast around towards Qayrawan, which lay inland to the south of Sousse. It was something he never imagined he would ever do – to visit the foreign outpost of an enemy. Still, it was a remarkable land out here, to be sure.

To the south, its dry, arid terrain was home to those wonderful ships of the desert, the camels. To the north, sheep grazed freely on its flat, green, fertile plains while goats wandered along its steep slopes which gave way to wild woods. These were home to the Barbary macaques, those curious, playful primates. They lived amongst the evergreen oaks and giant cedars that clothed the mountain ranges. Stretching along the length of the continent, these same highlands separated the great Sahara Desert from the coasts of the Mediterranean and Atlantic seas.

From where Julian stood now, he couldn't see the coast or the sparkling Mediterranean Sea, but even so he could picture in his mind his galley boat. It was moored out on the calm, azure waters near the old port of Sousse (just a few hours trek by horse from Qayrawan through the lush green forests). On board his galley his loyal crew would be waiting for his return. Julian was here to meet with the governor of the Muslim province of North Africa. His name was Musa Ibn Nusayr.

Before the Umayyads had arrived here the land had been under Roman control. Qayrawan had been known as the town of Kamuniya, which had once long ago housed a Roman garrison. The city of Qayrawan had been raised on the ruins of this ancient town. Now it was like a busy hive, a major military encampment for the Umayyads. It had also become an important launch point to further their expeditions throughout *Al-Maghreb*. Now, *if they wanted to*, they could even go northwards, beyond the Straits towards Iberia. Julian's eyes narrowed, silently contemplating over this thought.

He had an important task ahead of him. He knew that. His eyes were still fixed where he had imagined the coast to be, but his mind now conjured another place beyond it. A land that lay across the shimmering Straits from his own province of Ceuta – the Visigoth Kingdom of Iberia to which he had vowed his fealty.

As always, *that* thought fulminated in his mind as Florinda's letter swam before his eyes. His heart turned to stone from the savagery of betrayal. How much he had misjudged the new Visigoth king. Only he himself knew; his jaws clenched.

Toledo was the capital of the Visigoth kingdom. Florinda was his beloved daughter and like all daughters and sons of royal blood, nobility and rich personages across the kingdom, she had been sent there to the royal court. The sons were trained to master all military expertise. They were promoted and advanced, marked by favour of their king, under whose watchful eyes they flourished, only later to be appointed to command posts within the king's army. Daughters on the other hand, were educated in the ways of the nobility and the etiquettes of courtly life.

As any father might have secretly cherished for his daughter, Julian had (like a fool) great hopes for Florinda in Toledo. He had wished that during her time at court Florinda would come to marry and form a grand alliance from amongst one of the noble houses within the kingdom. But it was never meant to be, for dreams are often spun on the most fragile of threads. One winter's morning not too long ago, the arrival of a letter had ripped his world apart, tearing down his hopes with it.

He had read the parchment a hundred times over since the day he first beheld it. Its words were by now etched into his memory. Each time he recalled them, his pain and grief were as bitter as the first time he had read it:

My dearest father,

In trust and good faith did you hand your Florinda to the care and custody of one who calls himself king and protector, yet he has proven to be a man of neither honour nor conscience. I write to tell you that you have been betrayed as no father should ever be betrayed. I beg you to find some means to remove me from Court, whose walls have closed about me and become my prison.

Father I am a watched and followed. The king has forbidden me to speak to you or anyone of my plight. I fear for my life and yours. You have been mistaken in your judgment of him. This king is nothing less than a tyrant. There is an unspeakable cruelty and injustice being inflicted across his domain if I could but tell you. You should know now that I am but one among his latest victims in a long list of crimes he has committed against his people.

I write this note to you with no certain means of knowing whether it will ever fall into your hands, yet I do so in the hope that it is not in vain. I pray that the bearer of this message reaches you safely and is rewarded well for his courage. Help me father.

From the hand of your desperate daughter,

Florinda.

Julian's face tightened and his fingers clenched into a firm fist. He stared blindly out over the distance in grim silence now, still oblivious to the

rich beauty of Qayrawan. Lurking in the depths
of his eyes was the desire for justice and revenge.
Florinda's estimation of King Roderick's character
was right.

Julian had been a valuable and trusted minister
in the previous government of King Wittiza, who
happened to also be his father in-law. Julian
himself had married King Wittiza's daughter. He
had been left appalled when the royal household
and Wittiza's sons were ruthlessly ousted by Roderick. Julian had already come to know what
Roderick was like during Wittiza's reign. Both
callous and selfish, Roderick wasn't worthy of such
office, but such was the status quo that when
Roderick became king Julian had no other choice
but to keep his opinions to himself.

For years he had resisted and fought for the
control of Ceuta in the name of his king and
country. Was *this* mistreatment of his daughter to
be the reward for his services now? Within the
space of a day Julian, beside himself with rage, had
set out across the Straits to travel at all speed across
Iberia towards the Visigoth capital, Toledo. His
sole purpose was to remove Florinda (come what
may) out of the clutches and reach of this despot
king.

Throughout the journey, his mind also worked
relentlessly to mastermind, plot and plan Roderick's downfall. Breathing the fresh, clean air,
whenever he slowed his pace, so as not to exhaust
his steed, his eyes drifted across the acres of varied
plains, rich with golden cereal, sweet clusters of
grapes and olives. Poor peasants stooped low

amongst the straggling crops or else plucked tirelessly away at the vines, driven out of the cities to work in the countryside under the Visigoth's oppressive feudal laws.

The Goths were a Germanic elite. They had arrived from the north and conquered these lands during the fifth century. For too long Julian had turned a blind eye to all that happened about him. After two hundred years of rule, Julian was now of the opinion that the time was ripe for change.

The city of Toledo was fortified by high walls and was itself built on a granite hill. It was surrounded on three sides by a bend of the river Tagus. Its silvery waters flowed gently through the heart of Castilla to Portucale and out into the Atlantic Ocean. Over the river stood a magnificent bridge with a solitary arch supported by large stone piers on both sides of the river. On arrival at Toledo, Julian headed straight for the palace. He tore across the bridge of Tagus and amid a thunder of hooves arrived at the palace gates.

Having dismounted and left his horse at the stables he sprung with hasty strides, up a flight of wide stone steps taking them two at a time. They opened into a great courtyard, lined with columns on all sides. He soon made his way through a colonnade and entered a hall that was both austere and cold despite the few flickering, flamed sconces that lit where the sun failed to reach. Gargoyle like figures danced while grotesques stared back at him mockingly from behind the chilling shadows that fell over the columns and wall carvings.

It was from here he found himself ushered by

a courtier towards the throne room for an audience with the king. As he followed behind a
pompous red-faced attendant, they passed
through several chambers, all richly furnished
from floor to ceiling with priceless furniture and
relics. The odd woollen tapestry embellished the
plain stone walls, each telling their own story.

Through an open door to one side, he caught
a fleeting glimpse of the lavish banqueting hall
adjacent to the throne room. During ceremonial
occasions, the long, solid wooden banqueting table
was laden with all manner of delicious delicacies
on golden plates, silver goblets and ornamental
dishes; all worth a king's ransom.

Soon, Julian's arrival was announced by a
heavy-set doorman with a coarse, stentorian voice
that rang out and echoed around the chamber.
Upon hearing his name, the king's brow furrowed
as he looked put out, making obvious his displea-
sure at witnessing Julian's unexpected arrival.
Julian recalled how he had found Roderick
perched indulgently on his throne of gold, decorated with the carved legs of a lion.

A golden crown nestled upon his long golden
mane. The Goths grew their hair long as a matter
of pride, deeming it to befit their rank and station
in life. Parted down the middle, it fell on either
side of his head to below his shoulders, lying over
lavish robes of gold silk brocade, trimmed at the
hem with a fur band. The king was a middle-aged
man, powerfully built, yet with a distinct paunch
from a life of self-indulgence.

"Count Julian, this is a surprise!" said the king.

"I had not thought to expect to see you here at court this time of year," he drawled. A frown nestled between a pair of cool blue eyes, set beneath heavy eyebrows.

"Surely this is neither the right time nor an occasion that necessitates our meeting like this? I trust there is nothing amiss – is all well in our province of Ceuta?"

"Forgive me, Sire, for the intrusion," said Julian, suppressing the inner rage that had ignited now that he stood before Roderick, his heart pounding hard against his chest. "You are right we have no official engagement between us so to speak – and rest assured, all is well at Ceuta," he quickly continued, though his mind calculated otherwise, *'for the present moment that is – but not for long!'*

"Alas, it is but a personal matter that brings me to court."

"Personal, you say?" replied the king tersely. For the first time a look of curiosity passed across his haughty features. Watching him from beneath half hooded eyes, Roderick began to wonder if Julian was here because he suspected the improper treatment of his daughter. Swift to interpret Roderick's reaction, Julian moved to allay any suspicion.

"My wife, as you know, has been ill for some time, Sire, but recently she has taken a turn for the worse. She is desirous to see Florinda again. I fear it may be for the last time…" entreated Julian, his face masked with worry.

As he had hoped, Julian watched with satisfaction as Roderick's demeanour relaxed. After a moment's pause, Roderick spoke.

"It is a shame. Queen Egilona of course will be disappointed. She'll be loath to lose Florinda's company – she is well liked at court. But under the circumstances Julian, I see Florinda must accompany you back home," replied Roderick begrudgingly. At the back of his mind the king believed Florinda would reveal nothing incriminating about her time at court. She wouldn't dare if she valued her honour, not to mention her life, and that of her father.

"I am most grateful to you, Sire," said Julian as the lines on his face faded away, relieved that at least one problem seemed solved. He listened intently as Roderick gave orders for Florinda's departure from the palace, all the while fearful the king might have a change of heart at any moment. When Julian was finally ready to leave, Roderick made a sudden unexpected request that bemused him for a moment.

Roderick had, at least, a high regard for Julian as a merchant, if not as a member of his office. Julian was famous for bringing back from Africa some of the most superb horses, hawks and fine produce to come out of that continent.

"Julian, seeing as you are here, a thought has just come to my mind," said Roderick eagerly as he leaned forward on his throne. "I have a request to make of you. On your next visit it would please me were you to bring me a pair of those fine swift hawks. They do amuse me so!"

Julian wondered at the perfidy of the royal request. Only Roderick could act in such a deceitful manner towards him and then behave so innocently, expecting favours from him, adding insult to injury.

'*Yet* – could any request be more fitting?' thought Julian to himself with grim satisfaction. He schooled his face into a beguiling smile.

"Of course, Sire – I shall not rest until I bring you such hawks the likes of which you have never seen before in your life!" exclaimed Julian with a dramatic show of hand.

For a moment Roderick hesitated. Just for a second, he could have sworn he had gleaned some flicker of emotion behind Julian's dark eyes that made him feel uneasy. Yet it came and left so quickly that before he could wonder over it, he brushed the feeling aside. Roderick laughed lightly, convinced he had imagined it all as nothing more than a trick of the light.

Julian inclined his head graciously. He withdrew without so much as turning his back on the king (as he dearly wished to do, but all in good time). He moved away leaving the king watching thoughtfully after him, conscious of his crown that for some reason seemed to weigh uncomfortably upon his head.

Suddenly the soft sound of a door closing and swift returning footsteps brought Julian out of the memory of his last meeting with King Roderick and back within the walls of the *Dar al-Imara* in Qayrawan. He spun around and quickly abandoned his position by the window to see the Arab secretary hurriedly making his way towards him, his long white robe billowing about him.

Julian had solved his first problem when he had brought Florinda home safely to Ceuta. His mouth set into a hard line. Now there lay a more formidable task ahead of him. The king had asked for hawks and *that* was exactly what he intended to bring him. As he eagerly watched the Arab secretary advancing, his mind beheld the vision of the mighty Umayyad army that had descended upon this region of *Al-Maghreb*. Its arrival had transformed the place in a way he had never thought possible.

Only Julian's province had so far remained outside the Umayyad's reach. Ceuta acted as a buffer between the Umayyads and the rest of the Visigoth kingdom. But now, Julian would seek advantageous conditions for himself and for his people, before taking a step back. No longer would he stand between the Umayyad's army and his province of Ceuta. But the bigger question whirling in his mind was would they go further afield? Would they press on beyond the Straits and bring about the downfall of a tyrant king? Nothing would give Julian more pleasure than to meet Roderick one day over the length of his sword.

"Count Julian," addressed the Arab secretary, his sharp eyes raised firmly to meet his, "Musa Ibn Nusayr will speak with you now."

MUSA IBN NUSAYR

Governor of North Africa, 710 CE, 91 AH

JULIAN followed the Arab secretary through the same high arched door from which he had just seen him emerge. It was the door he knew that led to the audience chamber where Julian would meet the Governor of North Africa. His mind was reeling at the thought of the impending meeting, but also over the unusual request that the secretary had made moments earlier, before they stepped through the door. It had left Julian feeling suddenly unsure of himself.

"Count Julian, you may not be accustomed to or familiar with our laws and ways, but I would kindly ask you that upon meeting the Governor, you refrain from bowing," said the Arab secretary firmly but politely. "Allah the Almighty has forbidden us from prostrating before any human being. Prostrations and bowing are for none but Allah, may only He be glorified and exalted."

Count Julian looked surprised, so alien was this notion to his own traditions. Still, he inclined his head and agreed to this request.

Now as he was led through the audience chamber, his nose was met with a sudden rush of the earthy, aromatic, sweet scent of frankincense as it mingled with the air. At the far end of the chamber, he soon became aware of the figure of a man. Julian's eyebrows lifted curiously on first impressions. He was dressed in simple white robes, with a turban wrapped about his head (much like the secretary's own clothes). Julian also noticed to his surprise that such a notable man as he should be seated on nothing more elaborate than simple cushions.

Discreetly flanking either side of him, half concealed in the shadows against the back wall, stood his guards. They were dressed in the familiar military garb of the Umayyads.

Then it struck him. Julian's eyes widened as he marvelled at the sight of the Governor. He made a startling contrast to the vision of Roderick's arrogant repose upon his bejewelled throne. In fact, there was none of the pomp or ceremony to be found here at Qayrawan, as there was at the court of Toledo. Nor was there any cold opulence to its surroundings. Instead, only a warmth reflected from the humble, earthy stone walls as they glowed under the brilliant sunlight that flooded in from a nearby window.

As Julian approached him, his pulse quickened. He was suddenly assailed by a feeling of uncertainty. He felt self-conscious and unsure of what to say or do. How was he to address this man? He clearly had the bearing of a leader and the physique of a seasoned warrior. His distinguished features were set upon a face framed at the chin by a neat beard, with bristles of henna-red. As Julian drew closer to him with every footstep, their sound ringing in his ears, he could see Musa Ibn Nusayr was regarding him with bright, inquisitive, intelligent eyes.

Not for the first time Julian began to wonder over the stories whispered about the Umayyads. It was said their rule brought harmony, peace and prosperity between communities, even if they differed in faith. From all that he had heard and seen since entering Qayrawan, he could well believe it. It only added to his own growing sense of respect for them.

If Julian was appraising the scene unfolding before him with curiosity, so too was Musa Ibn Nusayr.

'So, this was Count Ilyan! A senior, high-ranking official in the Visigoth court and Commander of the garrison of Ceuta, the only fort in North Africa to have resisted and remained outside of Umayyad control so far,' mused Musa, his shrewd eyes scrutinising the visitor up and down.

From the moment the Umayyad Caliph Al-Walid had sent him to continue with their advance into this region, the Muslims had reached as far as Morocco. Yet there still remained the coastal city of Ceuta, governed by people loyal to the Visigoth king. Musa Ibn Nusayr had found Ceuta to have shown much resistance. Despite the siege they had laid around the small city, their efforts had come to no avail and the reason lay with *this* man, known to them as Ilyan (the Arabic for Julian) now walking towards him.

Ilyan was dressed in his full regalia. He wore a Gothic tunic of fine, fawn linen lined at the hem with fur band over which was draped a dark woollen cloak. Only his sword and scabbard were missing from his attire. These had been removed at the gates under instruction of Musa's guards before he was allowed entry into the *Dar al-Imara*. His hair was long, mousy brown and hanging loose over his broad shoulders. His skin was coarse, tanned and weather-beaten, as was to be expected of a sailor who had spent much time at sea.

Musa Ibn Nusayr knew of Ilyan as a skilful mariner with a fleet of galleys that repeatedly crossed the Straits for food and supplies from the Visigoth kingdom. It was this very advantage they had that had rendered the Umayyad siege around Ceuta ineffective. Yet now, by the decree of Allah, Ilyan had arrived unexpectedly on his doorstep, claiming to come in peace.

With a guarded smile, Musa Ibn Nusayr invited Ilyan to sit down. A servant soon appeared at his elbow, offering Ilyan a small decorative cup of sweet tea. It was a familiar drink that was said to have been introduced to these parts by the Phoenicians long ago. Ilyan found the warm drink strangely refreshing, as it began to slake his thirst from heat of the day.

Musa Ibn Nusayr watched Ilyan gratefully accept their hospitality, slowly sipping the brew before he spoke.

"Count Ilyan," began Musa coming directly to the point. "What brings you to Qayrawan?"

Ilyan looked at Musa Ibn Nusayr for a long

moment before he began to speak. Some instinct
inside him told Ilyan that this man before him
could be trusted. Musa listened quietly as Ilyan
began to recount the tales of King Roderick's
treachery. The visitor talked of Roderick's cruelty
towards his people, and the crimes he committed
against them, including his own daughter's suffering at his hands.

Such were Ilyan's vivid tales of injustice across
the Visigoth kingdom, that Musa was reminded
of the plight of another persecuted people. He
remembered the poor, vulnerable souls, who had
lived not so long ago in the time of the Prophet
Muhammad.

They too had been hounded men, women and
children of Makkah and the other tribes of Arabia,
who had embraced Islam. They had been neither
able to escape at first, nor to protect themselves
from the clutches of those who would hurt them.
They too had been forced to endure many hardships. Yet the more he listened, the more Musa
intuitively knew why Ilyan had come. His next
words revealed themselves to be just as he anticipated.

"King Roderick has a hardened heart. He's not
fit to rule his people," said Ilyan frankly, leaning
forward in his seat. "I have always heard how your
part of the world thrives more in peace and
prosperity. With your mighty army it would be
nothing for you to come to Iberia and remove this
tyrant from his throne ..." entreated Ilyan, laying
bare his plans. He proceeded to provide Musa with
a tempting list of the merits of doing so.

"Only think, Iberia is a vast kingdom, ripe for your picking – filled with treasures of all kinds," said Ilyan, his eyes shining and words brimming over with pride. "It is a country rich in groves, gardens, beautiful rivers and land yielding exotic fruits and plants of every description. Their castles are strong and a sight to behold.

"Did you know that wheat can be stored underground for a number of years without its decaying?" continued Ilyan, his enticing description ringing about the walls of the audience chamber.

Ilyan had heard of families who had included wheat as inheritance, passing it down from father to son like any other valuable commodity, all because of their ability to preserve it.

Musa clasped his hands together thoughtfully as he surveyed Ilyan's anxious face. This wasn't the first time the notion of crossing the sea had presented itself to the Umayyads. His eyes strayed thoughtfully past Ilyan's shoulder seeking the window behind him.

It was another glorious day. Outside, enveloped by the golden sunshine was the mosque built by Uqbah Ibn Nafi al-Fihri. Years before, he was the one who had laid the foundation stones upon which this great city of Qayrawan was built.

It was said that Uqbah had bravely crossed the lands of central north and north-western Africa; from Libya, Tunisia, Algeria and then on to Morocco. When he finally reached the farthest edge of the known world, he came face to face with the great Atlantic Ocean. Uqbah plunged straight into the sea and spurred his battle horse forward into the rolling waves until he could go no further. Lifting his hands in the air, he had cried out longingly, beseeching his Maker:

"Oh Allah, if the sea had not prevented me, I would have galloped on forever like Alexander the Great, upholding your faith!"

Musa knew the Straits Ilyan spoke of. Unlike the great Atlantic Ocean that had halted Uqbah, the Straits were but a short stretch of sea that separated the citadel of Christianity in Europe on one side, from the land of Islam in North Africa on the other. In Damascus, the Umayyads were already putting their heads together trying to find a way of taking Constantinople, the capital of the Roman Empire. They had set their sights and hearts upon that land. Eager was their desire to grasp the blessed rank promised by the Prophet, blessings and peace be upon him, to those who would reach Constantinople. Speaking of them, the Prophet had said, *"Verily you shall conquer Constantinople. What a wonderful leader will her leader be, and what a wonderful army will that army be!"*

It just so happened that the only way to reach Constantinople was either from the south through Anatolia, or from the north after passing through the lands of Iberia and across southern Europe. When Musa had been sent to North Africa, he had also been instructed to explore the possibility of reaching Constantinople through Europe after crossing the Straits. But such had been the turn of events in *Al-Maghreb* that he had not yet looked to what lay beyond the Straits. Instead, he had been distracted.

*Musa Ibn Nusayr listened quietly as Ilyan began to recount the
tales of King Roderick's treachery*

Much of Musa's time had been spent in defence against the Romans. He had also been busy spreading the Prophet's teachings amongst the Berbers. Allah had commanded that there is no compulsion in religion and Musa Ibn Nusayr knew this only too well. There was no better example for him than that of his own father, Nusayr.

As a young boy Nusayr had been raised in Christian monasteries and had been set on the path to becoming a monk. But when Khalid Ibn Al-Walid overcame his town of Ayn At-Tamir, it was to change the course of Nusayr's life completely. Living alongside the Muslims, Musa's intelligent father Nusayr had been moved by the new religion. He couldn't help it. He quickly found himself, like so many others, willingly entering its fold.

Musa had been inspired by his father's life. He too wished to see the same conviction that his father had experienced, blossoming in the hearts of the Berber people. So, Musa had worked tirelessly among the local population. He hoped that by appealing to their minds and sense of reasoning, many a heart would willingly open to its message, and so they did – in droves. Some even went so far as to enter his army as soldiers and officers.

As to the matter of successfully overthrowing the Visigoth kingdom – Ilyan was right on that score! Musa had by now amassed not only an army of considerable might, but he had also established a small but highly skilled naval fleet. Even as they spoke, in the busy dockyards of the port of Tunis, more ships were being built under his orders. Their purpose was to protect the Umayyads against amphibious attacks along their coastline.

The Romans were always under their noses, raiding their shores. Musa had intended the ships for defence in seaborne battles, or to cut off supply routes. He had never actually envisaged using them as a means to expand their territory. But now... Musa smoothed his red beard between his fingers as he pondered over the possibility.

To cross the Straits as Ilyan suggested was not a difficult task, except that time might not be on their side. The building of ships takes many months, and a full armada was still far from being completed.

Ilyan sat with a rigid back, trying to read Musa's expression, but his face was an impenetrable mask. He wondered if there was anything more he could say that could convince the man before him. Yet Musa was a man endowed with a sharp mind and wit, experienced in the art of diplomacy as well as warfare. He had been born during the reign of the second Caliph Umar Ibn Al-Khattab, a faithful companion of the Prophet Muhammad. Musa had sat amongst those who had known the Prophet and acquired their wisdom. So, in that moment Musa thought it unwise to throw caution to the wind, however sweet its course may seem to be.

"I don't doubt that what you tell me is the truth, Count Ilyan," said Musa Ibn Nusayr finally, his eyes holding Ilyan's anxious ones. "But you must understand that I have to be cautious for the sake of my people, and the dangers they may encounter at sea.

"You wish us to enter a country with which we are not in the least bit familiar and from which we are separated by an intervening sea. This while you, Ilyan, are bound to your king by the common ties of your religion and laws …"

"With all due respect Governor Musa," interrupted Ilyan, wincing at his words, unable to stomach the connection, "Roderick is a usurper – he is no king of mine! Nor is he of his people's choosing!"

"Be that as it may," continued Musa shaking his head gravely. "You forget that there is still the matter of your being united to your countryfolk as well – whether through ties of kinship, customs or by the practice of the same faith."

Ilyan pursed his lips. He could see Musa's line of reasoning and yet he could not counter the argument. His shoulders sunk slowly with disappointment. This was a terrible blow. He had failed. How would he ever look Florinda in the eyes again? The pain of failure consumed Ilyan like fire, but Musa continued to regard Ilyan with guarded interest.

"Count Ilyan, perhaps there is a way forward…" ventured Musa, having watched the wave of emotions wash over the nobleman's face. Ilyan sat up straight, his eyes alight with a sudden curiosity and renewed hope.

"I have a proposition that could settle this matter that lies between us. Return to your people. Gather your vassals and partisans and cross the Straits in person. Make an incursion into the territory of King Roderick as an enemy. When you have done so, then will it be the time for us to follow in your footsteps if we can, *insha'Allah*," said Musa.

As though a cloud had lifted, Ilyan's face lit up and a smile spread across his weary face, now overcome with relief. He could hardly believe the words he had just heard – and just when he had thought all was at an end.

"I accept your terms!" said Ilyan, feeling the tension flow from his body as his limbs relaxed.

After their agreement, Ilyan rose to his feet and took his leave. There was a light spring to his footsteps now as he made his way briskly back through the audience chamber and into the hall. All the while, he was conscious of the feeling that an immense weight had been lifted from his shoulders.

Musa Ibn Nusayr sat quietly for a long time after, his thoughts turning over the extraordinary meeting with Count Ilyan. They were interrupted finally when his young secretary hurried back into the audience chamber, having shown Count Ilyan his way out. Now Musa knew what he must do.

"Bilal, has our guest left?" asked Musa from beneath half closed eyes.

"He has – he rides as we speak at great speed away from our walls," said Bilal confidently clutching a parchment in his hand. Musa smiled to himself, as he noted the blank parchment. His secretary could always be relied upon to know what was needed to be done next.

Bilal was a shrewd, intelligent young man and a good judge of character. He had acquired his post as secretary owing to his good traits of thoroughness, honesty and trustworthiness, which bespoke his *taqwa*. For nothing else would do but that Musa Ibn Nusayr should surround himself with such people who were either endowed of religious knowledge or the most righteous of character.

"And what did you make of this meeting – and of our visitor?" asked Musa of the younger man curiously. Bilal's brow furrowed thoughtfully.

"I sense that Count Ilyan speaks the truth," said Bilal slowly after considering the question for a moment. "I do believe that across the Straits the conditions are not as they ought to be – and how can they be, when a man is left to rule according to his own whims and desires? There can only follow pain and suffering for his people."

Bilal paused for a moment and saw to his delight that Musa Ibn Nusayr was listening with interest, nodding profusely. Emboldened, he continued to offer his opinion, eager as he was to make a good impression.

"I was just thinking, *Sayyid*," said Bilal earnestly, "this may be a momentous opportunity for us, *insha'Allah*. If Ilyan, a high-ranking official of the kingdom is so disaffected by his ruler, then it stands to reason that others may feel the same way too. Surely it could only be to our advantage if we were to help them?"

"I agree," said Musa Ibn Nusayr, nodding his head. He looked at the parchment in Bilal's hand and gestured to him to sit down. Musa Ibn Nusayr settled down to dictate a letter to the Caliph (just as Bilal had anticipated) and appraise him of all that had passed between Ilyan and himself. His intention was to seek the Caliph's permission to cross the Straits and enter the Visigoth kingdom.

In the name of Allah, the Merciful,
the Compassionate.

To the Caliph Al-Walid Ibn 'Abdal-Malik, in the city of Damascus, from Musa Ibn Nusayr, Governor in the province of North Africa, Qayrawan.

Peace be upon you and the mercy of Allah. All praises be to Allah, Lord of the Worlds, and may blessings and peace be upon His final Messenger Muhammad, and likewise upon the family of the Prophet and his companions.

As for what follows, Oh Commander of the faithful, today I was visited by one who calls himself Count Ilyan. He is the Governor of Ceuta, a province in North Africa of the Visigoth kingdom of Iberia we call Andalus, which, as you well know, lies on the very doorstep of our domain ...

TARIF IBN MALIK AND THE ISLAND

Summer of 710 CE, 91 AH

THE lateen sail cracked out like a wing expanding into the clear blue sky, as the spine of the boat arched against the sea. As the wind lifted, the swell carried the boat further into the Straits on a course away from the coast of Tangiers. The solitary figure of a man stood at the prow. He looked back for a moment, one last time as the familiar coastline slipped away into the far distance. The breathtakingly beautiful Rif mountains that rose up from the sea, seeking the sky, slowly shrank away almost disappearing beneath the crests of the deep turquoise waves.

Tarif Ibn Malik felt the warmth of the wind blowing across his face. It had been some months since he had been summoned by Musa Ibn Nusayr to Qayrawan.

"Tarif, you understand what you must do!" Musa had said.

"Gather a small force and cross the Straits towards the shores of Andalus and learn what you can about this land and its people."

Once Caliph Al-Walid had received word from Musa Ibn Nusayr, the Caliph had accepted Ilyan's proposal, but not without caution. Although he had given Musa permission to enter Andalus, Al-Walid had also added a proviso: Musa had to first dispatch a light troop to explore the land. He was eager to know the true extent and strength of Roderick's army. That, and to ensure that their own army would not be betrayed by Ilyan, although any fear of possible betrayal was far from Musa Ibn Nusayr's mind.

Ilyan had followed through with his promise. A few weeks after their meeting, Ilyan had gathered his forces and entered Andalus, raiding the territory near its shores. He had returned to Qayrawan laden with a trove of treasures and captives so as to assure, in Musa Ibn Nusayr's mind at least, that there could be no possible reconciliation to be had between Ilyan and Roderick. After all, he had now entered Andalus as a foe.

Encouraged by Ilyan's foray, Musa Ibn Nusayr lost no time. He summoned one of his best men to lead a fleet – a Berber and new Muslim by the name of Tarif Ibn Malik Abu Zahrah.

With his instructions, Tarif left the city of Qayrawan and boarded a *maraqib* that was waiting for him at the old port of Sousse. He sailed along the coastline of North Africa towards Tangiers. There he put together an army of four hundred stalwart men on foot and a hundred of his swiftest cavalry, to be ferried across on a small flotilla of boats.

After weeks of preparing, they finally cast off.

It was early one morning when the wind was sure to be fresh, as the sky lightened to a pale glow, sweeping away the last remnants of darkness. Theirs was to be a vital scouting expedition to Andalus.

A sudden flicker of movement along the horizon now caught Tarif's attention. He smiled as he spied a pod of dolphins leaping high out of the sea. Like elegant scimitars they hung momentarily in the sultry air before plunging back into the waves. Seeking attention, they frolicked playfully in a flood of froth that slipped over their glossy, granite backs. Then in a matter of moments these gentle beasts of the sea dived below into the cold, dark depths and disappeared out of sight as if they had been nothing more than a figment of his imagination.

Tarif looked away, his smile quickly fading as he thought how life for humans was far from play and amusement. His mind, weighed down by the heavy burden of their mission, soon shifted back to their journey as they sailed the Straits towards an island on the southern tip of Andalus. As the boat turned to starboard, it moved on a course away from the Atlantic Ocean, that great span of mysterious waters that people liked to call 'The Sea of Darkness and Fog.' It was the very same gateway, beyond the Pillars of Hercules, into the unknown world that had been beyond Uqbah Ibn Nafi al-Fihri's reach. Following close at their tail were three other boats, each eager to keep up their pace.

Then after a time, as was to be expected of her

capricious mood, the wind dropped and the sea fell calm. The sail fell limp and listless about the solitary mast that speared skywards. At the high stern post, a tell-tale long pennant that streamed readily in the direction of the wind fell exhausted. The waves that once broke noisily were now so still that they clung to the wooden sides of the boat.

In the belly of the boat rose the coarse voice of the Master of the Sailors, bellowing out loud. It was time for the crew to run out the oars. Lifting them from their stows, the men below deck began to power the long wooden oars with a decided will. They settled into a rhythm, continuing their momentum through the calm waters that parted easily beneath the bow of the boat. Tarif turned his head sharply now as a new voice reached his ears.

"*Sayyid!*"

It was his young lieutenant calling out to him from across the weather deck. Seeing Humayun, Tarif nodded at once and quickly left the prow where he had been standing for the past half hour. He was a tall, brawny man who carried himself with an unmistakeable air of dignity and forbearance. Humayun watched as Tarif manoeuvred his way through the busy upper deck towards him just as a young sailor swept past, greeting him warmly. Tarif smiled and replied with some words of encouragement. The youth bobbed his head in return with a broad grin, before clambering up the ratlines for a better view out to sea.

"Nu'man *Ra'is* says he's free now," said Humayun, as Tarif came to stop beside him. "Everything's ready, just as you asked."

Tarif nodded, his keen, dark eyes appraising Humayun's words with approval. He had been eagerly waiting for this moment to be able to speak to the busy Boat Master. Together they walked to the stern of the boat where on a raised platform stood a small awning. It had been set up on deck to afford some respite from the full glare of the Mediterranean sun. Beneath the awning was the squat burly figure of the Boat Master. He stood before a wooden table on which there lay strewn a number of maps. Of particular interest to him was a curious old rutter, recently removed from its oilskin. It was spread wide open over the other maps, ready for Tarif's inspection.

Tarif warmly greeted the Boat Master with *salaams* and a courteous nod borne out of a mark of respect for the other.

A Damascene like many of the boat's crewmen, Nu'man *Ra'is* was one of Musa Ibn Nusayr's best navigators in his small but highly trained fleet. He was used to patrolling and protecting their coast-lines, yet now they had been put to a different task. Still, Tarif could rest assured in the knowledge that they were in the capable hands of Nu'man *Ra'is*, a distinguished mariner whose reputation held true.

"What do you have for me?" asked Tarif eagerly looking at Nu'man *Ra'is* on the other side of the table as he stood hunched over the map. A coarse, weather beaten finger traced a line moving along the waters of the Straits from North Africa on one side and then stopped short over a spot close to the coastline of Andalus.

"This is the narrowest part of the Straits and at the end of it is an island – Isla de Andalus," said Nu'man *Ra'is*, tapping the location of what looked like a small, lonely island detached from the mainland. Tarif's turbaned head bent forward, inspecting it thoughtfully. Then after a moment, a frown settled on his hard, sculpted features. Something was troubling him. Humayun had been watching eagerly from the wings when he caught the sight of the frown.

"How are the men holding up?" asked Tarif, with a look of concern in his eyes. He knew his men, a brave mixture of mostly Berber and a handful of Arab warriors. They would be sailing (some for the first time) into what could only be described as the treacherous unknown. Relieved that the question was nothing more serious, Humayun threw him a hopeful smile.

"*Alhamdulillah*, they're good, strong men. They rely on Allah and invoke His help and protection," replied Humayun encouragingly. Tarif's handsome features relaxed into a smile, pleased to hear as much.

"May Allah accept their *du'a* and grant us success – *Ameen*," said Tarif.

The crew had placed their trust in Allah, and it sufficed them to do so. *Insha'Allah*, they would brave the difficulties and hardships that awaited them at sea or upon setting foot on that strange, still landmass in the far distance towards which they were sailing. It was bathed in the morning light now, rising out of the water like a great fortification on the horizon.

Prompted by Tarif's *du'a*, Humayun couldn't

help but look across at the sea, her waves gently lapping against the hull. He was excited. He had never sailed before and what a wonderous thing it was to behold Allah's creation, from the crest and fall of the gentle waves, to the taste of the salty sea air rising up through his nostrils to the back of his throat. Even the sound of the early morning cry of the seagulls was exhilarating. Humayun could clearly hear the piercing sound of their squawks, for once not drowned out by the gusty sigh of the wind. The levanters had died down now – and in that moment, he remembered that he had called Tarif for another purpose.

"*Sayyid*, Ya'qub says the winds will pick up quickly enough, especially as we get closer to the island – they are known for it, so the local fishermen say," repeated Humayun rather dubiously. His eyes fell thoughtfully on the young Iberian prisoner he spoke of who had been brought aboard with them, sent from Qayrawan. Since coming into their custody he had to admit Jacob (or Ya'qub, as he had come to be known by the Umayyads) had been no trouble so far. He had proved to be intelligent, hardworking and seemed knowledgeable enough.

"The boy's probably right," said Nu'man *Ra'is*, folding his large arms across his chest, a flicker of interest passing over his otherwise impassive, sun-tanned face. "A fisherman knows his own part of the world."

"But that's if you *trust* Ya'qub of course," added Humayun as an afterthought, nodding his head towards the figure of the Iberian youth.

Jacob was an inhabitant of Iberia. He was sitting in a corner against a barrel on the wide deck of the stern. The heat was slowly rising, so he gratefully drank down the water being offered to him by a Damascene crewman clutching a long, deep ladle and water container in his hands. In the next moment the crewman refilled his container with cool water from a barrel and disappeared down the companionway leading below deck to seek out his brothers. Fifty parched oarsmen waited patiently, sitting on their thwarts in pairs, eager to quench the thirst from their hard work, for hard work it was down below.

Their bearded faces were bathed in perspiration, as their feet pressed hard against the footrests. Their backs rose off their seats under a strain as hands held fast to the oars. Their broad muscular arms heaved mightily as they flexed and extended in a synchronised motion, sinking the oars in and out of the flat, still sea. Tarif Ibn Malik considered Jacob for a moment, turning over Humayun's concerns in his head.

"It's not just a matter of trust, Humayun," said Tarif finally. "We have an agreement. *Insha'Allah*, if he guides us to where we need to go, he'll be freed. It's in his own interest as much as ours," said Tarif firmly, watching curiously as the young Iberian stood up to stretch his legs. Jacob was tall, young and from his simple rags, it was clear that he was a peasant. Tarif couldn't help but marvel at the difference in his appearance to that of everyone else on board the boat, so much so that his mind reflected momentarily on the speech of his Lord:

"*Among His Signs is the creation of the heavens and the earth and the variety of your languages and colours. There are certainly Signs in that for every being.*"

Well Jacob *was* clearly unlike the others. For a start, he had sandy hair and eyes as grey as the sea after a storm.

"Besides," continued Tarif, "Ilyan says there's no love lost between Ya'qub and the Visigoth kingdom."

This much was certain. Jacob was one of the captives brought back by Count Julian after he had raided Andalus at Musa Ibn Nusayr's request. Julian and his men had stormed through the field in which Jacob and his brother had been working since dawn. Their intrusion was by no means a surprise. Many a time before, when Jacob (or any peasant who worked the lands, for that matter) had spotted Visigoth troops passing through the vicinity, he would rush to hide. It was out of the fear of the hard labour and the exactions they would be made to suffer at their hands.

The Visigoth troops were mean and could wreak havoc. They trampled on crops and seized fruits and produce, right from under everyone's noses. If that was all they had to endure, they could perhaps have made do with their lot in life, but the peasants were often physically attacked to boot.

This particular year had been no different. It was the reaping season and fatigue had numbed their senses. Jacob's normally sharp instincts for survival had for once let him down. He had missed the sight of Julian's troops advancing through a sea of parting crops. Caught unawares, Jacob found himself surrounded – although mercifully his brother had managed to take flight in time. A struggle had ensued, but it was to no avail. Jacob was trapped. The next thing he knew, rough hands were clamped about him. They tied him up and thrust him on board a galley boat bound for North Africa, a strange, unknown land to him, which lay on the other side of the Straits.

Tarif's voice carried along the deck now as he summoned Jacob, calling him under the shelter of the awning. Jacob hastened towards him, his eyes fixed on Tarif's face. It was a face that neither evoked fear nor hate in Jacob's heart, but only wonder and curiosity. Could such goodness among human beings really exist in a world where he had come to know only cruelty and contempt?

It had been some months now since Jacob had been taken from Iberia. Yet incredibly, he was within sight of the shores of his home once more. He also faced the prospect of earning his freedom, but still his mind was elsewhere. In the intervening time that had passed, so much had happened to him. He had seen and learned a great many things since the day he was captured by Julian and was left at Qayrawan.

At first, he had been petrified, frightened out of his wits on arriving in a foreign land. He was quickly handed over to the custody of strangers. Yet no sooner had he beheld them than he realised that no harm would befall him at their hands. For the first time in his life, he was treated well, so well at times that he forgot that he was now a slave. They fed him good food, clothed him well and even made him bathe – frequently at that!

Slavery was entrenched in the fabric of most societies, yet he knew of no slave back home in Iberia that received such kindness and good treatment. Nor had he ever heard of the prospect of a slave being able to buy their own freedom or to be released so readily as it was done here amongst the Muslims and quite often at that. Their faith encouraged this generosity as a means to reparation of wrong actions and being granted a place in Paradise.

Never in his wildest dreams had Jacob imagined that what had begun as a terrifying event could have catapulted him into an adventure such as this. Time and again, he had wondered curiously about the people with whom he was travelling, people who showed compassion and mercy to their fellow human beings, even towards a captive like himself. If Humayun could read minds and delve into hearts, he would surely have been relieved to know the truth of where Jacob's feelings lay. He had come to hold the Muslims with genuine high regard.

"You asked for me, *Sayyid*?" said Jacob as he stepped under the welcoming, cool shade of the awning. Tarif's turbaned head was bent busily over a map, his forefinger tracing the crudely drawn coastline of Andalus. As his fingertip reached the southernmost part, it came to rest on the island close to the mainland, the same one that Nu'man *Ra'is* had just pointed out.

"Tell me more about this place. Did you say they use it as a store – is that all?"

Jacob scratched his head thoughtfully.

"Yes sometimes – for storing weapons and equipment. It's also where they can, on occasion, launch their boats too," he revealed. "But you know, if it's the glitter of gold you seek, then it's not the island you'll want. You ought to go inland and seek out the town of Julia Loza. You'll find a garrison there – it's only a few hours trek through the hills and countryside." As Jacob spoke, he could picture in his head the hoard of sacks swelling with coins from the Visigoths' tax collections.

Tarif was silent. Jacob knew nothing about their mission, but the news of a garrison intrigued him. It was imperative they learned as much as they could about King Roderick's army, both about their capability and strength – and without having to delve deep into Andalus at this stage. A garrison like that could certainly shed more light. Tarif made a mental note of Jacob's information against the basic map before him. Up until now the crudely drawn map had revealed little more to him than the changing shape and winding curves along the coastline collected by cartographers over time.

"Have your people ever been to Andalus before?" asked Jacob as he dropped his head to one side curiously.

"Yes. There were a few excursions in the past, *alhamdulillah*," admitted Tarif (although nothing like what they were doing right now, he thought to himself). To Humayun, who was listening intently beside him, the news of previous excursions came as a complete surprise. Till now, he had been gladly under the impression that they were going to be the first Muslims to land in Andalus. His face fell suddenly.

"Were there really others before us?" asked Humayun incredulously. His voice couldn't hide the fact that he was slightly piqued by the news, but his curiosity was aroused nonetheless.

"There were. Over sixty years ago, during the rule of Uthman, the *Caliph ar-Rashid*, may Allah be pleased with him, the early Muslims set foot upon this land," revealed Tarif Ibn Malik with a slight smile.

"There were two separate occasions that I know of on which they travelled to the south-eastern peninsula, but from what I gather, it was more in the nature of exploration," he continued. "Like most mariners eventually do, they disembarked on Andalus in search of fresh food and water and in order to replenish the provisions on board their boats."

Reading the disappointment in Humayun's face, Tarif gave him a more sympathetic smile. Humayun had really hoped to be among the first of the Muslims to set foot in Andalus. He was an eager young Berber, strong, agile and intelligent. He had kept a cool head in battles and that had seen to him rising very quickly up through the ranks, even at such a young age.

Standing six-foot-tall, he wasn't much older than Jacob. A new Muslim and a youth full of life, it was to be expected that Humayun was keen to serve. *He* might have been disappointed, but Tarif was nonetheless pleased with his young officer. He liked to see enthusiasm and eagerness in his men.

Just then, the boat lurched suddenly and the rigging rattled as the sails billowed out under a strong gust of wind. Tarif's hand flew out to protect the charts, as they began to flutter and almost blow off the table. Galvanised into action, Nu'man *Ra'is* left the shelter of the awning with a sudden sense of urgency, knowing that it would require all hands on deck.

The boat had entered the waters near the island and was about to sail hard into strong winds. All around them a commotion beset the boat as she heeled to the wind with the creaking and groaning of her cordage and planks. Voices rose above the wind, issuing commands to protect the boat and make the most of the gusts. Sails once unfurled were reefed. The boat moved with a new lease of life, slicing through the waves. Somewhere nearby on deck, a crewman's cry could be heard praying earnestly, a *du'a* upon his lips as the winds blew harder, *"Oh Allah! We seek from You the good of this wind and the good of what it has been commanded ..."*

"Subhana'Allah," uttered Tarif after he caught his breath on the cusp of the levanter. The sea had changed now, rolling as the wind decorated the waves with white crests. He smiled to himself, as his face lit up with satisfaction. It wouldn't be too long now till they reached the island. As the boat rose and fell over the choppy waters, they finally drew close to the landfall they sought.

They followed the island around, away from the great white waves of the Atlantic Ocean that broke crushingly over its shores. Instead, they sought the waters of the Mediterranean Sea on the other side of the island that lay by contrast like a brilliantly blue millpond. As they approached land, oars were run out and the boats were brought into shoal waters for easy beaching.

A boarding ladder was secured over the side of the boat. Tarif eased himself over the bulwark and touched down with a splash into the water. Some of the younger men, eager to disembark, vaulted impatiently over the bow of the boat landing on the sand. Restless feet relished the feel of the firm earth beneath them, glad to be ashore once more. Conscious of their mission, heavy footfalls sank into the glorious white sands. The beach lay littered with colourful treasures brought up from the sea, basking under the hot Iberian sun. The island was a beautiful paradise of dense emerald-green foliage and tall trees, but Tarif wasn't taken in by all of its apparent beauty and innocence. Danger could yet lurk in this most perfect paradise.

"Mind how you go and secure the beach!" ordered Tarif Ibn Malik as his men fanned out across the sands, scouring for any danger. Once satisfied that there was no imminent threat to his troops, Tarif soon ordered the rest of his men off the boats.

"We'll not be staying long here," he warned.

"Recover from the voyage as you will and take care not to be seen – but move on we shall, *insha'Allah*. It's the mainland we seek!" said Tarif pointing to the coastline of Andalus just a short distance away from the island.

*"It's the mainland we seek!" said Tarif pointing
to the coastline of Andalus*

If there was time, thought Tarif, on their return they would explore the stores of the island Jacob had spoken of. There was much to be learned here too. But right now, he was keen that they remained unseen by those on the mainland, or even the garrison at Julia Loza, ahead of their arrival. For in his mind, it was the garrison he had firmly set his sights on.

As Tarif's men rested, the sun soon reached its zenith in the clear blue sky above. They made ablution in some nearby swelling springs and performed their *dhuhr* prayers. Soon after, they returned to their boats and sailed towards the mainland, just within sight of the island.

The boat carved a smooth path until it finally came to rest outside the sand reef. The lush green land that swathed Andalus loomed before them. As Tarif's eyes roved over the shingle beach and the cedar trees beyond, he wondered warily what they would find after setting foot on this new land. Was it a land of desolate inhabitants and woe, as Ilyan would have them believe – or were they walking into a perilous trap?

5

A PEASANT'S TALE
OF WOE

"**W**E'VE not seen anyone since we left the beach – you don't think that strange, *Sayyid*?" asked Humayun, throwing Tarif Ibn Malik a puzzled look.

He rode his horse clutching the bridle tight with one hand. The other was just pushing back a low branch that scratched at his head. They had not long left their boats behind under a careful anchor watch of a few men who stood on the bows guarding the flotilla. Tarif and his men had quickly stepped from the shingle and moved inland through the dense woods.

"I expect they saw us coming when we were still out at sea," replied Tarif as he reined in his horse. His handsome chestnut Barb responded, coming to a halt. It soon began snuffling eagerly among the dead pine needles that littered the ground.

Tarif looked about him curiously, taking in the scenery. There was a mountain of green on either side of him. Mixed with it was a palette of rich, colourful, wildflowers. There were tulips and indigenous irises that could be found nowhere else but in Iberia. Overhead, patrolling high in the sky was a honey buzzard. It circled about, then suddenly swooped low to claim its prey.

Andalus was every bit as beautiful as Ilyan had described it. All around, Tarif's men now traversed through the pine trees and oak woodlands. Some were on foot, leaning on their spears from time to time, while others rode on horseback. Jacob had called this place Mellaria, home to an old Roman settlement, long since deserted. He was amongst those on foot now, following close behind, when he overheard Humayun. Jacob wasn't in the least bit surprised and suspected much the same as Tarif did.

"The peasants are as meek as mice!" he said wiping away the sweat from his brow with the back of his hand. Beads had broken out over his forehead like a rash as the heat of the day was rising fast.

"Hiding comes second nature when you live in these parts. They're no strangers to raids and attacks – you can be sure they've gone to ground somewhere. You're as much a threat to them as any raider or encounter with Visigoth troops!" said Jacob with a quick glance at Tarif and his men.

Tarif was sitting astride his horse and both he and his men cut an impressive sight. It left no doubt in Jacob's mind that the serfs had fled at the very sight of them.

"We're not here to harm the peasants – it is forbidden – it's not our way!" said Tarif firmly.

"Well, they don't know that!" laughed Jacob.

Tarif expected as much. All the same, he wasn't prepared to overlook the fact that a peasant could all too easily reveal their presence to the Visigoth soldiers, whatever Jacob might say. The temptation of a reward for the poor could lend them courage to seek out the Goths. Tarif's eyes looked upon his cavalry ahead as they spaced themselves out in front, meandering through the trees. Amongst them Tarif spotted two of his best men who were scouts.

"Abdullah! Mustafa!" shouted Tarif, summoning them both to attention.

Hearing his call, the pair quickly detached from the rest of the men. Abdullah was the first to haul his battle horse round on its haunches and Mustafa followed closely behind him. Before long they drew up beside Tarif.

Beneath his thick eyebrows, Abdullah's keen eyes searched his face questioningly. Abdullah was a stocky man with the build of an ox. He wore a hooded burnous that rested upon his broad shoulders and draped down his back, over which he had slung his longbow. Mustafa was a tall, burly man, his head covered by a simple winding cloth twisted about it. Both men were armed with broad swords, their straight blades blinking under the sun.

"Go ahead of us and locate the garrison," instructed Tarif as they both listened attentively. "Observe the militia's movements and find out what you can about them. We don't want to walk into an ambush – understood?"

They nodded, knowing what was at stake. The success of their mission depended upon them and Tarif had confidence in his scouts' resourcefulness and skills. They were both excellent swordsmen, with swift reflexes that allowed them to move with blinding speed. Together they had outwitted many an opponent in their time. Both men were confident in their own abilities as well as the other's. Between the two of them, they were a force to be reckoned with. At any sign of trouble ahead, Abdullah and Mustafa could be relied upon to warn them.

"Leave it to us, *Sayyid* – we'll find the garrison," said Abdullah, lifting his chin.

"You can depend on us, *insha'Allah*," said Mustafa, adding his own show of support.

"But the peasants aren't loyal," persisted Jacob, stepping forward to stand in front of Tarif's horse. "They're not likely to warn anyone up at the garrison."

"That may well be, Ya'qub – but that's not to say that soldiers or spies haven't been posted by the Goths themselves to keep an eye on the shores," pointed out Tarif, brushing aside Jacob's assurances and trying to shift the focus away from the peasants.

Tarif was yet to formulate his own opinion about the local serfs. Until they crossed paths with some of them and he witnessed their reception through his own eyes, Tarif was inclined to reserve all judgment about them. Although in his heart, he sincerely hoped that they wouldn't meet any along the way. Besides, he also had to consider the possibility of lookouts along the shore as a genuine threat. Meeting the Goths was simply a matter of time.

"For all we know the king's lookouts may already be halfway to the garrison as we speak, with a head start over us!" added Humayun.

"Precisely!" agreed Tarif, his lips forming a grim line. "We have to be ready for all possible outcomes!" Although, if the truth be known, Tarif's instincts told him that the Goths were still blissfully unaware of their arrival on their shores, for now at least.

Jacob swallowed hard as he suddenly paled. Tarif was right. He had forgotten all about the lookouts. He could imagine nothing worse than being discovered and overcome by the Goths and for him to be found amongst Tarif's men.

"Ya'qub, how far is the garrison from here?" asked Tarif suddenly.

"Not far – especially on horse," replied Jacob.

"Good – give my men the directions they need so they can be on their way!"

The scouts slipped off their horses and gathered around Jacob.

"Don't go holding anything back boy!" warned Abdullah playfully. "Or else Mustafa here will go after your share of the rations if he finds that you sent us on a wild goose chase!"

Jacob grinned, not in the least bit intimidated by the burly scouts. This strange journey had thrown them together in each other's company. The scouts had been the ones instructed to take him to Tangiers from Qayrawan to join Tarif's reconnaissance mission. Jacob had come to know and like them well, as they did him in return. The scouts lowered themselves to the ground, each on one knee, and listened attentively. Jacob described the route they should take, using a makeshift map which he scratched on the earth with a stick.

Shortly after, Abdullah and Mustafa nodded their heads, satisfied with his directions. They remounted their horses and then with a sharp click of the tongue and dig of their heels they were off, urging their horses forward. Leaving their party behind, the scouts soon disappeared into the thick woods and undergrowth that closed about them.

Tarif scuffed away all traces of the map on the ground. Then he and his men continued to move on through the woodland at an even pace. With eyes peeled in their new surroundings, their ears picked out every sound that revealed itself, from the sigh of the wind to the crack of a twig. They continued along their route for another hour until the shadows began to lengthen and the sun lost its brilliance, as it began its descent in the sky. The summer days were long, and it was still some hours until sunset.

The men briefly stopped to rest and pray their *asr salat*. They took turns, as a group stood by on guard whilst the other purified themselves making *wudu* from a nearby cool spring.

The *muadhin's* deep voice called the *adhan* which carried in the air around the men. Then the troop fell into hushed lines behind Tarif's lead. In front of him was a spear he had staked to the ground as a *sutra*. They all faced the direction of that far distant sacred land, the Holy City of Makkah, home of the Kaaba. Humayun's strong voice rose as he recited the *iqamah*, a little faster, as is the *sunnah*, than the *adhan* – "*hasten to the prayer... hasten to success...*"

Jacob in the meantime stepped back to shelter under a pine tree. From there he watched the movements of the *jama'at* at a discreet distance, in a pensive mood. He liked to watch the Muslims in prayer, with its natural rhythm of standing, bowing, lowering themselves to their knees to go into prostration, then standing again in cyclic turns, sitting after the first two cycles and at the end of the prayer. No matter what they were doing, sleeping, travelling or tilling the fields, when the time came to pray, they put the world and its cares on one side and were still: to Allah they turned, as though the Last Hour was upon them.

Before, Jacob had rarely thought about prayers. He had seen his brother and foster parents pray often. Sometimes like the Goths and at other times in a strange way and in another tongue which he didn't recognise and which was different to that of the Goths. Once, when he had asked them about it as a child, silent but knowing looks had passed between his foster parents. Their eyes spoke of a fear that their lips dare not confess. Later, as he grew older, they finally talked about the prayers which they were too scared to share outside the walls of their home for fear of the Goths. Yet now, never was Jacob's curiosity more roused than by the way Tarif and his men prayed so diligently five times a day.

The prayer came to an end as Tarif Ibn Malik turned his head from right to left, his men following behind him together with the same movements. Tarif then raised both his hands in supplication, making *du'a*. At the close, he wiped his hands over his face and ran them down his short thick beard and on to his chest over his heart.

Before long they resumed their journey, once more slipping in and out between the tall trees. They soon arrived on the outskirts of what appeared to be a small, deserted settlement. To pass through it would be the quickest and most direct route to take.

"Be on your guard!" instructed Tarif, his eyes moving shrewdly over the smokeless holes that served for chimneys. Steeling themselves for an ambush, they cautiously approached the seemingly abandoned grey sprawl of homes. The dwellings stood on walls made of mud, clay and straw, covered with thatched roofs. Tarif wasn't concerned, confident that Abdullah and Mustafa must have passed by the settlement already.

If the settlement had been occupied, or at any sign of trouble here, they would have already got wind of it by now – of that he was certain. Still, for anyone else it might have been all too easy a thing to become complacent, but not Tarif. He chose to act with due caution – better to be on the safe side, he mused.

His men fanned out to search the sleepy settlement. They weaved their way in and out from house to house, finding that they had been reduced to nothing more than empty shells, devoid of their owners. Tarif's men were ready at a moment's notice to raise the alarm and forewarn of any awaiting hidden plot to attack. It didn't take long to discover that the peasants had chosen flight rather than to make a stand and meet them with an armed reception (which was the last thing they wanted). For Tarif, this was the first positive sign.

Fires had been doused to cinders, with the cooking pots left over them still filled with their unserved contents. The smell of wood, smoke and stews, made of legumes or a porridge the peasants called *pulte* mingled in the air. It was made from coarsely ground wheat to which mashed legumes had been added, producing a hearty, earthy aroma that lingered. The occasional game was found still skewered and hung over a once lit fire, still oozing occasionally with drippings of fat.

Figs, pears and sliced pomegranates lay abandoned on plates. Doors had been left thrown wide open, creaking and moaning as they swung on their hinges in the breeze. The peasants had certainly left in a hurry.

"Clear!" shouted a soldier.

"Clear on this side too!" came confirmation from every direction around them.

"There's nobody here, *Sayyid* – only geese, goats and sheep," confirmed Humayun as he drew his horse beside Tarif's.

Tarif nodded with a look of relief.

"Let's keep going. We only have a couple of hours of daylight left and I want to reach the garrison before nightfall *insha'Allah*," he said as he glanced at the sky above.

Humayun nodded, his eyes bright with satisfaction. He couldn't have been more pleased by the ease with which they had reached thus far and without incident. He was about to say so to Tarif when he suddenly froze at the sound of a disturbance. Hands flew to the hilts of swords as Tarif, Humayun and a few nearby soldiers moved stealthily to the ready.

At the edge of the woods came the sound of chattering voices accompanied by the distinct noise of snapping twigs that grew louder and louder as the strangers approached. Suddenly shadows stretched along the ground as two Iberian figures emerged from behind the pine trees.

A pair of round childish eyes peeped out from over a pile of firewood cradled in scrawny arms. His companion, an apple-cheeked boy, just a few years older, carried his prized game proudly slung over his shoulders. It was a rabbit he had trapped and caught earlier in the day. At the sight of Tarif's men their jaws dropped, their chores quickly forgotten. The firewood which the youngest boy had been carrying cascaded to the ground. He squeaked in fright and flew to hide behind the elder boy who was no less timorous than he.

"Stay your blades!" roared a voice suddenly breaking the silence. "It's alright – it's just boys!" continued the voice, at which shoulders sunk back gratefully.

"Where's Ya'qub – find Ya'qub and bring him here, quickly!" commanded Tarif urgently as he looked about him at his men. Jacob wasn't far. His hand shot up in the air as he rushed forward, materialising out of the sea of faces.

"Here – I'm here!" came his breathless reply.

"We're strangers to them but you are familiar," said Tarif gesturing kindly towards the two boys huddled together. "Tell them we mean no harm and send them on their away!"

"And tell them to inform their families to keep away for the time being – it will be safer for them. I have a feeling these young'uns will know where to find them." Tarif smiled as his hand slipped inside a saddle bag that was slung over his horse. Within moments he produced a succulent orange. Smiling, he tossed it to the elder of the two boys, who caught it deftly in the palms of his hands and surprised, broke into a smile. Tarif turned his horse and rode away. His men followed suit and quickly dispersed, leaving a bewildered Jacob behind to tend to the young boys.

Jacob passed on Tarif's words of advice to the awed pair. Too dumfounded to say anything, the boys simply nodded. Then within the blink of an eye, the pair scampered away and disappeared amongst the pine trees.

Humayun dismounted. Leading his horse Shabhah by the reins, he came to stand beside Jacob just in time to see the boys disappear into the wood.

"What is it? – you look troubled," asked Humayun glancing at Jacob as he stood pensively, wrapped in his thoughts. Jacob turned to look at Humayun curiously.

"It's nothing – I'm just surprised that's all. I'm

glad you let them go back to their families," said Jacob frankly, "but why did you do it?"

"Because the Prophet, blessings and peace be upon him, forbade us from harming the inno-cent," said Humayun firmly. "Women, children and the old alike, and even men who do not fight," he continued as he held out a shiny red apple for Shabhah, while his other hand gently stroked her muzzle.

"You're not worried they'll go to the Goths?" asked Jacob.

"No, if they reveal us to the Goths we can only hope to be long gone before they take any action to seek us out," replied Humayun.

Jacob digested this piece of information silently for a moment.

"The Goths wouldn't have been so merciful!" said Jacob slowly.

"Then it's just as well the boys found us, *alhamdulillah*, and *not* the Goths when they wan-dered back to the settlement," said Humayun gravely, although his eyes were alight with amuse-ment.

Jacob smiled and nodded his head. He had to agree. It seemed like not a day passed by when he didn't learn something new about the Muslims that left him surprised or speechless with wonder. Their ways were so different from those of the Visigoths. Jacob had grown to like Humayun for his sense of humour and gracious manners. He was easy to talk to, maybe more so because of their closeness in age.

Jacob ran his hand thoughtfully over the back

of Shabhah's neck, smoothing out her velvety grey coat. To see the young Iberian boys run away had affected him so, more than Humayun could possibly realise.

"You know, I was five years old when the Goths took me and my brother away from our parents," revealed Jacob suddenly. Humayun looked up sharply, Shabhah forgotten for a moment. His attention fixed on Jacob seriously. He was still busy making a fuss over Shabhah, but there was no mistaking the pain in Jacob's voice, or the anger that smouldered behind his eyes.

"Why were you taken?" asked Humayun quietly.

"There was a revolt being planned – back then – against King Egica," explained Jacob. "But before it could be carried out, it was discovered.

"I still remember it as though it happened yesterday," he continued, his eyes on the horse but his mind far away.

"The Goth soldiers burst into our home one morning. They took my brother and me to be raised as Visigoths, but as for my parents – they were enslaved for their role in the plot."

For the most part, Jacob's childhood memories were hazy except for this one lucid memory that stuck in his mind: the deafening sound of splintering wood as the front door flew wide open; a table violently overturned, pans and plates clattering as they fell against the hard flagstone floor – all around earthen pots lying shattered to pieces; the piercing screams of his mother and defiant shouts of his father echoing out from behind a shield of crimson knuckles; the vision of scarlet cloaked soldiers, swooping all around him like ravaging flames. Jacob's home, once a safe haven, now long since gone, still haunted his memories.

"Where are your parents now?" asked Humayun, although he had his suspicions how the story would end.

"I don't know," said Jacob simply shrugging his shoulders. "Never saw 'em again after that day."

Incensed by the revolt, King Egica had been determined to punish. Once his parents were discovered by the Goths to be Jews, their property was seized and confiscated. They themselves were taken away and condemned to a bitter life of slavery.

"I have my brother at least. The Goths didn't achieve all that they set out to do that day!" continued Jacob almost proudly.

"What do you mean?" asked Humayun.

Jacob broke into an impish grin.

"*We* escaped!" he said triumphantly. "The Goths got careless on the journey to the monastery – at least that's where I think they were taking us. They didn't tie us up properly. After dusk came, they soon fell into a deep slumber. My brother managed to wriggle his wrists out of the ropes and untie his feet. Then he set about untying me," grinned Jacob, still reeling from the memory of their escape. The young captives had got the better of the Goth soldiers whilst they were fast asleep.

His brother untethered their captors' horses and released them into the open, so the Goths couldn't pursue them. Jacob and his brother had fled. For days they had wandered through the woods until their foster parents found them. They were simple serfs, a childless couple who recognised the boys to be from among their own people. Jacob and his brother soon found a new home with them. Humayun was about to ask more about Jacob's life, but the words died on his lips. There was a loud thundering clap of hooves that drew everyone's attention. Approaching at a full gallop, were the scouts on their horses whose long manes could be seen flowing back in the wind by their break-neck speed.

Humayun swung round to see Abdullah and Mustafa's return. The scouts were certainly kicking up a cloud of red dust in their wake. The distance closed and they soon rode up beside Tarif Ibn Malik, leaning forward eagerly in their saddles while their horses recovered from their wild gallop, puffing and grunting as they flicked their tails in the air. Humayun and Jacob could hear their triumphant voices ringing out.

"We found the garrison at Julia Loza!" Abdullah said, smiling broadly.

"It's not very far from here, just beyond that hill we came down from," added Mustafa. His eyes twinkled with delight. "They don't know we're here yet – the Goth are sloth!"

Far from satisfied, Tarif narrowed his eyes. But for how much longer, he wondered? It was getting late in the day and he needed to see the garrison before dark. He had to see for himself what they were up against.

"Come on everyone, let's move on!" ordered Tarif eagerly.

Waved forward by the scouts, Tarif Ibn Malik and his men quickly left the settlement. They crested a low hill and saw a rich valley spread out before them on the other side. Fortunately for them, the cover of the trees that studded the hills offered protection for Tarif and his men, who could remain unseen from any prying eyes.

Julia Loza had once been an old Roman settlement. Now it was a small, enclosed town that stood to no particular plan. It contained only whitewashed houses, warehouses and an olive press that had been built on a chosen spot of land at the will of its owners. Tarif listened intently, as Mustafa and Abdullah described the garrison that was stationed at the edge of the town while they rode.

As the sun dipped towards the hills, long shadows stretched across the valley like dark strips of sooty rags smudging the earth. Soon Tarif left his men behind with strict instructions at a carefully chosen concealed campsite, their horses tethered to the old oak trees.

"Post sentries to keep watch," he ordered his men, determined to stay hidden. "Remember no campfires, or lamps to be lit and whatever you do keep the horses quiet!"

It was the middle of the lunar month and he was confident in the knowledge that as the evening drew in, the moonlight would suffice. Led by the scouts, Tarif and Humayun then continued on foot along a steep, rough trodden path on the side of a hill, mostly used by goat herders. As Julia Loza came into view, they dropped to the ground. Laying on their bellies, they wormed their way forward, making their way towards the ridge.

Looking over they soon saw a purple valley below. Their eyes rested on the town, taking in the location of the houses and every twist and turn of its warren of alleys. Finally, they managed to carefully observe the position of the fortified garrison. They noted every detail about it that they were able to, before it was swallowed up by the darkness.

Tarif Ibn Malik could see its battlements silhouetted against the rose gold sky. Stationed on them were Visigoth soldiers preparing for the night watch. Blessed with keen eyes, sharp over distance, he watched them with great interest, not wishing to miss a single detail. From judging their weapons to estimating their physical strength, he knew that anything he saw on this trip could be useful in the days and months ahead. Beside him he could hear Mustafa and Abdullah stirring. With lowered voices they both recounted their findings from earlier in the day. They described the guards' movements and routines, and the frequency with which they went about their regular rounds.

"They take turns guarding, but mostly they police the town," said Mustafa.

"And what about their numbers?" asked Tarif.

"It's small. Maybe three hundred or so men," replied Abdullah.

Once the night fell, flamed sconces began to glow gently along the garrison's stone walls. It was a reminder that it was too late in the day to do anything else now but camp. Tarif ordered Mustafa and Abdullah to stay put and keep watch through the night. In a dark valley, it was easy for enemies to move through or hide in its shadows. He then signalled to Humayun and they quietly slipped away to return to their camp. At his orders, Tarif and his men took turns resting beneath the cover of the night, overlooked only by a bright silvery moon. They waited for the dawn to approach, when the white thread of light appears distinct from the black thread of the dark night sky. Until then his men needed to conserve all their energy.

Tarif knew what the morrow might bring, for a garrison like the one in the valley below was sure to have its own scouts and lookouts. So as the first signs of light emerged, they soon stirred to offer their *fajr* prayers. As always when in a military situation, they took turns in two groups. While one prayed the other stood watch over them. When the sun finally rose and lit up the sky, while the words of their morning *dhikr* still lay fresh upon their lips, a sudden flash of movement between the trees alerted Tarif. His scouts had returned with news.

"*Sayyid*, there's a small troop of Goths coming this way!" shouted Abdullah, a meaningful urgency in his voice. Tarif nodded and quickly mobilised his men. All eyes looked towards the woods.

The sudden alarmed flight of birds and voices from between the trees signalled the closing

Their eyes rested on the town

proximity of their enemy. Then they appeared. Grizzly men in dark woollen cloaks, their hands clutched swords and peculiar coffin-shaped shields. They wore Gothic tunics with hems trimmed with fur bands. Their long golden or tawny manes fell unruly over their shoulders on either side. They looked like wild barbary lions.

Hard eyes stared back at Tarif's troop from behind a ragged shield wall; their hands itching at the hilts of their swords. Tarif and his men braced for the attack. A shrill battle cry broke out. Arrows whipped through the air and the silence between the two unwavering sides was broken.

6

THE WITNESS

THE Goths lunged forward wielding their weapons. Jacob was standing behind Tarif's men. His blood ran cold at the sight of the grisly Goths. In an instant, his instincts rose to survive. As Tarif's men advanced, Jacob lingered back. Just a few feet away from him there stood a mighty oak, its branches reaching upwards towards the sky. He had slept beneath its canopy during the night.

Jacob had climbed trees all his life. He pulled himself up by a low branch and swiftly began his ascent, between fits of ragged breath. He looked down for a moment. Panic seized him by the throat and he gasped. He had been seen. Below stood a Goth soldier drawing back the creaking string of his bow, his arrow notched. Then came a whipping sound, followed by the ominous crack of splintering wood. Narrowly missing his ankle, the arrow thunked into the bark and juddered.

Jacob swallowed hard. Spurred on by the will to survive (for he wasn't ready to die – not just yet) he kept moving. His heart hammered in his chest as he climbed higher and higher. Suddenly his arm grabbed a loose branch that gave way cracking ominously beneath his grip. He slipped and lost his footing. About to tumble perilously to the ground, he flailed his arms wildly to stop his fall. Managing to grasp onto another branch just below, he hovered in the air for a moment, teetering. Too afraid to take a breath, he reached out with his free arm and grabbed on to the trunk, easing himself up. It was a narrow escape. He carried on climbing, until the dense foliage cocooned him out of sight.

Sitting on a thick oak bough with his legs hanging limply on either side, Jacob's head fell back against the trunk. His chest heaved up and down painfully as he battled to regain his breath. Down below, a bitter skirmish was playing out to the sound of a deafening din.

Swords clashed. Shields collided. All around him it seemed, Jacob could hear shrill whinnying and the shriek of battle horses. Some reared upwards on their hind legs, or else struck powerful blows from their kicks whilst others trampled over the earth as men swarmed around them like angry ants. The soldiers fought in close combat with what sounded like the ferocity of lions, grunting and growling.

In the thick of it all, Jacob suddenly caught sight of Tarif, Humayun and the scouts. They were all nearby amongst the cavalry, high on their horses. Their swords flashing and scintillating through the air in a display of deadly strikes, swinging down hard from left to right and right to left in sweeping arcs. They had the advantage. The bulk of the Visigoth troops were infantry soldiers. Only few from amongst them, mostly nobles, came out on horseback. They moved slowly, burdened by their heavier breastplates, swords and battle axes.

Tarif's foot soldiers did much to hold back the battle line of the Goths, but it was his cavalry that wrought havoc upon them from their elevated positions. It was easier to defend from the top of a horse than to stand on the ground and face a half-ton battle horse carrying an armed man looming high above.

Jacob watched with widened eyes, numbed by the chaos around him. He could see Humayun as he swung his horse in hard and blocked the path of a Goth soldier as he homed in to strike. All around, men fought feverishly. Suddenly Jacob caught a movement in the corner of his eye. He gasped as he saw the ugly glint of a spearhead draw back, ready to be thrust into the air by yet another Goth. Humayun had unwittingly placed himself in the path of the spear when he had intercepted the previous Goth soldier. Realising Humayun to be in grave danger, Jacob reacted in an instant.

"*HUMAYUN – LOOK OUT!*" he shouted at the top of his lungs.

His voice carried over the sound of the skirmish raging below. Whether Humayun heard him, or some inner instinct roused him to the impending threat, his eyes flew in the direction of the Goth soldier. Just as the gleaming spear was loosed from the enemy's hands, Humayun hauled his horse

His heart hammered in his chest as he climbed higher and higher

round on its haunches. His shield swung out and cut short the path of the spearhead.

Jacob held his breath, but as Humayun escaped miraculously unscathed, he expelled the air from his lungs, giving way to the heady feeling of relief as it washed over him. He admired Humayun for his courage and chivalry. Never had Humayun mistreated him – not even once. In return, Jacob could no more wish to see him (or for that matter any of Tarif's men) come to any harm.

How long they fought he couldn't say, but Jacob remained still in his high vantage point. Nestled away in the safety of the tree, he waited out of sight. Some time passed until the noise of the storm and strife that had swirled about him finally died down. Shouts were silenced. The aimless volleys of whirring arrows ceased and the abandoned Visigoth spears stood still, staked to the ground. Some of their owners sat alongside them, hunched in defeat, faces in hands, shaking their heads in disappointment. Jacob soon realised that most of the Visigoths, with the sudden shock of being overcome by Tarif's superior forces, had abandoned their weapons and fled without look-ing back. Victory in this skirmish lay firmly at the feet of Tarif's men.

Jacob watched eagerly as Tarif Ibn Malik ordered his men to tend to their injured and gather the captives together.

"Be careful, their wounds might harm them yet!" warned Tarif, but to his relief he soon learned that only a few of his men had been injured, none seriously, only a handful who had received nothing more than cuts and bruises. Knowing full well the gravity of abandoning the battlefield, his men had stood their ground, unlike those on the other side. Miraculously the clash had been short and had looked far worse than it really was. Amazingly, there was no loss of life on either side; mostly because many of the Goths had quickly disbanded and taken off in fright.

After a time, Jacob felt a numbing calm steal over him. Somewhere between a cluster of leaves below he heard a familiar voice call out to him.

"Ya'qub! Are you coming down, or do you plan to stay up there till dusk?" shouted Humayun. He grinned, the whites of his teeth showing as he reined in his horse below the great oak tree. Humayun squinted up through the branches at the sun as it beat down upon him. He could make out Jacob's scrawny shape hidden amongst its foliage. Even after the skirmish had ended Jacob had remained where he was, too stunned to do anything, but Humayun's call jolted him back to his senses.

Unsteadily at first, he clambered down the tree, his eyes never leaving the Visigoth soldiers for a moment. Some critical part of his mind couldn't quite believe that the Goths could be defeated. Yet there they were brought to surrender, looking forlorn with weeping wounds. Not even the town's folk of Julia Loza came out to their aid, nor did they care to show pity for the Goths' defeat, so despised were they by the townspeople.

Word had quickly spread like the wind. The arrival of Tarif's troops and the ensuing confrontation that was taking place outside their town was on everyone's lips. Still the peasants stayed put in their homes. Locked away behind closed doors they kept watch, peeping out from the other side of their shuttered windows. They had determined their position (saying, 'it's naught to do with us').

Only a handful of inquisitive youths ventured out to peer from behind walls, corners or hide behind trees, eager to gather some morsel of news. When the skirmish had finally finished, they too couldn't believe the Goths were defeated. The townsfolk finally emerged from their hideouts. With the curious relief and realisation that they themselves were not under threat, they welcomed Tarif's men without any cause for fear. Offering them food for nourishment and reward, they greeted the newcomers warmly.

Having achieved their objectives, Tarif and his men left the garrison town behind, prisoners in tow. They made light of the return journey, as they now knew their way back. Before long they found themselves standing on the shingle beach once again, where their boats had been moored the whole time, awaiting their return.

"Round up the prisoners, quickly!" ordered Tarif Ibn Malik as he watched the *maraqibs* on the water slew to one side at the hands of the prevailing wind. It was past midday. In the distance the shores of North Africa beckoned – and he was eager for the boats to be getting underway.

"You call 'em handsome? *Subhana'Allah* Mustafa, they're the filthiest creatures I've ever seen!" complained Abdullah pinching his nose with disdain at the olfactory assault. He was busy manoeuvring a prisoner into place behind a small line of defeated Visigoth soldiers who hadn't managed to escape. As Abdullah prodded him ahead to join the line, he caught another whiff of sour sweat, only this time Abdullah recoiled and gagged.

The prisoners were stood, shackled and scowling, some revealing their crooked and mottled teeth as they waited on the shingle beach ready to board the *maraqibs*. Their wounds had been tended to and one or two had had their clothing replaced if torn or too badly soiled from the skirmish.

Tarif's men were taking a lead from the Prophet Muhammad's example, when after the battle of Badr, he had ordered the Muslims to treat their prisoners well. A companion, Jabir, once described how al-Abbas, who did not have a shirt on, was taken prisoner. The Prophet looked for a shirt for him. It turned out that a shirt of Abdullah Ibn Ubayy was the right size, so the Prophet gave it to al-Abbas to wear, and compensated Abdullah Ibn Ubayy with his own shirt.

A crisp, salty air drifted in from the sea and mingled with the heavy scent of perfumed oil worn by Tarif's men that lingered in the air like the sweetest of nectar. However, they did little to mask the smell of the Goths.

Even for Jacob their appearance came as an

unpleasant shock, not to mention a revelation. It had been months since he had last set eyes upon a Visigoth soldier and somehow, he couldn't remember ever being as repulsed by their repugnant malodour as he was now. It struck Jacob that living amongst the Muslims and adopting their wholesome regime of cleanliness made his nasal functions appreciate what he had not been able to appreciate before. Quite simply, the Goths reeked. More sobering was the thought that he himself probably did too a year ago!

He looked at their grim faces now. Never had he been more terrified in the whole of his life as he had been at dawn when they attacked. Nor in his wildest dreams had Jacob imagined that he would see the Visigoths defeated so completely.

As Jacob stood on the beach now, he watched with dispassionate eyes as the few Visigoth captives were led away by Tarif's men and taken on board one of the *maraqibs*. Along with them went sacks and small caskets of booty made up of coins and precious objects that had all fallen into their hands. The Goths had been on their way to a repository in the neighbouring town of Carteia to deliver to their treasury.

They had been oblivious to the fact that Tarif's troops lay camped on the hill above. No sooner had the Goths stumbled upon them, than they had attacked Tarif Ibn Malik and his men, fearing an ambush by a band of robbers. Little did they realise, until it was too late, that they had encountered a force that was far greater and better equipped than their own.

Jacob continued to watch, his eyes fixed on the prisoners with mounting interest until Humayun joined beside him. After a few moments silence Jacob turned his head to look at Tarif Ibn Malik's second in command. He stood quietly with pensive eyes as though contemplating the captured men, but Jacob wasn't fooled. He knew what was to come. His work was done – and his services were no longer needed. In the next moment, Humayun's carefully chosen words proved he was right.

"You've upheld your end of the bargain by taking us to the Goths," he said, finally breaking the silence between them as he turned to look at Jacob. "So now it is our turn. You are free to go – so go back to your home, my friend," he said warmly.

Nearby, now busy shifting a small wooden casket of gold coins were Mustafa and Abdullah. As Humayun's words reached their ears, Mustafa stopped suddenly and caught Abdullah's eyes. The scouts had grown fond of the young Iberian since he had joined their crew, just as much as Jacob had grown fond of them. The lad had shown mettle, and both men would be sorry to see him go.

Thrown together as they had been since Qayrawan, the scouts had been the ones to bring Jacob to Tangiers. As such, they had spent much time sitting around campfires with him. Jacob had listened to their life of adventures and their travels to the battles they had fought together in far flung lands. But a promise was a promise.

Jacob's heart sank as he turned back to look at the Goths, his eyes weary. The prospect of gaining his freedom didn't fill Jacob with as much joy as he once thought it might. Humayun studied the young man's face with surprise. He had not missed his downcast expression, nor the light now gone from his eyes.

"What is it? – I should have thought you'd be pleased," asked Humayun, lifting an eyebrow with surprise. "I was expecting to see the back of you disappearing through those trees, desperate to be rid of us and to be with your family."

A ghost of a smile flitted across Jacob's face. If only that were true, he thought. Suddenly in that moment, it came to him. He knew what he really wanted. In fact, if he was honest with himself, he had known it for some time now. He spun round to face Humayun squarely.

"Take me back – I want to go back with you all!" pleaded Jacob. Humayun looked at him astonished.

"I don't understand – what about your brother, your home?" asked Humayun surprised by Jacob's request. "Don't you want to be with them again?"

"*Don't you see* – there's nothing here for me," replied Jacob, throwing his hands helplessly out and around him. "This *isn't* my home. It is only a place of misery for both my brother and me," continued Jacob in a desperate bid to make his case before Humayun. He was eager for him to understand. "I can't help or protect my brother while we live here, but there's a chance for me – for both of us across the Straits. I can help him from there, but also..." Jacob paused for a moment; his eyes fixed on Humayun's face.

"There's something else – something more important than that, which is why you have to take me back…"

"What do you mean?" asked Humayun, his forehead furrowing.

"Would you abandon your brother amongst wolves?" asked Jacob.

Humayun stiffened.

"Never!" he said. Humayun's eyes widened, with a growing realisation kindling in their depths.

Living amongst the Muslims, not a day seemed to have gone by that Jacob had not witnessed amongst the Berbers eager souls who came forward to do what he was about to do. Just a few simple words, nothing more, but an affirmation that awakened their hearts and souls from slumber and transformed their lives into ones full of purpose and meaning.

Jacob opened his mouth and took a breath, as deep as a newborn baby when it draws its first breath of life. Then he uttered the words that he had heard time and time again over the past months:

"I bear witness that there is no god except Allah, and I bear witness that Muhammad is the Messenger of Allah."

Humayun's eyes looked probingly into the young Iberian's face as he listened to the familiar words of the *shahada* effortlessly pass over his tongue. Then there followed a moment of stunned silence, broken only by the sounds of the faint rolling sea and the gulls cawing high above their heads.

"Do you say this because you fear we'll not take you back with us? You should know, even had you not said the *shahada* – I would have promised you safe passage over the Straits," said Humayun. He was torn between the joy of hearing the *shahada* uttered from the Iberian's lips; at the same time, he needed Jacob to know they would still be willing to help him, even if he had not embraced Islam. There could be no compulsion to enter the *deen*.

"I know," said Jacob, quickly holding up his hand to prevent Humayun from saying anything more. "I've known you all too long to know that when you give your word you honour it. You speak the truth and give alms to those who are in need of it," smiled Jacob. "But all the same, *akhi* – I'd sooner leave these shores as your brother than anything else," said Jacob firmly, for *iman* had entered his heart – and only Allah guides whom he wills.

"From now on, I'll call myself Ya'qub, as you've all been calling me these past months," affirmed Ya'qub decisively.

A sudden loud crash and jingle of coins from a casket falling to earth, followed by a blast of laughter, caught Ya'qub's ear. Before he could think or say anything more, he was mobbed by the two scouts. Abdullah locked his burly arms about him and hoisted him up off the ground and into the air, whilst Mustafa stood beside him, face beaming, rejoicing with the words of *takbir* that sprang from his lips in glee.

"What took you so long, *akhi*?" asked Mustafa. Ya'qub, by now returned to solid ground, stood looking up at Abdullah's towering form, his face wreathed in smiles.

"Didn't I say it would end so – *insha'Allah*," said Abdullah heartily nudging his great big elbow into Mustafa's ribs. Ya'qub returned a questioning smile.

"I don't understand – how could you know that?"

"I knew it – *subhana'Allah* – back at the settlement. None of us had eaten for hours. But *you* could have eaten the food – the game roasting over the fire. I saw the hunger in your eyes the same as any man. You reached out for it but then you stopped – and I wondered why. I couldn't help but hope it would end this way, *subhana'Allah*!"

Ya'qub looked surprised. He had never realised that anyone had seen his dilemma. He couldn't understand his own feelings back then, but now he understood. For all the familiarity of his old life around him, he had felt different ever since they had landed ashore. He had changed. Even in his old peasant clothes which he now wore, washed and darned, he felt uncomfortable and out of place. He missed his fine new tunic, burnous and the turban his master had given him. They had kept him cool on the hottest of days. He tried to frame his thoughts into words.

"I was hungry ..." confessed Ya'qub, his brows knit together now wondering over his own actions, "but *subhana'Allah* I couldn't do it. I couldn't bring myself to take what was not mine and eat that which had not been slaughtered in the name of Allah," explained Ya'qub. His answer earned him an approving look from Humayun, who had stood by watching, amused up until now, unable to offer his own felicitations.

"Come back to Qayrawan with us *akhi* and you can eat as much as you like," he said, welcoming Ya'qub in a warm embrace. Feeling a lump stuck in his throat, Ya'qub just nodded, too overcome with emotion.

Then from a distance, Tarif Ibn Malik's command reached their ears. The *maraqibs* were ready to move out laden with most of their men, the captives and the booty. A short time later, as Ya'qub saw the shores of Andalus recede into the distance, some intuition told him that this was only the beginning. He watched curiously as Tarif stood at the bow looking back at the coast of Andalus. A look of satisfaction slowly settled upon his face and there was determination behind his smile. This was no ordinary journey. Ya'qub had a feeling inside him that said he was standing on the brink of something momentous.

7

FORMULATING A PLAN

City of Qayrawan, 710 CE, 91 AH

A SWEET, fragrant scent percolated through the air, filling the audience room at the *Dar al-Imara*. A curious circle of men sat in deep deliberation. Among them was a wise man, a valiant soldier, a rich merchant and a humble seafarer.

"Are you saying there wasn't much resistance?" quizzed Musa, his fingers closing around a gold coin pulled from the small casket presented to him by Tarif Ibn Malik. It was a sample from the spoils brought back from their successful foray into Andalus. Musa turned the golden coin over between his fingers, examining it with great interest, imprinted as it was with the mintmarks of a citadel across the Straits.

"Only a little, *Sayyid*, nothing significant – if you would like to call it that," replied Tarif Ibn Malik. "*Alhamdulillah*, no men were lost on either side during the confrontation – only minor and superficial wounds."

He paused to pick up a drink called *nabidh*

presented to him now on a tray by a servant. Tarif
took a fortifying sip of it, remembering it had been
a favourite of the Prophet. It was a cool, sweet,
delicious drink made of dates soaked in water,
both refreshing and appetising, that soon washed
away the tiredness he felt. The long journey by
sea, then by land with rarely a meaningful break
in between had taken its toll. Yet Tarif Ibn Malik
had felt it necessary to keep pressing on in his
eagerness to quickly return to Qayrawan.

"What little resistance there was lasted for only
a short time," he gladly continued to report. "The
Goths quickly decided they were no match for us.
Most turned on their heels and fled in fright."

"*Subhana'Allah*," praised Musa raising his hands.
Nothing could have pleased him more than to
hear that his men had arrived safely back, without
realisation of the fear of loss of life in battle or
drowning in the waters of the Straits. Caliph
Al-Walid was bound to be relieved of any concerns
he may have harboured. Musa was almost certain
now that this news could only sway the Caliph
towards pursuing further campaigns into Andalus.

"And the peasants – what of the peasants?
Surely some of them came out to support the
Goths?" continued Musa, hardly able to contain
his curiosity. Tarif broke into a smile.

"Oh, they came out to meet us eventually,
Sayyid – but not armed with weapons, if that's what
you mean," revealed Tarif. "Their arms only
carried jugs of water and baskets full of fruits and
bread! For most of the time we were there, they
hid from us. They only came out after the confron-

tation was over to *greet* us – and warmly at that, *alhamdulillah*."

Tarif leaned eagerly forward on his cushioned seat.

"*Sayyid*, I think you'll find we hold an advantage over the Goths with our cavalry," he said, looking at the older man seriously. "It is what I feel secured our success that day. The Goths came out and fought on foot. And from what I could ascertain from our surveillance, their ranks are mostly numbered by infantrymen. They were sluggish and often ill-disciplined," Tarif Ibn Malik added, aware on the other hand he had full confidence in the Umayyad cavalry. They were highly skilled and versatile. If it came to it, they were also well capable of dismounting and fighting defensively on foot in ranks.

"In that case tell me more about the land – what is this country like?" asked Musa eagerly clasping his hands together, all ears.

"There are hills to the north and an abundance of pleasant green pastures, some cultivated with the most exotic fruits I've ever seen. We mostly kept to the woods if we could, to keep out of the way," said Tarif before gratefully downing the last remaining drops of the sweet *nabidh*.

"But there are roads and they're reasonably passable," continued Tarif, thinking this was only to be expected. He described seeing roads that had been skilfully laid out by Roman engineers long ago. From what he could see they had been maintained well enough over time.

Musa sat quietly, pausing to absorb the information and to gather his thoughts on all that he had heard.

Nearby sat Ilyan, holding a cup of sweet, aromatic tea. He listened anxiously to the conversation passing between the two men. A shoot of hope burgeoned in his chest as Ilyan looked from Musa's thoughtful face to Tarif's animated one. Months had passed agonisingly by, waiting and wondering against all hope. Ilyan had returned from his own raid as promised bringing captives and booty as proof of his own commitment. This was nothing when he knew he would be prepared to give up all he had if it meant he could see justice served.

News had reached him through the trusted eyes and ears of his agents of business in Andalus. They had told him that a reconnaissance party sent out by Musa had set foot on their shores. After this Ilyan couldn't have been more optimistic about being closer to reaching his goal. It was what he might have expected to have done himself if he was in Musa's shoes, rather than take his word for the state of affairs that lay across the other side of Straits. But he had borne it with patience. Ilyan had hoped the mission would prove successful and lead to something larger and more full scale later.

As he watched Musa fall into a meditative silence, the moment felt right to press his case.

"You see how it is – it *is* as I described it to be. I have neither exaggerated nor hidden anything from you," said Ilyan. "You have a superior force with your cavalry and a sizable one at that. Now is the time to move – to take Andalus. I have it on good authority through my sources there, who tell me tensions are more heightened than ever before in the kingdom. There is talk that Roderick is planning to lead his armies to the North, near the city of Pamplona – to purge the rebellion amongst the Basque people," revealed Ilyan.

Among other things, Ilyan made it his business to keep abreast of the power struggles that ensued across the kingdom and its sons. It was thanks to his own resourceful agents of business, who had assured him that conditions were ripe for a strike if anyone cared to do so.

"These are dark days upon us my friend," so said one of Ilyan's longest acquainted friends and agents. "When a people despise their king as much as they do, the people *will* look for a light to lead them out of their misery." Ilyan knew he was right and didn't hesitate to recommend Musa to do so.

Musa observed Ilyan thoughtfully for a moment from beneath half closed eyes.

"It is not as simple as that, Count Ilyan," he said finally shaking his head. "To take across a large force which includes men *and* horses will not be an easy feat to achieve overnight," continued Musa. "Our boats are nowhere near completion, let alone capable of taking on such a cargo!"

"Is that not so, Hani?" asked Musa turning to look at the far side of the circle at a small figure. He sat so quiet and unassuming, that Ilyan only for the first time became aware of his presence. A thin, wiry young man who had not thus far taken part in the proceedings, sat on a cushion wearing distinctive workman's clothes with a voluminous pouched apron hung over his front. A turbaned, dark, curly-haired head with bright, intelligent eyes now lifted to meet Musa's enquiring gaze.

"Yes, *Sayyid* – our existing *maraqibs* are too small," replied Hani dutifully, in a quiet yet confident voice, "but when you commissioned their construction, you did ask for a fleet of *shalandiyyat* that were small and fast. They're capable of protecting against amphibious attacks along our shorelines. They have the ability to outmanoeuvre and outsmart any marauding fleet of Roman *dromon*," continued Hani in the unmistakable voice of one who took great pride in his work – and it was to be expected. After all, Hani came from a family with a long line of seafarers, boat builders and naval architects among them.

Hani had been born in Alexandria, one of the ancient lands of Egypt. Like his forefathers who had built up the thriving city ports of Alexandria, Hani had inherited invaluable skills and the knowledge of ship building. Where once the Egyptians had built boats for their Roman masters, when the Muslims arrived in the land (as in Syria before) they inherited their shipyards. They quickly drew from the traditions and talents of its local seafaring community.

It was not surprising since the Prophet once said to a companion when he awoke from a nap, smiling, "I dreamt that some people from among my community were sailing on this sea like kings on thrones."

In fact, it was Uthman, the third rightly guided Caliph who quickly saw the strategic importance of using the sea. He allowed the first of the Muslims' ships to set sail after the winter of 28 AH to the island of Cyprus. There a treaty was made with its people who agreed to keep the Muslims informed of their Roman enemy's movements so that they were better able to protect their lands in Syria.

So it was that in time, between the ports of Syria and Egypt came the birth of the Muslim navy, with the building of gallant fleets to rival any of those of the Romans as they did in the Battle of the Masts, rising from the sea as the victors despite being outnumbered by the ships of Emperor Constans II.

Hailing from the dockyards of Egypt, Hani the boat builder had an ingenious mind, a keen eye for detail and a flair for design. So, it wasn't too long before his talents were quickly spotted. With the Umayyad territories, now far flung and rapidly expanding, it was an exciting time to be living in for any restless young man with a thirst for travel and seeing new places.

With a culture that thrived in pooling together all of its knowledge and resources, Hani soon found himself promoted and applying his talents elsewhere. He had been sent to the port of Tunis to help build Musa Ibn Nusayr's new fleet.

"Forgive me, *Sayyid*," said Hani suddenly as his eyes filled his anxious face. "I designed for you boats with sails that point high into the wind," he continued earnestly. "They glide fast riding the waves, but they weren't built to a specification of transporting large numbers of cavalry and infantrymen." Musa looked at the young man before him and read the disappointment in his eyes.

"You have nothing to apologise for Hani," said Musa quickly. "You've delivered what I asked of you and with admirable skill. Your ingenuity, *masha'Allah*, has left me only pleased with your services," smiled Musa at the young protégé. "May I remind you Hani, it is thanks to your boats that my son Abdullah even reached the Balearic Islands and established a treaty with its people."

Hani, the modest young man that he was, could only smile and heave a sigh of relief. He inclined his head, in gratitude. His cheeks reddened, mollified by the unexpected compliment.

"All good is from Allah," he said humbly before continuing. "But *Sayyid*, if it is boats you need to transport a large army of men and horses then I can do it. It will need time – many months – or more than a year maybe depending on the manpower, resources and funds. The existing *shalandiyyat* cannot be adapted. But the new *maraqibs* you ordered that we are building now – they can still be changed to meet the specification you require."

On the edge of his seat, Ilyan was listening attentively. Having now perceived the whole situation to be as it was, he was gladly moved to make a suggestion.

"If your boats are not ready, take mine! I have four large merchant galleys. They are moored at my port and await at your disposal," said Ilyan.

At this offer a sudden protracted silence followed. Tarif Ibn Malik and Hani looked from Musa's serene face to Ilyan's anxious one. For Ilyan, it was as if time had stood painfully still. He searched Musa's face for some sign, until finally he spoke.

"Thank you Ilyan, for your generous offer," replied Musa. "Please allow me some time to think over your proposal." Ilyan sighed and nodded his head as he acquiesced to this request. He had done all that he could. Not wishing to rush matters, he realised things would have to remain to be seen. Feeling it the right time to step back he rose from his cushion to take his leave. Taking his cue, Musa's trusted secretary promptly stepped forward to usher the Count out of the audience chamber.

As the door closed behind their parting guest, Musa turned to look at his two associates.

"Ilyan offers us his boats – what do you think of that?" asked Musa.

"*Sayyid,* if I may be permitted to say so," ventured Hani, "Ilyan's galleys would be a better option to explore if you cannot wait. They're large and equipped with cargo holds," he continued, tentatively thinking over the convenience and ease it would be to use a merchant boat. Ilyan had already established a successful trade of taking horses, among many other goods across the Straits.

"I agree with Hani," said Tarif Ibn Malik nodding his head fervently. "It would also buy us time. Merchant galleys of Andalus and Cueta move back and forth across the Straits all the time. It will not raise any suspicion if the boats are ferrying to and fro, dropping our men off. For a sizable force it will take weeks to transport everyone – so the less conspicuous we are the better," insisted Tarif, holding Musa's gaze in earnest.

If Tarif Ibn Malik had learned anything from their foray, it was that their unfamiliar looking boats made the locals aware of their arrival. The last thing they would want was to alert them too soon, especially Roderick's lookouts. To witness a large-scale force coming, even before they had had the chance to disembark would be a mistake.

Tarif only hoped that by now if Roderick had been told about his foray into the South, he would put it down to a harmless raid and nothing more serious to worry about. After all, Ya'qub, his young Iberian guide had said that raids happened all the time in that neck of the woods, like any other place.

Musa listened attentively as a plan began to materialise in his head.

"While I *am* prepared to wait for my own boats to be constructed, the offer of Ilyan's boats is a tempting one," he mused after a moment, stroking his beard. "Using his boats would only be necessary if you believe Roderick is planning to go north. If this *is* the right time, then to delay would be folly – did you by any chance verify what the king's activities were during the recent foray?" asked Musa raising a thoughtful eyebrow.

"I did – Count Ilyan is right. If you'll recall, you allowed me to take one of the captives brought back by Ilyan from his own raid on Andalus. The young Iberian proved to be an effective guide and by the grace of Allah by the end of our journey he took the *shahada*," revealed Tarif to the immense delight of Musa, whose face lit up as he praised Allah in response. Musa heard how Ya'qub had helped by allaying the fears of the local peasants, who in turn began to trust them.

Musa listened as Tarif continued to describe how they spoke to the captured Goths. Along with the testimonies they took from the local peasants, he could verify all that Ilyan had said regarding the king's plans was true. By the time the Umayyad men reached the shores of Andalus, Roderick should be deep in the North. He might even be compromised, his men being weak and tired from putting down the rebellion in the North. It would be even more so if he then had to travel all the way down to the South to meet them.

Musa nodded his head in quiet deliberation. Satisfied, he now had an accurate picture, and all the information he needed to present to the Caliph.

"I will have to lay out this plan and its merits for Caliph Al-Walid's approval," said Musa finally before beginning to summarise. "But I'm thinking Hani – you and your men do what you can to make use of Ilyan's boats while continuing to build our own *maraqibs* to the new specification. To begin with we will send an initial army of seven thousand men in Ilyan's boats. They will go in however many trips it takes to get them across – at least they will be shipped incognito. Should reinforcements be needed later, our new boats will be ready and better equipped for transport and battle if need be, *insha'Allah*."

There was a sudden, discreet cough at the door. It was Bilal, Musa's able and trusted secretary who had returned. The men turned to look in his direction.

"*Sayyid*, the General has arrived and wishes to offer his greetings. Should I show him in now?" asked Bilal. All at once Musa's eyes lit up and with his hand he eagerly motioned for his next visitor to be brought in.

Bilal slipped around the door only to return seconds later in the company of a young Berber. Standing tall, a fine, broad shouldered, personable man entered the room. His sharp, inquisitive gaze instantly locked upon Musa within the circle of men. As Tarif Ibn Malik immediately recognised the newcomer, he broke into a broad smile at the sight of this notable and most favoured of guests. Right now, he would have given anything to be in his shoes.

"*As-salamu alaikum wa rahmatullahi wa baraka-tahu* – you asked for me *Sayyid*?" enquired the firm, deep voice of the visitor.

"*Wa alaikum as-salam wa rahmatullahi wa barakatuhu* – welcome Tariq, welcome," replied Musa quickly rising from his seat, more pleased than he could say. He appraised the young man fondly as he came to stand in front of him. Musa Ibn Nusayr looked deep into the dark penetrating eyes of Tariq Ibn Ziyad. This was the man whom he had chosen to lead the seven thousand brave men of the Umayyad army into the land of Andalus.

8

QASIM AND HISHAM

Tangiers, 711 CE, Rajab, 92 AH

'O Allah make (the months of) *Rajab* and *Sha'ban* blessed for us
and enable us to reach Ramadan'
The Prophet's prayer

THE invitation was sent out. Recruitment of volunteers began in earnest during the months that followed Musa's meeting. Caliph Al-Walid's approval for the advancement upon Andalus had been given. Mostly Berber and a few Arab men arrived from far and wide across North Africa. Tangiers was built on the slopes of a chalky limestone hill, spread between the western opening to the Mediterranean Sea and the glorious Rif mountains. It was a garrison town and its activity bustled more than usual after the invitation had been extended.

Qasim looked about him with wide eyes and wonder.

"We're a long way from home, Warda!" he whispered softly to his horse beside him. Warda agreed. She tossed her flaming chestnut head and replied with a gentle nicker. He smoothed her neck soothingly, conscious of the loud cacophony of sounds all around them. It was a far cry from their sleepy Berber village with its dear ramshackle sprawl of simple dwellings they called home. The pair had left it behind in Tlemcen, near the banks of the river Tafna.

Tangiers wasn't anything like Qasim expected it to be (although what he had expected to find, he wasn't quite sure of either). It was an all too bewildering experience for him. He had never before travelled this far away from home. Wheedling vendors called out to him now from every direction, eager to show off their goods and wares.

It was of course nothing unusual for those who lived in this prosperous town in the north-western most tip of the Umayyad lands. Tangiers was quickly growing into a promising, industrious town, producing anything from leathers, decorative rugs and intricately carved furniture to the best weapons a man could forge.

In the hot heat of the day the air mingled heavily with smells of food cooking, tanned leather hides hanging out to dry, burnished weaponry and smelting metal from a nearby smithy. Qasim stood now with nothing more than a light satchel bag neatly strapped to Warda beside him. It contained all of his worldly belongings. In it, he carried all that he needed for his long journey ahead.

There were a few items of clothing, his hauberk, bowstrings (including some spare), leather cuffs, packing needles, linen threads, an awl, scissors, Warda's nose bag and her feed-basket. These were just some of the things that the recruiting officer who had arrived at his sleepy village early one morning had advised him to bring – although there had been one precarious moment when he thought Captain Waseem might actually refuse his services and turn him away.

Back in the village square in Tlemcen, Captain Waseem had read out the invitation from a scroll of vellum to a curious crowd after *jumu'ah*. It was always exciting when an emissary arrived, especially if they brought news or a message from the Caliph in Damascus. Qasim had been accompanied by his father who had come out in support of a son who eagerly rushed forth to present himself alongside a long line of other hopefuls.

The senior officer had frowned thoughtfully as he looked up and down at the father and then at the son. Qasim was a handsome lad with closely cropped raven hair and dark eyes. He was a strong, sturdy young man full of life. Yet Captain Waseem's eyes kept straying back towards Qasim's father as he stood quietly in the queue beside him, hunched over and frail.

Captain Waseem spoke to his father first, pressing a gentle, worried hand on the old man's thin shoulder before he asked for his name.

"*Ya* Abu Yasir," Captain Waseem began. "Your son's place is best served at your side. You're old and weak and have rights over him. Take him back home with you," said the recruiting officer compassionately. Qasim's heart sank at these words until his father spoke up.

"*Sayyid*, Allah has blessed me with many sons

and daughters, *alhamdulillah*. This is Qasim and he's not the eldest. I have two older sons than he, one who is my right hand and the other my left, while the other younger two sons still cling to my knees, but not for long the way they grow up fast!" he chuckled with the pride of a father written all over his old, wrinkled face.

"If it pleases you *Sayyid*, Qasim may go. I can part with him – he is restless here and eager to spread his wings and go seek his rewards elsewhere."

Satisfied over the old man's welfare, Captain Waseem nodded his head and Qasim quickly found himself in receipt of a barrage of instructions, one of which was to go to Tangiers and present himself at the barracks.

Wandering his way now through the strange, labyrinthine alleys of Tangiers, Qasim led Warda past a tanning yard. Then following a dirt track, he soon found himself in front of the famous harbour. There he was assailed by more new sounds. Boats creaked on the water, sailors shouted out orders over the heads of other sailors and traders stood by squabbling over some urgent matter of commerce that needed their attention. Between the mosaic of interlocking sails of the moored boats bobbing up and down along the quay, Qasim's keen eyes came to rest on the distant horizon.

Despite the sun beating down on him, he could see the hazy outline of a solid landmass that lay across the blue shimmering Straits. His heart skipped a beat as he stood for moment, mesmerised, his mind recalling all that he could about what Captain Waseem had said about a land in turmoil.

"That's Andalus..." said a friendly voice suddenly intruding upon his thoughts. Qasim turned his head to find a stranger standing beside him.

"... or Hispania Ulterior if you like, as the Romans call it," continued the stranger, looking across the Straits with a pair of searching eyes from beneath a pointed hood.

"Here to join too, are you?" asked the stranger turning to look at him with a warm smile. Even before an answer could be given, a quick glance from Qasim to Warda and his belongings had told him all he needed to know.

"To bring down a wicked king across the Straits," said the man now as he began to shake off the dust from the folds of his shabby burnous. It was draped over his broad shoulders and made an adequate cover for the leather plate and soft white tunic that lay hidden beneath, protecting them from the sand and dust in the air.

Qasim nodded his head in reply as he watched the man with as much curiosity in return (almost certain that he was an Arab and not Berber). The man pulled back his hood to reveal a thatch of dark hair and pale skin over an arresting face. He had passed his early youth, but was yet to reach maturity. A pair of hazel brown eyes speckled with golden flecks looked back at him warmly. In his hands the stranger carried a bag not unlike his own, while an unstrung bow with its quiver was slung carelessly over his back.

"*As-salamu alaikum* – my name's Hisham," said the man as he extended a friendly hand to take Qasim's and then back to rest across his heart in the familiar customary way of greeting.

"*Wa alaikum as-salam*, I'm Qasim," replied the young Berber as he watched Hisham eagerly turn his attention next towards Warda. He began to smooth down a white patch of forelock, the only part of her coat that was not otherwise a glorious shade of chestnut.

"You've a fine horse here, Qasim," said Hisham with an approving smile that warmed Qasim to him immediately. With a compliment like that he couldn't help it. Warda was his most prized possession.

"The Prophet himself, may Allah bless him and grant him peace said, 'The most favoured horses are the sorrel,'" continued Hisham wistfully, admiring her shiny coat as he scratched playfully behind Warda's ears. "What's her name?"

"Warda Hamra – but I call her Warda for short. I've had her since she were a foal, *alhamdulillah*," replied Qasim proudly. Warda was a fine Barbary horse with high withers and short back. She had both strength and stamina that could see her gallop easily at great pace.

"I need a mount like yours for myself. I just got off the boat from Sousse. What you see on me is all that I possess – and I'll need a horse if I'm to go there!" said Hisham nodding his head towards the shadowy shoreline across the Straits.

"I saw some good ones for sale when I was searching for the barracks – back at the market square in town," offered Qasim as he followed Hisham's gaze back across the Straits. Hisham would definitely need a horse, and he remembered walking past a great gathering of noisy men in the square. They had been eagerly vying each other over bids for the best horses.

"The *barracks*?" exclaimed Hisham with a lift of his brows. "Ah, you won't find them in the middle of town," he said shaking his head knowingly. "I tell you what, you take me to these *good* horses you saw – not sure if they're going to have any left like yours by now – and I'll take you to the barracks after that, *insha'Allah*. Do we have a deal?" asked Hisham good humouredly.

Qasim agreed immediately, having no wish to wander about the crowded town in a futile search. Retracing his steps over the dirt track, they made their way towards the market square.

"So where are you from?" asked Hisham presently, having taken the young Berber under his wing.

"From a small village – in Tlemcen," replied Qasim. Hisham turned to look at him in surprise.

"*Tlemcen*! Then do you know our General, Tariq Ibn Ziyad? He's from your village, is he not?"

"He is, but I never knew him – that is, I was just a boy before he left," replied Qasim with an undisguised admiration in his voice. Tariq was somewhat of a local hero. When news reached them of his success, no one in the village expected anything less of him. Tariq was known for his *iman* and enthusiasm for inspiring faith in the hearts of people. It was only a matter of time before Tariq's skills and exceptional character were noticed. It was certainly appreciated by Musa Ibn Nusayr, who quickly saw Tariq moving up the ranks.

"I remember him well. The boys in village – we all looked up to him," said Qasim enthusiastically. In those days Tariq had been a teenager.

"None of us were surprised really," continued Qasim. "Tariq was strong, fast on his feet. He had the courage of a Barbary lion. He could wrestle you down to the ground with his bare hands, even back then! It would've all been wasted if he'd stayed back home as a goat herder in Tlemcen," blurted Qasim, shaking his head indignantly.

Hisham's shoulders heaved with laughter.

"And what's wrong with being a goat herder?" he asked as he turned his head to look hard at Qasim, amusement still warm in his eyes. "You'd do well to remember that Allah made all of His Prophets shepherds. They all cared for their flocks, *even* the Prophet Muhammad himself at one time, when he lived in Makkah, may Allah bless him and grant him peace."

Qasim looked slightly abashed. He didn't mean to look down so, but he couldn't imagine that sort of life for himself or see how it could reap rewards.

"My brothers Yasir and Farooq are both shepherds," offered Qasim, almost apologetically. He knew both of them could happily spend hours on their father's land keeping a watchful eye on the herd. Qasim never quite understood how they managed to do that. It was nothing more than endless hours stretching out, filled with boredom, and only the bleating sheep for conversation.

He would much rather have spent his days riding Warda, teaching her tricks or training her, which is just what he did most days. With two older brothers, there was little call for Qasim to do much aside from his daily chores. But between Yasir and Farooq, their father's farm had flourished under their capable hands.

As Hisham continued to look at Qasim, he saw in him an all too familiar desire. He had seen it in so many good men before, including himself. It was the insatiable zeal to labour for the rewards of the afterlife.

"When a person seeks the pleasure of Allah, *all* lawful roads can lead to rewards – some more than others – but the promise of reward awaits for all, nonetheless," said Hisham as they continued to walk side by side.

"There's much patience to be learned from nurturing, guiding and protecting a flock, Qasim. We achieve little if we cannot reach our fullest potential in life through being patient – even when in battle. Do you know what Khalid Ibn Al-Walid always used to say to his men?" asked Hisham of the younger man as he walked nimbly beside him, matching his own pace. Qasim shook his head.

"Patience is the highest virtue. Defeat is feebleness. Victory is only won by patience," replied Hisham. The wisdom behind what Hisham said suddenly dawned on Qasim, but something else occurred to him.

"Have *you* ever been a shepherd?" he asked suddenly suspicious.

Hisham broke into a smile.

"I have – when I was a boy and lived just outside Damascus."

"Is that where you're from?" asked Qasim curiously. Hisham nodded his head.

"I grew up in a village – much like your own by the sounds of it. As a boy, I helped my father with the animals until I was old enough to take them out to the pastures by myself," explained Hisham. In fact, it was during those solitary days that he had often sat for hours on end, memorising the Qur'an, as the animals quietly grazed. By the time Hisham was eleven, he had become a *hafidh* of Qur'an, having memorised the Book of Allah by heart.

His mother had been so proud of him, that at her insistence it wasn't too long after this that Hisham began to expand his learning of the *deen* of Islam under the great scholarly guides of the time. He sat at the feet of the *'ulama*, first in Damascus – and then as he grew older, chasing town after town, he sought the company of the blessed scholars and learned from them until he drew to the limits of his own ability. He could read and write well and had a sharp memory. And yet, while he had achieved a great deal, much more than most, he decided to change his path and turn his hand to something different.

The Umayyads were busy expanding frontiers and protecting their territories against the Roman army, as Islam spread fast across the region of

Al-Maghreb. Hisham soon found himself joining their ranks, this time chasing town after town and great cities, in pursuit of this worthy new cause.

"So, tell me more about yourself – so far I know you have two older brothers Yasir and Farooq, a farm and a fine horse," asked Hisham in an affable inquisition. The lines of his face were drawn up into a friendly smile. Blessed as he was with a sunny disposition, Hisham was always one to talk to people. He enjoyed nothing more than to learn about different lives and places during his travels.

Qasim willingly obliged him, having found a kindred spirit in his fellow traveller. As they continued making their way towards the market square, Hisham soon learned that Qasim came from a family of relatively new Muslims (much as he had suspected). Throughout his life, Qasim's father, Abu Yasir, had always been a spiritually inclined man. He had never put much stock in the superstitious practices indulged of so freely by his relatives and tribe.

He had been endowed with much common sense, quick intelligence and wisdom. These had either rubbed off on his own family, or else his offspring had simply inherited these traits by the grace of Allah. So, it was unsurprising that Abu Yasir's heart should have warmed to the new faith as soon as it arrived on their soil, along with his wife and their seven offspring (all of five sons and two daughters).

The two new companions walked beneath the scraggly trees, deep in conversation. They barely noticed that they had long since passed by the dirt track and the sprawling huts that pegged the landscape, entering through the gates of the town. Qasim and Hisham only became aware of their surroundings when a hubbub of shouting among a group of men caught their attention. They were busy arguing over a strong dappled horse with a long, flowing mane.

The pair had arrived in the market square. They stopped in front of an auction ring where horses of every colour and description paraded before their eyes, kicking up clouds of dust around them. Amongst them, some were old, some young, some lean, some strong, from Barbary horses to fine Arabian steeds; in ebony, roan, chestnut and white to choose from. Hisham began to search in earnest with Qasim close at hand.

Qasim turned his head in every direction, looking on with interest, except for when Hisham occasionally called upon him for his opinion. After almost an hour of hunting, during which time they were accosted by several beady-eyed, tenacious horse dealers, the clink of coins finally passed between their hands. Hisham had become the proud owner of a mare with a glossy black coat and white socks to match the white blaze on her forehead.

"Her name's Laylah," said Hisham, introducing his newly acquired mare to Qasim as she tossed her head, arching her glossy neck. "She's a bit skittish but I think it's just the noise of the crowds today that's making her so. Otherwise, she's as fine a horse as you can get around here, *alhamdulillah*," he continued with a note of satisfaction. Hisham

114

smoothed Laylah's forehead and then patted her gently on the neck to calm her. He uttered a grateful prayer under his breath;

"Oh Allah, I ask for the good in her and the good that You have created in her…"

"She's a fine horse – and a real bargain too, *alhamdulillah*," admitted Qasim, impressed by the way Hisham had handled the shrewd seller and purchase. The horse dealer was a short man, a bit on the stout side, with heavy eyebrows that knit together over a pair of perceptive eyes. Despite his diminutive stature beside Hisham's tall frame, the man had a gift of the gab that had seen him boldly haggle over the price for a good half hour. But Hisham had borne this with patience until they finally parted, both happy with their agreed sum.

Pleased with the new acquisition, Hisham and Qasim quickly left the market. By the time they had reached the barracks it was late afternoon when the shadows were lengthening across the land. Hisham smiled at the awestruck look upon Qasim's face. Qasim had never seen anything so spectacular as this, nor so many people gathered into one area. All around him it seemed, and as far as the eyes could see, were rows upon rows of pitched tents, with men ducking in and out of them every so often.

They were soon walking between the long lines of tents, past the smoking campfires and pots of stew or water bubbling away. After a time, they had reached the farthest edge of the camp. On a stretch of open land, drill practice was well under-way. Men scurried eagerly between two points

The pair had arrived in the market square

along the archery field, fully immersed in their exercises and target practice under the guidance of their drill master. In another part of the practice yard, the clanging sound of swords rang through the air as metal clashed with metal.

"The Visigoths should be worried," said Hisham as he watched the impressive display. Qasim followed his gaze and grinned. He couldn't have agreed with him more.

9

HORSE 'N' HAY

"**G**ET that stallion off my boat!" bellowed Ilyan's red-faced Boat Master. He was watching a noisy, spirited animal bucking his way up the boarding ramp, whilst his poor owner beside him struggled to keep him calm, as he desperately pulled him by his bridle towards the ship's hold.

"He's too wild! He'll kick holes right through the hull and we'll soon turn turtle!" shouted the Boat Master.

Humayun, Tarif Ibn Malik's first officer, stood by shaking his head wearily. They had marched for some days, leaving the thick heat and dust of Tangiers behind them. Without any opposition, they had finally entered Ceuta and camped just outside the port. Ilyan's boats lay docked there and had been made ready for their departure to Andalus. These past two weeks transportation had already begun in earnest, with boat loads of infantrymen and supplies. Now it was the turn of the cavalry and their horses. Leaving from the port of Ceuta was ideal. From here, it was but a short stretch of sea across the Straits and the most direct route to Andalus.

The boats could carve a smooth, straight course that was all too familiar a route to any observer on the other side of the Straits who cared to watch. Its short distance would also make for a quicker and more bearable journey, especially should any of the men succumb to seafaring sickness. After all, some of them would be sailing for the first time in their lives. On the day of their departure for Andalus, there was an air of expectation about them as they waited to board the boats near the quayside.

After months of planning, preparing and training, the thought that a temperamental horse could set them back from their task was disappointing. The last time they had set out was almost a year ago for the reconnaissance mission under Tarif Ibn Malik. Then there had been little trouble in the way of transporting men and horses across the Straits. Yet as Humayun now stood watching the colossal gathering of men and their horses at the docks, he had to acknowledge something. Unlike now, it was a far smaller and much more experienced force (including their horses) that they had to deal with back then.

It would take them weeks of going to and fro over the Straits in shifts, crossing in four large, sluggish boats compared to their smaller but faster *maraqibs*. Still, it wasn't every day that such huge numbers of men and horses needed to be transported. There were bound to be hiccups and one difficulty had just presented itself.

In spite of the rigours of training and discipline, many of the men and their horses were still new to the whole experience. Just then a man suddenly appeared at Humayun's side. It was Ya'qub the young Iberian guide and new Muslim (now a recruit himself). He whispered a message from Tarif Ibn Malik. Humayun acknowledged it with a nod before he turned his attention back to the stallion and his young master.

"*Akhi*, best choose a mare," called out Humayun to the still struggling young soldier, before ordering him and his horse off the boarding ramp. "Where we're going, we need the animals to be manageable and ones that can keep quiet. We can't afford for them to give us away to the enemy!"

"Yes *Sayyid*, sorry *Sayyid*," replied the soldier between flustered cheeks, "*Subhana'Allah*, he's never been any trouble before – not like this!"

Frustrated and disappointed, the young man hung his head as he led his unruly black stallion back down the ramp on to the jetty again. Only this time, the stallion trotted happily after him.

Nearby the waterfront, watching the spectacle unfold, Qasim couldn't help but throw Hisham a worried look.

"I don't know that Warda will be any better – what if she kicks up a fuss going on board too?" said Qasim. He could imagine nothing worse than being turned away like that. If the truth be known, stallion or not, any horse, as docile as they may be at the best of times, might find it hard to board a wooden vessel and then sail the high seas. A few steps away stood a like-minded soldier who having overheard Qasim, decided to unburden his own worries too.

"I'm sure Prophet Nuh, never had this problem! What are we going to do – how are we going to get our horses on board?" grumbled the soldier.

"You're wrong, *akhi*," replied Hisham to the soldier with a sympathetic yet reproachful look in his eyes.

"Prophet Nuh, may peace be upon him, *didn't* go without his own share of troubles and trials. It was the same for the Prophets before him and for those who came after him, and so shall we too not go without our own share," came Hisham's voice of reason. "We *will* do as Prophet Nuh did, *insha'Allah* – we'll do our best and put our trust in Allah!" said Hisham brightly. Then turning to Qasim, Hisham handed Laylah's reins over to him to watch for a moment.

"Don't worry, *akhi* – I have an idea," said Hisham, his bright eyes twinkling behind his grin. Before Qasim could say anything, Hisham was weaving his way in and out between the crowd of waiting soldiers. Before long he was striding along the jetty towards Humayun. Curiously, Qasim watched from afar as Hisham sought permission to speak.

Soon he was absorbed in a lengthy discussion with Tarif Ibn Malik's right-hand man, Humayun. Whatever the suggestion was, it clearly had Humayun intrigued. He stood listening thoughtfully. He rubbed his chin then moments later gave an enthusiastic nod of his head. Then in a matter of minutes there was a sudden burst of activity as

Humayun appeared to give out orders to some
nearby junior officers. Qasim was too far away to
be able to hear them clearly. What they were
devising would have to remain a mystery, but not
for long. A little while later Hisham was back at his
side again looking every bit pleased with himself.

"Well – don't keep me in suspense, *akhi*?"
demanded Qasim, by now aching to know what
was afoot. "Do you know how we can get the
horses on board?"

"I do," replied Hisham with a broad smile.
"With the help of a blindfold and some fresh hay,
I'm hoping they'll be champing at the bit all the
way up the boarding ramp!" said Hisham as he
pointed back to the jetty. By now the officers had
returned carrying bales of fresh hay between
them.

Qasim's eyes widened, fixing him with a bewildered stare. Before he could interrogate him
further, Hisham's hand hurriedly reached for his
bag. It lay slumped over Laylah's back. Even
though Qasim's mind was reeling with questions,
there was an urgency in Hisham that made him
hold back.

After a few moments of rifling through the bag,
Hisham finally pulled out a piece of cloth and
deftly began to rip it up into narrow strips. Out of
the corner of his eye, Qasim saw Humayun's hand
rise eagerly in the air summoning Hisham back to
the jetty. Hisham looked at Qasim with a grin.

"*Akhi* are you sure about this?" asked Qasim
finally, but he got no further as Hisham pressed a
reassuring hand on his shoulder.

"Trust me *akhi* – when we get to the boarding ramp, do as I say," ordered Hisham. Without another word he walked hurriedly away in the direction of the jetty. Qasim was left to follow nervously after him and Laylah, while leading Warda behind him.

Curious eyes turned towards them as they navigated through the crowds of men who parted before them, like the Red Sea, to make way. Qasim looked at the onlookers nervously, as they whispered amongst themselves, with their heads close together.

Young and self-conscious as he was, Qasim hated being the centre of attention of anything, unless it made him appear in a good light. The thought of being turned away in front of so many watchful eyes just didn't bear thinking about. With his brow glistening, he offered up a silent prayer and hoped all the while that Hisham knew what he was doing.

As they walked along the jetty Humayun's men were already hard at work. A scattered bed of golden hay lay over the ramp. The weather was fine and the sea breeze wafted the sweet, familiar smell of fresh hay around them, masking the salty air of the sea. He could sense Warda's growing excitement. She gently nickered beside him as she caught the whiff of hay when they approached the ramp.

Humayun was joined by the ship's Boat Master. They had been busily absorbed watching the men, but at the sight of Hisham, Qasim and their horses, the firm line of Humayun's mouth relaxed into a smile.

"We're counting on you both to make this

work," he said as he jerked his head around towards some cloaked figures, who until now had gone unnoticed. They were stood on the upper deck looking down, having fixed their attention on the two recruits. Hisham and Qasim followed the direction of his nod.

To Hisham's surprise and Qasim's dismay, they could see Tariq Ibn Ziyad, leaning against the side of the boat with both hands resting on the bulwark. Beside him to one side, stood Tarif Ibn Malik and on the other, Count Ilyan the Governor of Ceuta, who was watching on just as curiously as everyone else.

Qasim stood rooted to the spot. His mouth fell slightly open, as though he had been about to say something, but the words had become lost in his mouth at the sight of the familiar cloaked figures. Recovering from his shock, he found his voice momentarily.

"Is – is that...?" he tried to ask, but his voice tailed away as Qasim now stood beside Hisham, still watching the men watching them back.

"It is," replied Hisham, completely calm and composed at the prospect of being watched by an Umayyad general. Then he turned to look back at Humayun.

"If you would give us a moment, *Sayyid*, to prepare the horses," said Hisham, "we'll do our best to have them on board in next to no time, *insha'Allah!*" Humayun replied that they could take all the time they needed. Qasim finally wrenched his eyes away from Tariq Ibn Ziyad to look at Hisham.

"You're not worried?" he asked with wide eyes.

"Why – they're only men – what's the worst that can happen?" he replied, shrugging his shoulders as though for all the world they could have been anyone. But to Qasim, they weren't just anyone. Among them was Tariq Ibn Ziyad, his hero. Qasim looked uncomfortable as he watched him quietly for a few seconds. Hisham was too busy inspecting the strips of cloth to notice anything amiss.

"We might just look like fools in front of them, don't you think?" pressed Qasim, plucking up the courage to confess his worst fears. Hisham suddenly looked up and caught his eye.

"Or they might just respect us for trying, *insha'Allah*," he said encouragingly. Then with a teasing light in his eyes, he continued.

"Thanks *akhi*, your confidence in me is over-whelming," he laughed.

"*Subhana'Allah* I don't know how you can laugh at a time like this," said Qasim glancing nervously back up at Tariq Ibn Ziyad. He seemed to be still absorbed with watching their every move, whilst quietly conversing with Tarif Ibn Malik beside him. This was not how Qasim had imagined attempting to make a good first impression on Tariq Ibn Ziyad.

"I know what you're thinking, *akhi*," said Hisham after a moment, holding his gaze earnestly, "but Tariq Ibn Ziyad is a man like any other man – and a God fearing one at that. Not that it matters, but trust me, he'll think nothing but good of you for trying. Remember *akhi*, we don't seek the pleasure of people but rather the pleasure of

Allah – so put your hopes in Him and pray this idea works, *insha'Allah*."

Thinking it over quietly for a moment, Qasim realised Hisham was right.

"What d'you want me to do?" he asked suddenly as he drew in his chest, rising to the challenge.

"*Alhamdulillah*, that's the spirit," smiled Hisham approvingly as he reached his hand out to pat Warda gently on the neck. "Let's see if she takes to the ramp now, shall we?"

Qasim nodded his head, willing to give the plan a go.

"Take this while I hold Warda still," said Hisham pressing one of the strips of cloth into Qasim's hand. "Use it to cover her eyes."

Qasim's eyebrows flew up in surprise.

"You don't have to worry, *akhi*. She trusts you. You've been with her since she was young. I'm not so sure Laylah here will see eye to eye with me just yet," smiled Hisham as he patted Laylah. Qasim's lips curled at the corners. Even he had to acknowledge Hisham was right about Warda. She always responded to his call in a heartbeat, trusting and loyal as she was. Warda would follow him anywhere he went (except perhaps up a ramp so precariously close to the sea!).

He slowly manoeuvred Warda into position and stood before the boarding ramp. It was only a few feet away from him, but he placed himself between the horse and ramp, blocking Warda's view of it. His hand gently stroked her nose as he whispered bracing words of comfort.

"I have to cover your eyes, but only for a moment, I promise," he said softly. Warda seemed to understand as she nuzzled him back warmly. Slowly he smoothed her forelock and carefully slipped the blindfold over her eyes. Qasim heard the creaking wood of the jetty as footsteps came hurriedly up behind him. He looked over his shoulder. It was one of the young officers he had seen earlier carrying the bales of hay.

At closer quarters, Qasim looked at him in surprise. He looked Iberian, much like one of Count Ilyan's crew, only he was dressed differently. He wore a white turban wrapped about his sandy hair, with a burnous falling over his shoulders and friendly grey eyes that looked back at him inquisitively.

Ya'qub stopped beside Qasim. He *did* look very different now to how he had a year ago, after returning with Tarif Ibn Malik's reconnaissance crew as one of their new Muslim brethren. The most notable change in his appearance was the neat circle of golden hair beginning to grow around his mouth, in keeping with the *sunnah* of the Prophet. Still looking at him, Qasim could tell he was young and not much older than himself. When Ya'qub greeted him with a youthful energy and warm smile, he knew he had guessed right. Despite his own anxiousness over his situation, Qasim couldn't help but smile back as he returned his *salams*.

"Here take it," said Ya'qub holding out a generous fistful of fresh hay towards him. Qasim hesitated a moment and glanced back at Hisham only to see him eagerly prompting him to take the hay.

With Hisham's encouragement, Qasim gratefully grasped the golden hay from his hand.

"*Jazaka'Allahu khairan, akhi,*" he said.

"This should keep her happy, *insha'Allah,*" assured Ya'qub. "What's your name – and hers?"

"I'm Qasim – and this is Warda," he replied.

"I'm Ya'qub! Captain Humayun says no need to rush, so take it slowly – take it at Warda's pace."

Qasim nodded with relief and turned his attention back to Warda again. He tried not to think about the eyes that were locked upon him right now from all sides. Still continuing to talk softly, he waved the golden hay under Warda's mouth, his other hand firmly holding her reins. She nibbled at it eagerly, and slowly Qasim shuffled backwards a few steps, tempting her to follow in pursuit of her favourite feed.

Despite not being able to see, the one thing that Warda could be relied upon was to recognise the familiar sweet smell of hay from her young master's hand. Slowly one hoof followed after another, edging towards the ramp. There was only one precarious moment, when everyone held their breath for far too long. As Warda sensed the gentle rise of the ramp beneath her hooves, she paused and sniffed suspiciously at her feet. But with further prompting (and a bit of patience) from Qasim as he wafted her favourite fragrant fodder under her nose, she was soon back on track. Slowly she began to ascend the ramp.

'*Alhamdulillah, it's working,*' thought Qasim. He

caught his breath with a mixture of excitement and relief as they slowly made their way up the ramp. Having left Laylah behind at the jetty in Ya'qub's capable hands, Hisham walked silently beside Warda's head. Qasim had been so engrossed in his task, he had not even noticed him walking diligently by his side till now. Qasim caught his eye now and saw his face wreathed in smiles. They had done it! They had reached the opening and were moments from successfully boarding the boat at the stern and entering the hull.

A quick nudge from Hisham's elbow and an eager jerk of the head caught Qasim's attention. He suddenly realised that their success had not gone unnoticed. Tracking Hisham's gaze once more, Qasim was soon rewarded by the sight of a warm smile and nod of approval from Tariq Ibn Ziyad himself. Qasim could have leapt with joy. Instead, he contained his excitement. Settled on his face was a modest smile, framed between a pair of dimpled cheeks.

Finally, Tariq Ibn Ziyad and his companions moved away with relief, a new-found confidence bolstered in their men. It was never easy moving animals, a troop of horses no less.

Hisham thought the same as he looked at Qasim now, a mischievous light in his eyes.

"See, it pays to be patient – just like a shepherd..." teased Hisham with a wink. Qasim laughed and shook his head sheepishly.

"You can learn a thing or two about animals – like you can always rely on a horse's appetite – just like people!" laughed Hisham as they stepped into the ship and proceeded through the hull together.

"Did you know when Allah breathed the *ruh* into Adam and it reached to his eyes, he saw the fruits of Paradise?" Qasim shook his head in surprise just as they were greeted by the boat's Bosun who ushered them along in the right direction through the boat.

"When his soul entered his stomach," continued Hisham looking curiously about him, "he desired for food. Even before his soul had reached his legs, he jumped for it – *Subhana'Allah*! Allah says, 'Man is created of haste!'"

Qasim laughed.

"I get it *akhi*. I promise to be patient and never to mock a shepherd again!" grinned Qasim solemnly.

Hisham laughed.

"You know I don't mean to tease you, *akhi* – I only say it as a reminder to myself too. We should live by our hearts and minds, not by following our appetites. This is what separates us from the beasts, *alhamdulillah*," said Hisham giving him a friendly clap on the shoulder. He was glad to see Qasim restored to a happier mood than his earlier anxious one.

"So, what do you think – will the horses like it here?" asked Hisham. They were moving now along the aft bulkhead where a makeshift stable was to be found. That's what the Bosun had told them on boarding. Qasim had never been on a boat before. He looked about with wide eyed curiosity at the snake like coils of rope, planks of wood, rolls of sail cloth and the neatly piled sacks of foodstuff brought on board.

"Oh, I should think so, *insha'Allah*," smiled Qasim as the sudden waft of familiar fresh hay hit him from the direction of the stable.

After the success with Warda, it was more or less plain sailing getting the horses on board the boats. The few more spirited ones shied away at first, but in the end, their owners managed to coax them all aboard before the great exodus of men began in what remained of the daylight hours.

When the horizon turned translucent from the dipping sun, wayward stars began to peek through the heavens and gently encroach upon a sable sky. The men, horses and their supplies were all finally on board. Soon, under the cover of darkness, the flotilla of boats set sail, silently slipping through the silvery waters of the Straits, now under the watch of a luminous orb and a star strewn sky. A prayer hung at their lips.

With the name of Allah it sails and anchors. Surely my Lord is Most Forgiving, Very Merciful.

10

TARIQ IBN ZIYAD

BENIGHTED, the boats breasted upon a restless sea over the Straits. Tariq Ibn Ziyad threw his head back and let the air out of his lungs in exchange for the fresh salty air he now breathed in. His eyes fastened on the sails for a moment, high above his head. They bellied out as the hands of the wind toyed with them playfully, as a child does with sheets hung out to dry.

He ought to sleep, he kept thinking, but his mind was too preoccupied to shut down. Parts of the upper deck of Ilyan's boat were cast into the shadows, but he could still see the silhouettes of his men or the odd face dappled in silver under the moonlight. Most were fast asleep by now under a coverlet of stars, although occasionally, a low hum of voices and the odd burst of laughter was carried over the deck by the warm levants that all but drowned out the mellowing murmur of the sea.

Earlier in the day, loading the boats with men, horses, equipment and provisions had been a laborious task – more than they had expected it to be. It had been a long day, in a long week that was one of many weeks over many months of hard work.

Tariq Ibn Ziyad now realised that in fact, all his years of training had been leading him in preparation to this very point in time, in the place where he now stood.

From the moment Musa Ibn Nusayr had charged him with the command of over seven thousand men, Tariq Ibn Ziyad knew he was on the verge of something momentous. Still, he couldn't quite bring himself to put into words what this could mean, but it weighed heavy on his young shoulders. Instead, his thoughts continued to pitch and toss like the waves around him between all the things that needed to be done.

At just the age of twenty-three years, Musa Ibn Nusayr had seen fit to choose Tariq Ibn Ziyad for the task. It wasn't a difficult choice. Musa knew all there was to know about him. Tariq had come to him as a youth from the tribe of Ulhasa who lived by the side of the river Tafna. Both Tariq and his father were freed slaves and had embraced Islam.

Over the years Musa Ibn Nusayr had taken a great interest in the young Tariq, taking him under his wing and seeing to his education. The more he watched, the more delighted he grew, witnessing his natural wit, talents and skills outshine in the field.

It wasn't long before Tariq had gained Musa's trust and risen so high in his esteem that Musa had appointed Tariq as Governor of Tangiers on behalf of Caliph Al Walid. Musa knew enough of the young Berber's merits to acknowledge that Tariq was the best man for this responsibility. Tariq possessed all the key qualities which Musa considered necessary for their success. He was pious, clever and well capable of leading the Umayyad force against the Visigoth army.

There was the sweet hum of the breeze in the rigging and the lapping of the waves against the wooden hull, but it was the creaking of the ship's timbers beneath a soft footfall that now drew Tariq's attention. A familiar voice soon spoke beside him.

"*Subhana'Allah*, did you see the line of horses waiting at the dock? For a moment there I was worried!" said Tarif Ibn Malik as he joined him at the bulwark. Tariq's eyes shifted for a moment to look at Tarif Ibn Malik's strong profile silhouetted against the moonlight, before turning his eyes out to sea again.

"Surely, *akhi*, you and I have seen worse obstacles than this? We can only do our best and leave the rest to Allah," smiled Tariq.

"We have, but I can't say I knew at the time if it would be better or worse than anything we've dealt with before," replied Tarif retrospectively, before elaborating.

"All I know is that it was really uncomfortable when I had to flatly refuse Ilyan's help with boarding the horses onto the boats. You wouldn't believe how they do it!" he frowned.

Tariq looked away from the sea sharply. If the moon hadn't slipped momentarily behind a vagrant cloud, Tarif Ibn Malik would have seen him lift an eyebrow with surprise and concern. Tariq had been so busy for the most part supervising another part of the operations, whilst Tarif Ibn Malik had been charged with overseeing the horses. The only time Tariq had come to know of any trouble was when he had heard the Boat Master's dissenting cries ringing out and about the wharf over the antics of one rebellious, black stallion.

"I'll spare you the details, *astaghfirullah*," continued Tarif Ibn Malik, shaking his head, reluctant to elaborate any further, "but let's just say it's not done with kindness as the Prophet, blessings and peace be upon him, taught us to do." As he spoke, he recalled in his mind the words of the Prophet when he once entered a man's garden and saw a camel which was so emaciated that its backbone was almost touching its stomach.

When the camel saw the blessed Prophet, it began to weep, its eyes flowing with tears. The Prophet went over to it, patted it on its hump and gently stroked its head until it calmed down.

"Whose camel is this?" asked the Prophet. A youth stepped forward, saying, "It's mine, Oh Messenger of Allah!"

"Don't you fear Allah about this animal in your possession?" asked the Prophet. "This animal has complained to me that you have been starving and overworking it."

So, it was the Prophet's instruction to always bestow kindness upon all of Allah's creatures. This was exactly what Tarif expected from his own men when handling their horses.

"How did Count Ilyan take it – I hope you were *diplomatic* when you declined?" teased Tariq, knowing Tarif Ibn Malik's intolerance of cruelty of any kind.

"I was polite – but I can tell you, he was certainly surprised and even more so when he saw our men bring up the horses the way they finally did," smiled Tarif Ibn Malik. He remembered the look of amazement spreading across Count Ilyan's face as he watched Tariq's men pay so much thought and attention to the welfare of 'mere' horses.

When he had first revealed to Count Ilyan why he couldn't agree to Ilyan's methods, Ilyan had looked at him as though he had taken leave of his senses.

'Pity for the feelings of horses, whatever next?' Still, how quickly Ilyan had changed his mind after watching the horses come aboard. It gave him plenty of food for thought about the new *deen*.

"*Alhamdulillah*," smiled Tariq nodding his ahead in approval, thinking that for far too long has cruelty been normalised, and lain unchallenged.

"May kindness and enlightenment enter the hearts of people by the dozen, ameen..." he said in a quiet *du'a* beneath his breath.

"How are the horses faring?" asked Tariq, aloud now.

"So long as the boat doesn't heave and pitch too much, they're fine, *alhamdulillah,* and as comfortable as they can be on board. Otherwise, we can expect them to kick and make a fuss. Then

136

we'll all have to abandon our sleep and sit up with them through the night to calm and hold 'em steady," laughed Tarif Ibn Malik.

"Speaking of sleep, Tariq you should get some yourself," added Tarif Ibn Malik, all of a sudden serious. He looked over at Tariq, noting his weary eyes with concern. "You've barely slept these past few days. Your body has rights over you too. Ilyan's had a berth prepared for you, if you like."

Tariq smiled vaguely, but he knew in his heart that a man burdened with worries wrestles much with sleep at night. He quietly nodded his head.

"I'll try – but I expect you to wake me when we reach this island of yours," said Tariq with some humour and hope of changing the subject.

"*My* island – what island?" said Tarif Ibn Malik, a confused frown furrowing between his brows.

"Yes, *your* island – Tarif's Island – that's what your men from the reconnaissance are calling it. I only repeat what they say," said Tariq holding up his hands.

Tarif Ibn Malik's face relaxed into a smile.

"Oh, *that* island – *Subhana'Allah. Humph* – it's all nonsense – pay no attention to it," said Tarif rolling his eyes and shrugging it off.

"I don't know about that *akhi*, it has a good ring to it I think," laughed Tariq, his eyes alight with amusement. "*Alhamdulillah*, we have Musa's Mountain to one side and Tarif's Island on the other – it makes perfect sense!"

"I'll have no island named after me unless they give you an equivalent, *insha'Allah*!" retorted Tarif

Ibn Malik. Of course, he knew that this wouldn't happen through Tariq's own choice, being as modest as he was. Tarif Ibn Malik respected Tariq and would follow his lead on the field, as in life. For as long as he'd known him, he had never seen Tariq hanker for power, position or fame, as some men do.

Just then a commotion on the other side of the deck drew their attention. A terrible moaning reached their ears. It was Tarif Ibn Malik's scout, Abdullah. They could see his bulky frame under the fitful streams of moonlight flooding the deck. Jumping up from a small group of men who were sitting in a circle on the timbered deck, he made a dash for the side.

The group watched his flight with a mixture of pity and amusement, laughing quietly and shaking their heads. Both Tariq and Tarif Ibn Malik pulled away from the ship's side and soon gravitated towards them. Of the two, only Tarif Ibn Malik had an inkling of what was amiss.

At their approach the circle of men looked up. Among them was Mustafa (Abdullah's trusty companion), Humayun, Ya'qub and the two soldiers Qasim and Hisham who had successfully brought the horses on board.

Sitting in the circle, Qasim's smile suddenly froze on his face on seeing Tariq Ibn Ziyad approach them.

Just then Abdullah came staggering back looking unlike his usual cheery self. Had it been daylight, Tarif Ibn Malik felt sure he would have found Abdullah's face easily rivalling the green of the sea.

Instead in the moonlight his face glistened from sweat that was pouring down his face in rivulets.

"*Subhana'Allah*, Abdullah, surely" you should have found your sea legs by now?" teased Tarif Ibn Malik. "A strong ox like you – it grieves me to see the sea get the better of you."

"Forgive me *Sayyid*, I'm a soldier not a sailor," smiled Abdullah uneasily, putting on a brave face in a bad situation. "An old ox like me belongs on dry land with his legs firmly on the *gro* –" but before he could finish his words he made a grimace and was off again, almost colliding into the Bosun, who was coming their way carrying a hank of rope over his shoulder. As the Bosun swept past their circle he called out to them with a wide grin.

"Aye, he's a real landlubber alright," he said, nodding in Abdullah's direction. He laughed heartily before disappearing down the shadowy deck, his laughter still echoing into the night.

"Will he be alright?" asked Tariq Ibn Ziyad, with concern, for by now Abdullah's head had disappeared over the side of the boat.

"Don't worry *Sayyid*, it'll pass. He'll be fine as soon as we get off the boat – I'll take good care of him till then, *insha'Allah*," said Mustafa confidently rising to his feet.

"Tell Abdullah he can take my berth," offered Tariq Ibn Ziyad. "I'm good to sleep under the stars out here on deck – in fact, I'd prefer it really."

The scout bobbed his head in appreciation.

"I'll ask, but I think he's best staying put as close as he can to there – if you get my meaning," replied Mustafa gesturing towards the scout, still retching over the side of the boat.

"I should go to him, *Sayyid*," said Mustafa. Scooping up a waterskin in his hand, he walked away, feeling for his friend's plight. He uttered a grateful prayer beneath his breath. After all, Mustafa didn't care much for travelling by sea either and would have hated to fall sick like that himself.

"Mustafa's right – he'll be fine as soon as we land *insha'Allah*. It was the same story last time. If you were to look at him afterwards, you'd never have guessed he suffered from any sickness hours before that."

Relieved to hear it, Tariq nodded his head. He then turned his attention towards the remaining ring of men that included Humayun, Ya'qub, Hisham and Qasim.

"Humayun, I hear it was a good job done bringing the horses on board," he said looking at both Hisham and Qasim.

"*Alhamdulillah*, it was a success. But it's all down to the efforts of these two *Sayyid*. These here are Hisham and Qasim," smiled Humayun introducing the pair to the Umayyad General.

"*Jazaka'Allahu khairan* – it was cleverly carried out, well done to the both of you," said Tariq smiling at them.

"*Baraka'Allahu feeq, Sayyid*, but it was Hisham's idea really," admitted Qasim as he nervously addressed Tariq Ibn Ziyad. He couldn't sit by and take credit for what had been Hisham's idea and cleverness of mind.

"And *I*, *Sayyid*, couldn't have done it without

Qasim's help, and his horse Warda," quickly added Hisham.

"Well, either way, I was happy with what you *both* did – you saved us a lot of time and for that I'm very grateful, *alhamdulillah*," continued Tariq Ibn Ziyad. "Where are you both from?"

"I come from a small village outside of Damascus," replied Hisham.

"And I'm from Tlemcen," revealed Qasim.

"*Tlemcen* – but that's *my* village too!" exclaimed Tariq Ibn Ziyad, looking at Qasim closely. "Have we met before?"

"No, you left when I was still a boy, but I do remember seeing you around the village," said Qasim quickly.

"*Subhana'Allah* that was years ago. I haven't been home in so long – what's it like now?" asked Tariq. The lines of his face softened as he began to reminisce over the past.

"Oh, nothing's changed much – it's still the sleepy village you left behind, *alhamdulillah*," said Qasim wistfully. "They still fish in the river, the goats and sheep graze in its lands and once a week the best foods come out in the market after the *jumu'ah*."

"Tell me, do the boys still pester Umm Hamdi for the bread rolls at the end of the day after market?" asked Tariq Ibn Ziyad. Turning to look at Tarif Ibn Malik and Humayun, Tariq declared that Umm Hamdi was by far the best baker on both sides of the river Tafna.

"If you could smell the rolls now, your stomach would turn somersaults," said Tariq Ibn Ziyad, his eyes bright and full of fond memories of his home village.

"Not so much now," laughed Qasim, knowing exactly of whom Tariq was speaking. Not too long ago, he himself would have been one among the boys that regularly thronged around her stall, his eyes savouring with delight the twisted, flat, round aromatic breads that lay on display under the hot sun.

"*Alhamdulillah*, her business has been thriving these past few years. If the boys are good for the whole week, Umm Hamdi gives them a roll for a treat after *jumu'ah*!" revealed Qasim to Tariq's delight.

For a time, Tariq laughed and shook his head, listening and talking to Qasim. His mind was relieved for a few brief moments by the memories of a life so far removed from the one he was leading now. It was a far cry from the pressures and responsibilities that awaited him in the weeks and months to come. Finally, as the evening grew late, he left the circle of men to rest. Tarif Ibn Malik left too, to take up his watch duties, promising to wake Tariq Ibn Ziyad for the *fajr* prayer.

Abdullah didn't take his berth, but Tariq still chose to sleep on the weather deck like some of his men. He made ablution and prayed *tahajjud* beneath the night stars. He invoked Allah to give him strength and guidance for the great task that lay ahead of him. As he settled down to sleep, listening to the lullaby of the gentle wash of the waves against the hull, a *dhikr* flowed from his lips. His heart softened with a peaceful ease as he drifted off into a deep sleep.

His heart softened with a peaceful ease as he drifted off into a deep sleep

THE DREAM

SOMETHING wrenched Tariq from his slumber. He opened his eyes and blinked a few times in an effort to banish away the sleep. For a moment he couldn't think where he was. Then as his eyes fell upon the sails silhouetted high against a coral sky, he remembered with a start. It all came flooding back to him in a wave. He was on a boat bound for Andalus.

Then he heard it again. A voice calling out to him. Tariq sat up, listening intently. A voice had woken him from his sleep. He looked about him curiously wondering who it was, but the deck was empty, with not a single soul in sight. There was only a strange, empty quietness all around him, where not even the swish of the sea was to be heard, or the creaking of the deck or yardarm. It was too quiet. Where was everyone he wondered? He pushed his blanket aside and rose to his feet.

"Tarif? Humayun?" he called out, only to hear his own voice ringing back in his ears. Then he heard it again – he heard his name. It came from the side of the ship. A sudden thought struck at his heart with a piercing fear, '*Abdullah*!' Tariq tore across the deck, his mind screaming '*man over-board*'.

"*Abdullah*!" he shouted as he hurled himself against the bulwark, his breath coming in bursts and fits. "*Abdullah* where are you, *akhi*?" he called out over the sea again in a frenzy and then, he froze. Every limb, bone and hair in his body went rigid with a sudden realisation: he was still asleep – and in his fast asleep yet wide awake state, he beheld the face of a man with the noblest of countenances, the most blessed face he had ever seen. His heart trembled in awe. Even in his dream state of consciousness, he was aware in whose presence he stood. For as Tariq gazed upon the beloved face, there was no need for words of introduction, for he knew – he just knew. It was always known that the Prophet, may the blessings and peace be upon him had said, "Whoever sees me in a dream has truly seen me, for Satan cannot assume my form."

Tariq could see the Prophet so clearly – and he wasn't alone. There appeared around him suddenly the brave, beautiful men of the *Muhajirun* and the *Ansar*, may Allah be pleased with all of them. Then Tariq heard the Prophet's voice call out to him and say:

"Take courage, Oh Tariq, and go and accomplish what you have been destined to perform!"

Then the Prophet and his Companions set off with swords drawn and bows at the ready, across the glistening calm waters of the Straits towards the land of Andalus.

Tariq put out his hand to follow them, but in that moment his eyes flew wide open. He woke with a start, his face aglow, eyes welling with tears of dawning realisation and his heart swimming with mixed emotions. On one hand, his soul wept for having been torn away from his dream of being in the blessed Prophet's presence. On the other, his heart soared with joy, overwhelmed with a feeling of confidence. From here on, Tariq Ibn Ziyad knew that he could never be in any doubt of victory.

Tariq slowly pushed the blanket from him and walked over to the same side of the ship where he had seen the Prophet in his dream. Ahead of him, looming under the last of the fading moonlight as *fajr* approached, his eyes caught sight of a large promontory of rock that rose out from the sea like a giant. He began to laugh, his hands gripping the bulwark. Then he heard hurried footsteps coming up behind him. It was Tarif Ibn Malik.

"I was about to wake you, *Sayyid!* We've arrived. What is your command?" he asked. As Tariq Ibn Ziyad turned to look at him, Tarif Ibn Malik caught his breath in surprise. Upon the young Umayyad general's face was a smile like no other smile Tarif Ibn Malik had ever seen before. It revealed the whites of his teeth and filled his eyes with a determined new light.

12

LANDING

Early Morning on a Summer's Day, 711 CE
Sha'ban, 92 AH

THE boat was abuzz with the news. Hisham and Ya'qub were busy preparing to disembark when they heard an excited cry.

"Have you heard?" asked Qasim, as he dropped down to sit beside them, watching Hisham and Ya'qub close up their bags.

"Warda's decided she's a natural sailor after all, so she doesn't want to get off the boat!" teased Ya'qub.

"What? No!" laughed Qasim, shaking his head at the unlikely notion before continuing. "I've just been to see her – if anything she's a little restless and fed up."

During the voyage Ya'qub had come to know both Hisham and Qasim. Friendship had quickly blossomed between the three. Hisham said they were souls of a kind, like kindred spirits; souls that feel inexplicably drawn to other souls as if they had already known each other before they came into this world. Allah doesn't reveal much of the soul, but the Prophet did say, "Souls are like

147

conscripted soldiers; those whom they recognise, they get along with, and those whom they do not recognise, they will not get along with."

So, it was no surprise that the three men bonded quickly and were soon almost inseparable.

"I know how Warda feels, *akhi*. I think we're all fed up," said Ya'qub sighing glumly, equally frustrated by their situation. Since coming on board, time had seemed to crawl along at a painfully slow pace.

"I'm itching to be off this boat," he continued, complaining.

"Well at least you're not like her. She tried to nibble at me until I told her it wouldn't be for much longer," admitted Qasim, who was not used to being nipped by Warda. Most of the time she was as good as gold, but on the rare occasion if she became upset, she could show signs of a rebellious spirit – like she did now. It was only until he dangled her reins before her eyes that she flared her nostrils back with delight. It wouldn't be long before she felt the steady, dry land beneath her hooves, he had promised.

"So, what've you heard then?" asked Hisham steering the conversation back to Qasim's big news. His curiosity was aroused by Qasim's excitable mien and his sudden change of mood. Before he had left them earlier to see Warda, he had been in a melancholy way.

"It will be all over the boat soon," said Qasim, a light returning in his eyes.

"Tariq Ibn Ziyad dreamt of the Prophet, blessings and peace be upon him, in the night –

and that's not all!" revealed a jubilant Qasim, smiling broadly from cheek to cheek. "He saw him with his Companions – they all entered Andalus!"

"Ah, *he did* now, did he – *subhana'Allah*," said Hisham not in the least bit surprised to hear it. A feeling of relief rushed over him. Hisham lifted his hand in a supplication upon hearing of Tariq's dream saying, "*Be it good you receive and be it evil you guard against. May your dream be good for us and bad for our enemies.*"

Hisham's eyes cast out over the sea to look at the great rock of Andalus with its strange head of clouds. He knew that the news of the dream was exactly what the men needed to hear. A short time ago before Qasim had gone to look in on Warda, they had dropped anchor close by the strange rock. When the men had locked eyes on to it the mood had changed on board the boat.

Qasim had been perturbed by the sight of it under the fading moonlight.

"I don't like it!" he was moved to say, then shuddered.

"You get used to it, but I can see how it might appear to you," said Ya'qub as he stared thoughtfully at the land that he had once called his home. His brother David was out there somewhere – and in what condition he knew not. He had so much to say and so much to tell him. He only prayed he would be able to find him after being away for so long.

"If you ask me, it looks like that great beast of the sea which Ilyan's men talk of," said Qasim thinking of a whale. "Like the ones that swim between the edge of the Straits and the great Sea of Darkness and Fog."

Hisham stared at the rocky mountain for a moment. Qasim was right. It lay on its belly over the waters, then rose high like the broad, humped back of a whale. Thick, dense clouds hovered above it, looking as foamy as the spouting froth that erupted from the back of the great beast. In fact, under the fading night sky the promontory had taken on the same greyish blue hue as a whale's skin. Hisham began to smile.

"If it does look like a whale, then it is a good thing, *akhi*," he said, catching them by surprise.

"How could it be a good thing?" puzzled Qasim, with a frown between his eyes.

"Do you not know the story of the Prophet Yunus, may peace be upon him?" asked Hisham. Both Qasim and Ya'qub nodded, for even Ya'qub knew well the story of the Prophet Jonah (which was the name he knew Prophet Yunus by, back in his former life).

"He was sent to the people of Nineveh, but they rejected him, so he left them in anger, without Allah's permission," said Hisham, before the words of *Surah As-Saffat* flowed out from his heart and on to his lips:

"*Yunus too was one of the Messengers. When he ran away to the fully laden ship and cast lots and lost. Then the fish devoured him and he was to blame. Had it not been that he was a man who glorified Allah, he would have remained inside its belly until the Day they are raised again.*'"

150

Hisham gazed at the rock as though it was calling out to him with a warning.

"*Akhi* if you do see a whale, then let it remind you of the duties you have, just like Yunus – and what befell him when he fell short of fulfilling his duties."

As anger led Yunus to flee from his people, so could fear lead to flight. Both Ya'qub and Qasim looked at him quietly now as he encouraged them not to let their emotions hold them back. Both men did not shy away from the meaning behind his words. Still, Hisham knew what he asked of them was easier said than done. What lay ahead of them wasn't going to be easy. They knew that the Goths were ruthless – and they were both young and impetuous when it came to life.

Tariq's timely dream was both a blessing and a much-needed source of encouragement for the men who would need it going forward to face what awaited them ashore. His heart brimming over with gratitude, Hisham breathed a sigh of relief. Already Qasim and the other men on board looked relaxed, warm smiles returning to their lips in a way unlike before the news of the dream had reached them. Gone was the restlessness that had lurked in their eyes, now replaced by a light of hope and belief in certain success.

Suddenly footsteps thundered across the decking as a flurry of activity took hold of the boat. Mustafa the scout rushed by down the middle of the deck calling out to either side to make haste. The moment had finally come. Tariq Ibn Ziyad had ordered the men off the boats. Seizing their

They dropped anchor close by the strange rock

belongings, men seemed to be scurrying in every direction.

They had stopped over shallow waters. Qasim, Hisham and Ya'qub collected their horses and they were soon to be seen disembarking down the ramps. The horses were eager to leave the boat and descended happily as they eased themselves into the water.

Qasim's memories of that night they left the boats was a scattered collection of images in his mind that he would never forget.

Not long after, the serene scene around him changed to a more dramatic one. Qasim found himself in a sea that was thronging with activity. His heart beat tumultuously against his chest. All around there were men in their hundreds, all having emerged from Count Ilyan's four anchored boats. Some were being transported in small row boats, while some were on their feet. From a boat that managed to anchor close to the beach, men were able to alight and were now wading power-fully through the shoal waters in their glittering chainmail – but most were on horses, like him.

Warda waded through the white foam that crested the waves, while Qasim's eyes never strayed from the beach that lay to one side of the rock. The sea frothed with so many men in the water all at once. He gasped as it splashed and splattered from all directions, the cold spray stinging his face like a thousand needles. There were no rip tides or undertows to worry about here, as found in those western beaches of *Al-Maghreb* which were exposed to the Atlantic

Ocean, but still Qasim held on tight. Holding his breath, he braved the waters before him as the land slowly shelved beneath him and the sea shallowed still.

"That's it – good girl!" called out Qasim over and over again, as he encouraged Warda over the rumble of the rolling waves. If the men were making any noise or the horses were neighing, their sounds were masked by the sounds of the sea. As they soldiered on Qasim looked up at the sky as it turned itself over to the light.

Towering above to one side, the men were sheltered by the great promontory rock that had witnessed their ascent out of the water. Then for just a brief second, Qasim thought he caught a glimpse of movement from the corner of his eye. Lurking up there on the rock, taking cover amongst its wild flora on a ledge, a shadowy figure – 'no, maybe even two' – he thought. Perhaps they were animals, or maybe something else more sinister ... spies?

He turned his head again, craning his neck to take a closer look, but was disappointed. Instead, the lines of the rock face, old, worn and weather beaten with age looked down upon him kindly (for he feared the rock no longer). It was enough for him to believe it was the rock that eagerly searched for their arrival and no one else. He could see no signs of life, and who would be awake at this early hour of the morning in such a desolate place as this? Even as Qasim and Warda drew closer to the beach, he could sense a darkness and the air of gloom that hung over Andalus, pressing down on him. Despite the beauty of its beach, its sand and the lush vegetation, a pervading sadness persisted.

Ya'qub had told him all about the land in which he had grown up, its people and their lives. Qasim's father had once told him that when people suffer the very earth from which they were created also suffers. He could sense all of this now in the sadness around him. As Qasim looked at this land he knew that the Muslims could make a difference and make it a better place for those who lived in it.

Warda made light of the progress through the white water and soon Qasim became aware of someone standing by her head.

"Hold on, *akhi*!" cried Ya'qub as he pulled Warda's bridle and guided her out of the sea, to where the last of the waves lay exhausted over the golden sand. Qasim could feel Warda's hooves sinking into the soft sand. The beach was crawling with men and horses. Small boats slipped out of the sea and carved into the sand where they came to rest. It was a momentary respite as the men they carried jumped eagerly out before they could be launched back into the sea to collect and bring back yet more boat loads of men.

"We have to get off the beach quickly, *akhi*!" said Ya'qub with an urgency ringing in his voice. Qasim could see Humayun and the scouts, Mustafa and Abdullah also leading the men away from the beach.

Abdullah was slightly pale in the face but the longer he stood on firm land, the more he began to feel like his old self again. Although at that very moment, he looked rather irate, holding his turbaned head at the sight of monkeys swimming in the sea. One had just reached the shore. It shook out its caramel fur, spreading a shower of water before scurrying off towards the safety of the great Rock before it disappeared.

"Are those *monkeys*?" asked Qasim, staring incredulously at the Barbary macaque, a native species of his homeland.

"Yes – we had a few stowaways of the furry kind on board the boats!" grinned Ya'qub. "The monkeys caught the scent of our food stores and thought they'd come along for the ride."

Qasim burst into laughter as he watched another monkey ride a wave on to the shore and then run off on all fours, disappearing behind the Rock. In fact, they all seemed strangely drawn to the great Rock.

"Where's Hisham and Laylah?" asked Qasim suddenly serious. He scoured the beach, aware that he had not caught sight of either of them yet.

"They're alright, *alhamdulillah* – I left Hisham making a small fire so we can dry off quickly," replied Ya'qub. "Though we won't be needing it for long," he said as he pointed out that the sun was no different here in Andalus.

"It gets really hot in this part of the world, *alhamdulillah*, and you can expect to find the sirocco here too," laughed Ya'qub. "Warm winds will see us dry soon enough."

They continued to walk over the sand and were soon at the foot of a sheltered, wooded area close to the beach where the men were slowly gathering.

There they could lay under its cover, away from any prying eyes. Qasim suddenly remembered the feeling of being watched as he and Warda had emerged from the sea. The hairs on the nape of his neck tingled as he twisted around on his saddle to look back at the mountainous rock. A thought niggled at the back of his mind – that same feeling of being watched had returned.

He caught a flash of movement again on a ledge above him. Someone *was* up there watching them – he was sure of it now.

13

SPIES AROUND THE ROCK

"**B**EN *please* – we must go!" implored Bella. Her cry called out in a desperate plea on the ledge of the Rock looking out over the Straits.

Her lips quivered nervously as she tugged in vain at her brother's sleeve. She was trying to pull him back from the ledge and away from all that they were witnessing below. The beach was by now filling fast, crawling with men of a like she had never seen before.

Who were they? Why were they here? What did they want? Bella didn't really want to know and quickly banished away the thoughts racing around in her head, to the exclusion of one. All she cared about now was to be far, far away from this rocky mountain.

"Bella, who do you think they are? Do you think they're here to help us?" asked Ben with a mixture of excitement and hope in his voice. His eyes, fixed firmly on the beach, were taking in every detail of the men. He was trying to make sense of all that was happening down below.

"I don't know, and I don't care to find out either – so just come away from there *please!*" she insisted. Bella caught his hand in hers, this time hoping to pull him away, but Ben wrenched his fingers free from her hold.

"*No*, I'm not going!" he replied stubbornly.

"Listen to me Ben, we have to go," appealed his sister anxiously, her voice trembling to match the fear that was written all over her face. "You don't know if they're friend or foe and if the king's spies are on the Rock and they see us too, they'll think we're involved in all of this."

Despite being consumed with curiosity, Ben slowly began to see sense. Bella was right. Reluctantly, he stepped away from the ledge and the pair quickly made their way down the old dirt track, faster than they had ever done so before in their lives. All the while Ben's mind was replaying the scenes at the beach in his head. Some intuition in his gut told him they weren't foes. They reached home to find their parents had got up with the dawn as usual.

Mother had just finished cleaning the floors (one of Bella's chores), sluicing water out of the front door with her broomstick. Bella looked contrite as Mother pursed her lips, threw them both a reproachful stare and then without a word disappeared once more with a flounce of her skirts through the doorway to begin breakfast. Just then Father appeared from round the back of the house.

He had finished tending to his first chore of the day – looking in on the chickens in their coop. He was carrying freshly laid eggs in a basket when he saw Bella and Ben and promptly waved them towards the house. Bella quickly shot her brother a warning glance. They had already discussed it on the way back home. Neither of them was going to talk about what they had seen on the beach that morning to anyone, not even their parents.

"I don't want to worry them – the less they know the better," she said firmly.

Ben smiled at his sister with a look that said, 'I couldn't have agreed more,' – only he would have included Bella along with them too. He had no intention of letting the matter go. As soon as he had the chance, he was going to find out all that he could about the men on the beach. So as far as he was concerned, the sooner Bella forgot all about this morning, the better for him it would be.

Both Ben and Bella followed after their father into the house, explaining away their absence as nothing more than the need to enjoy a brisk walk before breakfast, only they had lost track of time. Soon after, they left for church. For once Ben sat wrapped in his thoughts and not angry or resentfully brooding. He was looking for all the world as vacant and as bored as any of the other worshippers who were dutifully gathered there.

It was left to Bella to carry the burden of being seen to be attentive to the old priest. As usual he stood on the carved wooden pulpit overlooking the nave, watching their family closely throughout his sermon. Although today his beady-eyed stare seemed to be paying more particular attention to her, as though he were plotting or planning

"Ben please – we must go!" implored Bella

something in his mind to expose her. Could it be that he had read the truth in her face? Was her guilt as an imposter more pronounced on her face today than usual, or had he seen right into her lost soul, she wondered?

Shifting uneasily in her seat Bella did her best to avert her gaze and look solemn. Ben sat beside her still oblivious to the priest's scrutiny, his mind busily turning over a dilemma that wasn't going to be easy. He knew he had to get to the beach, then find out where the men had camped. Thankfully, he had an inkling where that could be. The hardest part wasn't finding them but being able to slip away from his family unnoticed – especially by Bella.

They hadn't spoken about what they had seen since the morning. Bella seemed to have already recovered and quickly forgotten. It was no surprise really. Her life was spent surviving each day as it came, hoping to get through it in one piece. Her mind very rarely ventured ahead to ponder on what might happen tomorrow let alone in the distant future. Right now, the most pressing thing on Bella's mind was to protect her family at all costs from being discovered by the Goths. If only Ben could find an excuse or some errand to do.

Today was their day of rest – what possible excuse could he come up with to leave the house? Then an opportunity presented itself in a way he could never have planned better for himself. As they left the church to go home, Mother turned to Ben as they were leaving and whispered to him. She had just heard from a neighbour that Old Joshua was unwell.

"The poor man is getting on in years. He has no one to help him now," she clucked. Ben hid a furtive, knowing smile behind his hand. Only it was more like Old Joshua's excuse for getting out of church, he thought to himself. The old codger was as fit as a fiddle. Still Ben quickly put on a mask of concern.

"Ben, go see how he's doing. I'll give you some food to take – though goodness knows it won't be much, but it's something," she sighed sadly before moving ahead to walk beside Father.

An hour later, carrying a basket containing some simple broth and bread rolls, Ben arrived at Old Joshua's ramshackle hut. It was not too far from the beach. As he suspected, he found Old Joshua hale and hearty. More importantly he was safe. But then that's how things were with the old folk. The Goths didn't look into their lives so closely. In their eyes, they weren't as much of a threat to them as the young'uns and so mostly they let them be, even turning a blind eye to them skipping mass.

No sooner had Ben sat down on an old rickety chair, than Old Joshua's voice shook as he launched into his usual tirade, waving an angry fist in the air from time to time.

"They're all rotten, the whole lot of them!" he said bedamning the Visigoths for their injustice and for compelling him to live out a life sentence without any hope of release from his poverty. Inside, Ben was aching to share his news of the men on the beach with Old Joshua but thought the better of it and stayed quiet.

He liked Old Joshua, but he had a bad habit of carrying tales, although no one paid much attention to an old man's ramblings. Still, he didn't want to take a chance. Until he knew more about the strangers it was a secret not to be shared. Instead, he resolved to keep the information close to his chest. He didn't know why, but a feeling inside told him to. After spending a while with him, listening and watching, with Old Joshua gratefully slurping his way through Mother's vegetable broth, Ben finally took his leave. He promised to visit again.

Slipping out of the small, dilapidated dwelling he walked purposefully towards the shingled bay. Keeping close to the undergrowth so as not to be seen, he began his search for the men. He could see Ilyan's boats more clearly now from his vantage point. They were moored over the same waters where he had last seen them that morning from the Rock. They were definitely galley boats from Ceuta. In the daylight Ben could now clearly recognise their familiar colours and markings. Yet strangely the men he had seen landing this morning didn't look like they came from Ceuta.

The boats looked quietly unassuming now as they bobbed up and down on the gentle swell. All around them spears of light pierced the clouds and twirled on the turquoise waves, stretching endlessly away into a hazy horizon. Anyone watching from afar would think nothing of the boats, which were often seen carrying their goods and wares across the Straits between the shores of Ceuta and Iberia.

Yet it wouldn't be so if they chose to look more closely, perhaps while rambling in the woods, or crossing the beach. Then they would be sure to run into their foreign visitors. But Ben knew that it would be unlikely in this lonely part of the world to expect any of the peasants to be passing through. They would either be busy working in the fields during the day or else exhausted after their labours, tucked up in bed at night.

Despite his own chores, for the next few days Ben managed to sneak away under the guise of visiting Old Joshua. Having heard the noises and caught the distinctive sweet, exotic scent of perfume that wafted across from the visitors, he had soon discovered their camp. Ben continued to watch, curiously aware that new boat loads of men were arriving every day as their numbers swelled. It wasn't long before he realised something stupendous was taking place – something that was soon to transform their shores like never before.

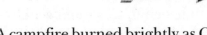

A campfire burned brightly as Qasim, Hisham and Ya'qub, along with the two scouts, sat languidly around it, savouring its warmth. Silhouetted behind them on a small plateau on the lower slopes of the Rock were pitched white and sometimes colourfully patterned tents. They had been in Andalus for more than a week now. Still, they were some weeks away from when the last of the seven thousand men were due to arrive on these shores, bringing an end to the relays of boats going backwards and forwards daily across the Straits. Until that time arrived, they had to make the most of the long summer days. As the days slipped by, much of them were spent in drill practice in preparation for the coming battles ahead.

Everyone knew what was to be expected as soon as the full retinue of Tariq's men had arrived. They would move up through the south of Andalus and make their presence known. No doubt there would be skirmishes along the way. Roderick's men were posted across many towns such as Gades and Julia Loza (where Tarif Ibn Malik had met his adversaries during his reconnaissance mission). The Goths were sure to come out to intercept them, but push on they would. Tariq Ibn Ziyad was determined to have the upper hand. He would reconnoitre the land and be the one to choose the ground on which to meet Roderick and his army.

The fire burned brightly and above it cooked skewered chickens, slaughtered earlier in the day in the *halal* tradition by Hisham. Food was in abundance for the time being, *alhamdulillah*. Even Warda and Laylah had no complaints with their noses sunk deep in their nose bags, filled with their rations of corn. Livestock and provisions had been brought over from Tangiers to keep the men and horses going until such a time came when they would need to live off the land they moved through, or else consume what they captured from their enemy.

They sat around the fire in good spirits eating, laughing and sometimes talking in earnest as friends do. It had been another long day of training and Hisham was busy teasing Qasim over his horsemanship skills. It began when Qasim moaned over his sore bones after attempting to vault up and over onto Warda's back whilst she cantered along, just like the Romans were known for doing. It was in fact a skill found among many who were used to working with horses, including the Muslims, both Arab and Berber.

Qasim had watched with giddy delight as he witnessed some of the men vaulting off the ground like acrobats during drill. Within seconds they landed astride in their seats, all the while their mounts continuing in motion. He knew instantly that it was something he wanted to learn. So ever since, Qasim had spent hours trying to master it. Instead, most times that Warda passed by him his hands missed her withers altogether. When he did catch them, he found himself not vaulting, but dragged across the earth, with ample bumps and bruises from having landed on his derriere more times than he cared to remember.

"You know what the trouble is – you don't trust Warda," said Hisham.

"What does it have to do with trust?" asked Qasim testily as he stared moodily at the flickering flames.

"Everything," added Mustafa the scout, turning his head like a wise old owl. "You need to trust your horse, and your horse needs to trust you."

"Mustafa's right," said Hisham shaking his head. "And it's a pity, because Warda obviously trusts you more than you trust her."

"What d'you mean?" said Qasim in sulky tones, feeling a little piqued by all the 'criticisms' being levelled his way.

"Well, Warda let you put a blind fold on her without a fuss and boarded the boat, but you're thinking she'll buck you off the second she comes past you," said Hisham.

Qasim quietly thought it over.

"So, you think I should just jump?" he asked after a moment.

"*Akhi*, I'd call it a leap of faith – but yes – Warda knows you won't hurt her, *insha'Allah*," said Hisham smiling sagely. He leaned back comfortably against a rock, folding his arm behind his head to rest.

"It might take a few tries, but she'll see what you're trying to do – clever they are, you know," added Mustafa before taking a large swig from his waterskin to wash down the delicious chicken Hisham had cooked. Qasim frowned as he digested their advice along with his share of what remained of the chicken he was now nibbling away on, forcing himself to eat. Suddenly there was a crackle of twigs and a muffled oath from somewhere behind a cluster of rocks nearby.

"Did you hear that?" whispered Ya'qub as his ears pricked up. He craned his neck to listen for a moment, as did everyone else.

Mustafa caught Abdullah's eye, who nodded back knowingly, as if reading his mind. Abdullah casually stood up to yawn and stretch his arms and legs. He then walked around the fire away from them while Mustafa brought his finger up to his lips to signal to the others to keep quiet. Minutes later there was the sound of a scuffle and a loud cry.

"Let me go – *let me go!*" bawled a voice as Abdullah appeared from behind the rocks, having approached them from the other side. Carrying him by the scruff of his neck, flailing and kicking out wildly with his arms and feet, Abdullah dropped Ben in front of the warm fire. He landed in a heap before them.

"*Subhana'Allah*, what's this?" asked Hisham in surprise, as the others eyed the newcomer curiously.

"*Alhamdulillah*, we have a guest – a young lad!" laughed Abdullah ruffling Ben's sandy hair, before returning to his seat against his favourite rock.

Ben gulped as he looked around him at the peering faces crowding about him now.

"What are you doing here?" asked Ya'qub rounding on the intruder. "Not spying on us, were you?"

Ben's eyes widened in consternation, suddenly aware of what his presence here might look like.

"No! I just wanted to see who you are – that's all," faltered Ben, his mouth quickly running dry. "I saw you arrive from the Rock."

"*Subhana'Allah*, I knew it!" cried Qasim, his eyes suddenly alight. "I thought someone was watching us from up there. Was that you near the cave?"

Ben nodded in surprise.

"Don't crowd him – leave the *boy* be, *akhi* – what's your name?" asked Hisham more kindly as he pushed past the others, holding a waterskin out towards him.

"Ben," he replied gratefully as his eyes locked on to it. He took the waterskin, eager to slake his thirst, but his eyes soon strayed to the large, flat breads, warming beside the fire in a basket. Ben couldn't help it – he was starving, and it smelt delicious. Following his gaze, Hisham picked up the bread, tore off a piece and gave it to him. Taking it greedily, Ben took a hungry bite out of it.

He hadn't eaten since breakfast. Most evenings this past week he had been able to get away after supper to watch Tariq's men. Today had been different. After his work in the fields, he had been so impatient that he had risked skipping his meals to come straight out to watch them. He wanted to see if Qasim had mastered mounting Warda on the move. After days of watching them, Ben was mesmerised by them all.

"Have you told anyone about us?" asked Ya'qub quickly. "Do they know we're here?"

"*No* – I told no one!" Ben assured him quickly, revealing that everyone in town still thought the galleys coming and going in the bay were just boats from Ceuta, going about their business as usual and nothing more.

Ya'qub nodded his head in relief, not that it mattered really. Enough of Tariq's men had arrived by now to be able to handle any resistance that came their way. What they sought now was to buy time and as much of it as they could, knowing that sooner or later they would be discovered. Besides, he believed the boy. They would have seen some sign of the Goths by now if he had exposed them all.

Sitting amongst the strangers close-up, Ben, chewing on his bread, looked at everyone curiously, especially Ya'qub. His eyes kept returning to him. Despite being dressed the same as Tariq's men Ya'qub looked unlike everyone else. He looked Iberian – he was sure of it. Still, there was something even more familiar about him, but he couldn't quite put his finger on what it was.

"I've heard the talk around the camp – it's true, isn't it? Do you come here to remove the king?" asked Ben, his eager eyes wide, shining with hope.

Ya'qub's expression suddenly softened a little as he looked at him with new eyes. He knew how Ben felt. He saw in him the same hatred that he himself had once carried living under the Goths.

"Would it matter to you if we did?" asked Hisham curiously.

"I can tell you this, there're many here that hate the king and would pledge to support you, just as I do now!" replied Ben, lifting his chin boldly.

Hisham smiled and looked at Abdullah.

"Well, that's good to know, but you're just a boy, so your silence would be enough all the same," laughed Abdullah.

Ben's face fell. Disappointed, he took an angry bite out of his bread – it was not what he wanted to hear. Naïve as he was, he couldn't help but wonder how it was that he could be considered old enough to work the fields and do chores, but too young to pick up a sword.

Reading his disappointment, Hisham had an idea that would make him feel useful.

"You could always keep us abreast of what goes on in town?" offered Hisham. It would be good, he thought, for them to know if they had been discovered.

"I'll do it!" said Ben, his eyes shining, jumping at the chance to help. He readily agreed and took on the task.

From then on, he made good his promise and continued to visit them regularly. Nothing would stop him now as each new day he raced to report to Abdullah the same news; the townsfolk were still blissfully unaware. Now that Ben was moving among them freely, he learned a good deal about the Muslims. Each day his respect for them grew as he watched their ways and manners with eager curiosity. Most of all he was in awe of their General, a young leader like no other he had ever seen.

Most days Tariq Ibn Ziyad took to walking through the camp, stopping from time to time. He liked to talk to his men, lifting their morale in a land that was totally foreign to them. Many of his men had been at one time nothing more than simple desert dwellers, used to the sand, sirocco and a simple life. This strange, new land on which they now stood was blessed with warm winds, but in them was an unfamiliar, sweet, subtle aroma of summer grass.

One late afternoon, Tariq was returning to his command tent. It was pitched strategically on the lower plateau of the mountain that also happened to enjoy breath-taking views over the bay. His eyes fell thoughtfully upon Ilyan's boats as they sat silently upon the glittering waters. He had just returned from talking to his men who were mostly in good spirits, but his mind kept returning to a piece of intelligence received only the day before. It had troubled him.

Mustafa and Abdullah had been out to explore an outpost said to be under the control of Count Theodomir. It was to him that Roderick had entrusted the defence of the frontier upon which Tariq's men now stood. From the scouts' observations, Count Theodomir was still none the wiser about their arrival. Still, he had a modest army that would soon be ready to come out and meet him. Tariq needed to announce their arrival in a spectacular way – one that would strike fear in their enemies' hearts and embolden his men.

'What could he do?' he wondered over and over again. Suddenly as if in a trance, Tariq froze, his eyes fixed on Ilyan's boats as they continued to sit serenely in the shoal waters. It was close to sunset. The deep red sun had moved behind the sails and enveloped them with its bright, burning light. It turned the sails and even the sea itself to a shimmering blaze of coral. Tariq Ibn Ziyad gasped. In that moment he knew exactly what he must do.

14

TARIQ'S MOUNTAIN

Summer of 711 CE, Ramadan, 92 AH

THE camp was abuzz with excitement. Tariq Ibn Ziyad had summoned everyone to gather near a natural platform on the mountainside before sunset. Nobody knew what it was about, except that it was *very* important. An announcement of some sort some said, while others speculated. Was it to be the moment they were waiting for, orders to march through the country? Or were they about to hear that their adversaries were marching towards them from all quarters?

At the appointed time Tariq stood waiting on the Rock. He was dressed in white, looking tall and as strong as the mountain he stood on. Behind him the dying sun slowly turned the sky, sea and the Rock a dusky rose. He watched as his men eagerly flocked together before him. It was an incredible sight to behold.

Crowds of men, some on the Rock, stretched back as far as the eye could see. There was a mood of excitement and restless expectancy in the air. By now all seven thousand men were finally

accounted for, safely ashore on this foreign land.
The last boat load of men had arrived only a few
days before. All men were by now rested and
adjusted to their new climes.

Just a few steps away from Tariq stood Tarif
Ibn Malik, clutching his bow, and Count Ilyan.
Both men watched quietly and contemplatively
from the wings.

Tariq took a quick glance at the sea in the
confident knowledge that by now his orders had
been put into action. Small boats of his men would
be waiting on the sand ready to set sail on his
signal. He meant to create an impact. It was
imperative that the execution of his plan was timed
to a tee.

Tariq lifted his hands in the air to give a signal
before the crowd of eager onlookers. The two
scouts Mustafa and Abdullah were on standby.
They acknowledged the sign and quickly turned
their horses on their haunches. They rode off in
the direction of the lower beach, a short distance
away, where Humayun waited ready to execute
the final stage of the plan.

Among Tariq's men stood Hisham, Qasim and
Ya'qub, watching the proceedings as curiously as
anyone else. Some moments later, Qasim was the
first to spot a commotion on the beach.

"Look! Over there – do you see the small boats
with men?" asked Qasim pointing out to sea. His
eyes narrowed over the distance.

"That's strange – where d'you think they're
going?"

Hisham followed his direction to discover small

dinghies loaded with men were being pushed out into the water ready to cast off. At the head of them, he recognised the tall familiar figure of Humayun.

"I don't know," said Hisham surprised. All around him a hum of whispering arose as the men noticed the boats sculling rapidly over the sunset waters.

"Looks like we're going to find out," exclaimed Ya'qub, with a sudden excitement in his voice. "Tariq's about to speak!"

Tariq had raised his hand again and drew everyone's attention.

"My men!" he began after praising Allah and asking for blessings and peace upon the Prophet and his Companions. His voice boomed out over them as it bounced off the ancient Rock, as good as any trumpet call.

"You know why we have come to this land. Nothing can save you now but the help of Allah, your bravery and your steadfastness. The sea is behind you and the enemy is before us," cried Tariq as his arm swept round to the sea. "The choice is a simple one. We must either conquer Andalus or perish in doing so."

As he finished speaking, he caught Tarif Ibn Malik's eye in a wordless command, who nodded in return. Tarif lifted his bow. It creaked under the strain as he pulled back hard on the bowstring. Then finally he let loose a flaming arrow, not long lit, which pierced the sky, momentarily illuminating its path over the bay before disappearing.

Out at sea, the men in the small boats had by

now surrounded Ilyan's four anchored galleys. Humayun, witnessing the ascent of the burning flare from the Rock, took his cue, as did the other men. Bows raised, a volley of burning arrows flew through the air at lightning speed, ripping and shredding the sails of Ilyan's galley boats.

A wave of gasps spread out over the land on which Tariq's men stood watching in awe. Then followed incredulous cries of, "*Subhana'Allah! Look they're burning the boats – they're burning the boats!*"

Transfixed, the men stared at the scarlet flames as they licked and hissed. Spreading quickly, they swallowed up the galleys, sparing nothing in their path, engulfing the sails, shells and skeletons within. The wind soon carried their heat and dropped it over the men on land like a warm blanket. As the fire took hold of the four boats, it lit up the sea to the twilight sky and the earth turned crimson before their eyes, as though the very gates of hell might have been thrown wide open.

The roaring flames and the shrieking, creaking cries of cracking timber called out to them now in a dreadful din. In return a few of Tariq's men raised their voices in glorifying Allah then more and then still more, until not one man was left standing who had not glorified their Lord.

Tariq smiled. When a fire is raging and eyes behold it, it was the Prophet's guidance to glorify Allah the Almighty as were his men doing now, with their words rising into the air, "*Allahu Akbar* – Allah is Greatest".

For Tariq it brought coolness to his eyes and a

moving confidence in his chest to see his men so emboldened. He knew it was no ordinary plan. Only a few days before Tariq and Count Ilyan had stood at this very same spot on the plateau looking out over the boats. He had summoned Ilyan to hear a proposal he had. One that he hoped would wake up the Visigoth kingdom and shake the very foundations beneath them. More importantly, he hoped it would kindle renewed courage in his own men too.

Tariq had looked at Ilyan seriously, feeling for words.

"Count Ilyan," he said finally and frankly, holding Ilyan's gaze. "I wish to burn your boats."

Ilyan stood shocked, not for the first time though. By now he was becoming all too accustomed to expect surprises in their company.

"Burn my boats?" repeated Ilyan slowly.

"Yes – but make no mistake, you shall be compensated, *insha'Allah*," Tariq quickly assured. "But I must burn the boats. I intend to send a clear message out to the Goths, and to bolster my men's confidence."

As Ilyan listened to Tariq's plan, inwardly he marvelled at the tenacious spirit of the young Umayyad General. It was a clever plan and if pulled off well would be sure to alarm the Visigoths. For Ilyan, anything that could threaten Roderick was a good thing. He needed no persuasion. At the mere thought of Roderick he was assailed by the memory of Florinda's plight and his blood boiled anew. He would have ransomed his entire wealth to have spared her that suffering, if only he had known what he knew now. Ilyan fixed a determined look on Tariq.

"When I came to Musa Ibn Nusayr, I offered to him all that I possess in order to seek justice," said Ilyan firmly. "So, I say to you now the same – do as you must so that I may see an end to Roderick's reign."

Tariq nodded his head.

"Thank you. I shall do my best, but victory will only come from Allah, if He so wills it," cautioned Tariq.

Having secured Ilyan's agreement, from there on Tariq had meticulously planned everything to the point where he now stood before his men. During the days that followed the crew and anything that could be salvaged had been removed to safety, away from what was to take place. Watching the raging fire now he drew relief from the knowledge that his plan had worked. Going forth on the morrow, whatever stood in their path, he and his men would be ready for it, *insha'Allah*.

"You've done well Tariq," said Tarif Ibn Malik after what felt like an almost interminable time of silence had passed between the two of them. He turned to look at Tariq Ibn Ziyad who stood thoughtfully beside him. His face was aglow from the light of the burning fires.

"I sense a change in the men already, *alhamdu-lillah* – they needed this – I see that now," said Tarif Ibn Malik as he threw him a warm look of respect.

"I don't mind admitting to you now, but I wasn't too sure when you first came to me with your crazy idea. But I see now there was method behind the madness," admitted Tarif Ibn Malik with a wide grin. He could never have mustered a plan as outlandish yet as ingenious as this. Tariq Ibn Ziyad had a brilliant mind when it came to stratagems of battle, as Musa Ibn Nusayr knew well.

"All good is from Allah, *akhi*," said Tariq quietly beside him, his thoughts far away as the flicker of flames reflected in his eyes. For anyone watching now, he thought, may the fire and the smoke be the signal that says, 'we are here to stay, God willing.' On the morrow it would be the first day of Ramadan and Tarif Ibn Malik would lead a division of the army around the bay to begin subduing the west.

He would take on towns such as White Port and Julia Loza, the very same town he had visited the previous year during his reconnaissance mission. Only this time, it would be to overcome and conquer. Meanwhile, Tariq Ibn Ziyad would head inland with the remaining men into the country of Count Theodomir, a Goth general who, according to Ilyan, had been entrusted by Roderick to defend the Goths' southern frontier.

Just as Allah had given the first Muslims victory at the battle of Badr during the holy month of Ramadan, Tariq had faith that victory would belong to them, as they too entered that same blessed month. Ramadan, whose beginning is mercy, whose middle is forgiveness and whose ending is freedom from the Fire.

From his vantage point on the Rock, Tariq's

eyes alighted on the new moon of Ramadan. It was a thin slip of a crescent, peeking out of a red sky, just above the horizon. He raised his hands in prayer on sighting it, just as the Prophet used to do.

"O Allah, bring it to us with felicity, faith, safety, and submission. My Lord and Your Lord is Allah," he said quietly.

Turning to Tarif Ibn Malik, Tariq gave the order to call for the *maghrib* prayer. Tarif's voice soon rang out across the bay as he called the *adhan*.

Beneath the watch of the Ramadan moon, the fire over the waters continued to rage late into the night, sending a dark fog inland. For a time, the men stood and watched, then slowly began to drift away with the ashen smoke as the fire raged on. Many, like Tariq, would sleep after the *taraweeh* prayers, then rise again and fall to their knees in prayer in that most sacred last third of the night. It is a time when Allah descends from His Throne to the lowest of the seven heavens to receive the prayers of those who call upon Him.

Among these were Hisham, Qasim and Ya'qub. Unable to sleep, they stayed up on the lower part of Tariq's Mountain ('*jabal Tariq*' as they had taken to calling it), drawing comfort from the curling fire of the burning boats, listening to their crackling flames. Soon it was time to eat their *suhur* of milk, dates and bread.

"Hisham, do you ever get scared?" asked Qasim staring at the fire, shadows dancing across his face in its flickering light.

"Yes – sometimes," said Hisham after a

moment. "It's in our nature to fear, but like most other instincts we have to struggle to overcome it."

"But *how* – how do you do it – how does one be brave?" asked Qasim. Hisham popped a date into his mouth, chewing it thoughtfully as he watched the flames, hot ribbons of light flickering in the breeze. He remembered the story of the Prophet Ibrahim, peace be upon him.

"It isn't easy – but you know, 'those who love Allah as Prophet Ibrahim did, do not fear,'" said Hisham looking at Qasim earnestly.

"When Ibrahim was catapulted by his people into the fire after he destroyed their idols, the flames were strong, but they did not burn him, because Allah the Almighty commanded, *'Oh fire! Be coolness and peace for Ibrahim.'*"

Sitting in sight of the burning boats, Hisham told the story of the courageous Prophet Ibrahim. How Ibrahim sat in the midst of the fire, glorifying and praising Allah. There was no room to feel fear or worry when his heart was only filled with trust in and love of Allah, fully submitting to Him. Allah does what is best for the believers and with this comes a sense of peace and comfort in their hearts.

Speaking of fear, there was a sudden loud sound, a piercing crack that made their hearts jump for a moment. Hisham broke off from the story he was telling. Part of the upper mast from the galley boat nearest to them was leaning pre-cariously before it collapsed as it broke asunder. Bright sparks fluttered momentarily in the air like fireflies as gasps drew again from the men while they watched the boats' destruction. The creaking and splintering of timber sizzling in the water immersed them in a dreadful din.

Even the Barbary monkeys who had made a new home for themselves on Tariq's Mountain came out to see what all the commotion was about. Shrieking and clapping they leapt about hysterically at the sight of the burning boats.

"Our fears are nothing but the whisperings of Shaytan playing on our insecurities," continued Hisham watching curiously as the debris of the mast slowly sank below the bubbling water, until it disappeared beneath the sea. "If you accept Allah's will and put your trust in Him you can cope with anything."

"Well, I hope the Goths are terrified watching this display!" exclaimed Ya'qub with a sense of satisfaction rising in his chest. "I wish I could see their faces when they look out of their windows and see this on their doorsteps," he grinned, thinking it was high time the Goths got what they deserved. Then the memory of his brother came flooding back. He wondered if David could see the fire. David had an inquisitive turn of mind and if the fire brought him out to have a look at it, the better it would be for Ya'qub. Otherwise, hunting for his brother in this land would be like looking for a needle in a haystack.

Ya'qub had always planned to start his search with their home, but it had been over a year since he had last seen it. A lot could have happened since then. He didn't even know if David still lived there; perhaps he had moved on. After Ilyan had captured Ya'qub, he couldn't see how his brother

The creaking and splintering of timber sizzling in the water immersed them in a dreadful din

could have managed the fields without him, to keep up with the exorbitant rent. What had happened to him, he wondered? David had always looked out for him. It was his turn now to do the same. Ya'qub fell silent, wrapped in his thoughts.

"Don't you worry, you'll find him, *akhi*, *insha'Allah*," said Hisham, recognising the pensive look in his eyes, as they glowed like embers. Ya'qub looked at him with a smile.

"I know – *insha'Allah*," he said confidently and went back to watching the fire.

Ben was running flat out, breathing hard as he cut through the grass as quick as his legs would carry him. All around him daylight was fading fast, and he needed to get home before dark, but the night was closing in rapidly. He had stayed out as long as he could, watching the burning boats in the bay. His eyes were still imprinted with the memory of the leaping flames rising high, heaped upon each other like a great bonfire. His ears still rang with Tariq's words, while his nose wrinkled up at the smell of smoke from the charred wood that was even now drifting inland as he fled from the scene overlooked by Tariq's Mountain.

His head was brimming with excitement. It was all out in the open now and all he could think of was what this could mean for his own family. Tariq's men were here to stay, preparing to meet the Visigoths. He could finally tell his family about what had been happening and reveal what he had held a secret for so long. With that thought, he was spurred on.

As Ben approached his home and saw the warm, welcoming familiar glow of the tallow lamps beaming through the windows as they burned, he slackened his pace a little. Then the front door suddenly swung wide open with such force it left the door shuddering on its hinges. A hooded figure came out, hurtling into him, knocking the wind out of him and almost sending him flying off his feet. It took Ben only seconds to realise who it was.

"*Bella!*" he cried holding her steady, as a tear-stained face lifted to meet his for a moment. Bella sobbed and then cried out in a terrible anguish, pushing him away from her. She darted down the dusty dirt track as though chased by demons, disappearing into the darkness.

"*Bella* – Bella what's wrong?" Ben cried after her. He would have turned on his heels, ready to pursue her, except he heard his father's voice calling out to him through the doorway.

"Leave her be," said Father in a voice so strange that it made Ben's heart sink with a feeling of dread.

"What is it – what's happened?" asked Ben moving towards him until in the light his father's face appeared before him; old, haggard and burdened. The lines on his face were pronounced such as he had never seen before.

"Your sister's … betrothed," said Father uneasily. Ben reeled back in confusion, wiping his hair back off his forehead as he tried to make sense of his father's words.

"*Betrothed* – to whom?" he asked in a voice as strange and strangled in his throat as his father's.

"He's a good man, from a good family and as well to do as you can get," said Father unable to meet Ben's eyes.

"Father, *who*?" said Ben, panic rising in his voice.

"It's done now. There's nothing more to do. Leander will make a good husband to your sister – so Father Martin says," revealed Ben's father pressing his temples.

"*Father Martin*!" said Ben slowly, in consternation.

"He came by today with the proposal on behalf of young Leander – it's to be settled," said Father in a resigned voice devoid of any hope as he hung his head in bitter shame.

"But Father you cannot be serious – it's forbidden – Leander is a –" began Ben, only to be silenced by his father's words that cut him like a whiplash.

"What would you have me do – we'll be dead in no time if we refuse!" snapped Ben's father. Looking at him now, Ben could see his father's tired eyes glistening over with unshed tears. It was no use. Any way they looked at it, Father Martin had them over a barrel. Bella was pretty, of marriageable age and Leander to all the world was an eligible match. To refuse would give rise to talk, when a married daughter could mean one less mouth to feed. Bella had been right all along. He had seen it in the priest's shrewd, calculating eyes only that afternoon, except Father hadn't fully understood it before. Naïve as he had been, it was clear to him now that this was a test and one that could expose them all.

"We're done for," said Father faintly, turning his face away, consumed in self-pity and despair for his family, as he leaned heavily against the lintel of the door for support. A sudden darkness threatened to overwhelm Ben, until a rush of acrid smoke in the air brought him back to his senses. It was as good as any smelling salts. Ben's breath came hard and fast as his fingers curled into a tight ball.

"You're wrong Father! Bella will *never* marry Leander," said Ben, his mouth set in a firm line.

"There'll be a war before there's any wedding!"

Father suddenly turned and his eyes flew back to meet Ben's, in consternation this time.

"What are you saying, boy?" questioned his father, looking sharply at Ben as though he had run mad. Surely Ben didn't mean to fight back?

"Father, I've something to tell you," said Ben with a meaningful voice full of hope. He pointed towards the far distance. In his grief his father had noticed nothing in the change of the air. Father followed the line of his pointing finger and his old eyes suddenly widened. Under the night sky, a beacon burned brilliantly bright.

15

NEWS SPREADS LIKE
FIRE . . .

SOMEONE else, at that very same moment as Ben's father, was witnessing the burning beacon. Far on the other side of the bay that looked across at Tariq's Mountain close to the town of Julia Loza, stood White Port. A night watchman on duty in a tower rubbed his eyes, blinking away their heaviness. He stared carefully again.

In the distance over the bay was a glare as bright as a mid-winter's bonfire. At first, he thought nothing of it when earlier in the evening it had been a soft glow, a reflection perhaps in the water from the setting sun. Whatever it was then, it earned little more than a passing glance from him before he continued to walk on. Keeping close to the walls he had finished his round of the tower. Then, as usual, he had waited quietly at his station, hoping to catch forty winks if he could before it was time for the next round.

Keeping watch was what he did most days, tediously trying to last out the long and lonely nights. As he leaned over closer now, his fingers dug into the spongy, moss-infested stone wall of the old turret. Straining his eyes over the distance, he stood in the same spot that he had occupied earlier, almost an hour ago.

What had been a soft glowing spot then had now definitely grown bigger, alarmingly bigger. It was fire. He was sure of it, especially against the black velvet of the night sky. Something large was burning out at sea, burning like a beacon, a warning, though why he should think so, he couldn't quite fathom. Then a disturbing thought entered his head, *burning boats* – not just one, but maybe more. He stepped back and gasped.

A vision of the merchant boats moored in the waters came flooding back to him. He was no stranger to them ferrying to and fro across the Straits between the prosperous lands of Iberia and Ceuta. He had grown as accustomed to seeing them as he was of the sea, the gulls and the shore's other comings and goings. Could it be that a boat had caught fire he wondered? It was late in the night and most people were asleep, yet he would have to report it. He quietly slipped away and hurriedly disappeared down a spiral stone stair-well.

The next day Bella was walking back from the orchard, her hands burdened by the weight of the heavy basket of oranges she was carrying. Even though the weave of it cut into her hands, the pain was nothing compared to the pain in her heart.

Rings of dark circles beneath her eyes marred her face from the restless night before.

After running away from Ben that evening, she had finally gone home and straight to bed, crying herself to sleep. The next morning, she left at the crack of dawn without any breakfast. She wanted to be left alone to her thoughts. How could it have come to this, she wondered over and over again. To have become betrothed to a man she loathed. The very thought of marriage to him made her skin crawl.

She had seen Leander often, especially at mass, trying to catch her attention, but she ignored him all the same. Polite and decent he may have been, but she could never contemplate his suit – not when there was such a gaping chasm between them.

She stopped suddenly, lowering the basket to the ground for a moment to ease the pain and numbness in her fingers. Wringing her hands in desperation, she stared blindly ahead, fresh tears threatening to fill her eyes once more as she imagined the life of misery ahead of her. Then a memory suddenly came to her. It was filled with longing for what could have been; a vision of laughter, games and a pair of childish blue eyes staring back at her.

David was her cousin. Although she didn't know it then while they played innocently as children, their betrothal had been agreed from the cradle. As soon as they grew up, their parents had hoped they would marry. What would he have been like now, if the Goths hadn't taken him and his family away?

Her mind drifted away until the sudden loud crack of a twig snapped her out of her thoughts. Someone was coming. She swept her lashes down in an effort to banish her tears. When they refused to escape, her fingers moved discreetly to brush them away from falling over her cheeks. Not waiting to look at who it was, Bella hastily picked up her basket, once more ready to flee, then she stiffened.

"Good afternoon, Bella," said a cheery but irritably familiar voice. "I hoped I'd see you today. I was just going to see your father when I saw you." Bella, not wishing to meet his eyes, averted her face, anger now rising within her. She had left home early knowing Leander would be coming to meet her father and she had no intention of being there. She had no stomach to meet him just yet.

"What do you want?" she replied coldly, busying herself with the basket.

"To talk to my betrothed of course – you do know we're to be married?" asked a confused Leander, coming to stand in front her, stopping her in her tracks. His long mousy hair was tied back at the nape revealing a wide brow and a thick line of dark eyebrows that now knit together over his question. To some, Leander might be considered a perfectly eligible match, but that meant nothing to Bella.

"I can't speak to you right now. I've chores to do," she said stiffly, still refusing to look at him. She would have moved past him only he stood before her, unwittingly barring her way on the narrow dirt track.

"Here let me help you with that, I'll carry it for you," offered Leander genially reaching for her basket, but Bella snatched it away.

"I don't need your help!" she said in a clipped voice. Leander's eyes suddenly narrowed as he looked at her thoughtfully. An uncomfortable silence passed between the two of them.

"You know Bella, when we're married, you'll have to honour and obey me," he said quietly. Bella couldn't help but shudder inwardly at those words that fell from his lips, full of intent. It was a reminder of everything she stood to lose.

"Yes, but you're not married yet," interrupted another familiar voice close by.

Leander swung his head round to see Ben smiling, standing near the trees beyond which lay their home.

"So, until then she has me to help her," continued Ben affably, despite the coolness in his eyes.

Bella had been holding her breath, but at the sight of her brother she sighed with relief. Seizing the opportunity, she slipped past a distracted Leander to stand beside her brother.

"Father's expecting you up at the house – if I were you, I wouldn't keep him waiting," said Ben politely as his eyes held Leander's. Ben wasn't afraid of him. Despite their difference in age the two young men stared at each other for a moment, locked in a battle of wills. Leander was first to break free from his gaze. He smiled benignly and walked past the two of them in the direction of their house, but not before playfully swiping an orange from Bella's basket.

They stared after him in mute silence and as Leander disappeared behind the trees, Bella finally dissolved into tears.

"Ben, what am I to do? I can't marry him!" said Bella in a voice both pathetic and ringing with panic.

"And you won't have to," grinned Ben, shaking his sister's shoulders, bringing her out of her hysterical state.

"Bella, there's been an army converging on the beach for weeks now and today they march through Iberia to meet Roderick. There is a battle coming!"

"*Those* men?" asked Bella, her sobbing stopped, suddenly giving way to a surprised gasp. Bella had forgotten all about the men on the beach.

"*Yes* – they mean us no harm and if Tariq Ibn Ziyad's men win, things will be different around here – you'll see! And *no one* can make you marry Leander if you don't want it," said Ben as he swung her off her feet.

Catching her breath for moment after finding herself firmly back on the ground, Bella looked up at her brother in a daze.

"I can't believe it – how can you be so sure? What if *they're* like the Goths?" she asked anxiously, through round wary eyes.

Then for the next few minutes she listened in an astonished silence as Ben talked of his encounters with Tariq's men. He spared her no detail in describing their chivalry and bravery, down to their extraordinary kindness towards him. Then he told her she needn't be scared or worried, for they treated womenfolk well.

A Muslim woman was allowed to inherit, with the right to handle and dispose of her own wealth as she pleased. When it came to marriage, a woman's consent was needed, and it could never be imposed upon her by force. Bella listened in wide-eyed wonder. She had never heard of such things before. It was too extraordinary to believe. Yet Ben knew the Muslims would do right by them. He had learned much about them, their Islamic faith and way of life in the hours he spent sitting in Hisham, Qasim and Ya'qub's company. In fact, Ben had only just now returned having spent the morning with Hisham and the others.

Father had come along with him, eager as he was to meet them. Tariq's men were all busy packing and preparing to move out. Hisham, Qasim, Ya'qub and the scouts among them would be following Tariq Ibn Ziyad deep into Theodomir's country while Tarif Ibn Malik, Humayun and a smaller troop of men headed out west towards White Port overlooking the other side of the bay. Ben had been sad at the thought of their parting. Tariq's men had become a big part of his life in the short space of time he had spent in their company. He had never known anyone like them before and there was no knowing when he would see them again.

Like him, Father had pledged his support to them. If all went well, the Muslims' newly acquired territory would be left in their absence under Father's safekeeping, together with a small garrison of men from Tariq's troop who would stay back. Aside from the Goths, Ben's father was a respected elder in the community and was likely to be an influential voice among them, with the remaining Muslim army guaranteeing security and protection from the Goths.

There would be many others only too willing to come out in support of Tariq's men, and not just from their own community. For almost two hundred years the early Visigoth kings had been Arian Christians who believed, like the Muslims, that Jesus was a human Prophet sent by God. And for a while this belief had been established by King Euric from the year 476 CE onwards, making it the official religion across their domain.

But all that had changed: over a century later, Recared the Visigoth king had converted to Catholicism and had then tried to force the rest of his kingdom to follow suit. With this change began the religious persecution of unitarian Arian Christians who refused to accept the Catholic belief of Jesus somehow being part of a divine trinity in which he featured at the same time as being both a mortal human and an indivisible part of the One Immortal God Who never eats, sleeps or dies.

Today there were still many unitarian Arian Christians left in Iberia and together with the Jewish population, they would be only too glad to see the back of the repressive trinitarian Visigoth rule over them.

Ben had never seen his father so happy, not in a long, long time. Father had looked torn, not knowing whether to cheer or cry tears of joy, but he shook the Muslims' hands with gratitude. As Ben finished, Bella burst into a new flood of tears, only this time out of sheer relief. Ben soon found himself locked in a bear hug with his sister. Excited, his eyes strayed over her shoulder to look back through the orchard in the direction where he knew the bay lay. Tariq's men would be leaving soon he thought, as a confident smile tugged at his lips. A wind of change was coming – and it was about to blow hard across the whole of Iberia.

Count Theodomir sat at his breakfast table. He had woken up in a disagreeable mood, perhaps from a bad dream, albeit one he couldn't remember. A superstitious man, Theodomir wondered if it was going to be one of those days when that irksome feeling niggling away at him spelled a bad omen for him. Impatiently, he tossed aside the missive from Roderick that he was reading. At least there was nothing in there to upset him. It was just more of the same, as the insufferable usurper divulged the latest news from his successful purge of the Basque rebels in the backwaters of their northern territories.

Lists reeled off the pages with names of leaders and traitors from among the rebellion, captured and accounted for. Along with the news were pages upon pages of self-praise and exaltation, all boasting of Roderick's success and the security he had established in his sovereign realm for years to come.

Quite honestly Theodomir couldn't have cared less about the machinations by which Roderick took the throne – just so long as his own lands and wealth remained intact and under *his* control. In any case, Roderick was king and it was his problem to bear, so better that *he* got his hands dirty in quashing any resistance. Theodomir, on the other hand, was only too pleased to watch over and defend his fortress in the South where his own precious lands lay.

He was just about to sink his teeth into a boiled egg when his peaceful breakfast was spoiled by loud, hurried footsteps and a noisy commotion brought about by the unceremonious arrival of a flustered soldier.

"What is the meaning of this?" thundered Theodomir over his interrupted breakfast, his face glaring as he brought his fist forcibly down upon the table, shaking its contents.

"Forgive me master –" said the man mustering his breath (and all his courage) to deliver the important news. Then finally with a distinct urgency, the words came tumbling out of his mouth.

"Sire, we're under attack – from across the sea!" he spluttered.

Theodomir froze. His expression was a perfect picture of astonishment at these words. A spasm twitched at the side of his round, purple face as he stared fixedly back at the soldier. For once, words failed him. Who would dare to cross into their dominions, he thought, as he sat in disbelief, floundering over the soldier's report? Finally, willing himself out of his confounded state, he looked at the man steadily.

"What do you mean we're under attack?" he demanded aghast, a vein now pulsating dangerously on his temple.

"One of the lookouts stationed at White Port reported a fire out at sea near the Rock," said the man hurriedly. "I went out to investigate – and master, the enemy, they were burning their *own* boats, every one of them!"

Theodomir's mouth fell agape. An almost ludicrous expression, somewhere between stunned disbelief and outrage possessed his haughty features. Nervously stealing a glance at Theodomir, the man continued to describe what he had seen: thousands upon thousands of strangers, foreign men, swarming around the Rock and on the surrounding beaches. There could be no mistaking the fact that they had set up camp (for some weeks now by the looks of it). For anyone watching, it was obvious that they had no plans to return from whence they had come, having burnt their boats to ashes. What was more, from all the intelligence he could glean, by first light they had been busy preparing to march through Iberia.

"Are you certain?" asked Theodomir as he laced his fingers together, trying to think hard. Roderick and a large portion of the Goth army were in the North and this unexpected situation was fraught with complications, more than he or even Roderick had ever imagined could happen while he was away.

"I saw it with my own eyes, Sire," persisted the soldier shaking his head in shock, as he recalled the vision of the burnt boats, now charred wrecks, bobbing lifelessly in the water. The sea and beaches were tinged black from falling ash and the once strong smell of acrid smoke that had led him to the discovery of the boats still lingered faintly in the air.

"When I left them, at least a third of their force appeared to be planning to head westward and make their way around the bay, but it's the rest of 'em master – I think they're preparing to come out our way!"

Count Theodomir rose wrathfully from his seat. He pushed his chair back so forcefully that it flew across the room, his breakfast in tow as his hands swept it off the table. The flying food narrowly missed the soldier as he ducked, shrinking back in fright.

"I'll not stand for this – gather every man we've got!" ordered Theodomir, his voice ringing off the stone walls. But his bravado belied the fear that was slowly creeping into his heart and soul. Tariq Ibn Ziyad's message had reached the first of its intended recipients, just in the manner he had hoped.

16

OLD MOTHER MAGDA

JUST as the soldier had described to Count Theodomir earlier that morning, the Umayyad camp was still thronging with noisy activity. It was past midday now. There was a cacophony of bleats, chomping and scuffling of horses' hooves and livestock. Men shouted out fresh orders at the tops of their voices. Tariq's men doused the campfires, packed away their tents and belongings and loaded them on to the backs of their horses in preparation for the long journey ahead.

There was no mistaking the frisson of excitement amongst the men now that they were finally leaving. They were about to exchange their temporary barracks, their home for these past few weeks, for the next adventure ahead in this strange, unfamiliar part of the world. Tarif Ibn Malik stood, arms folded, beneath the shelter of an ancient elm tree whose thick trunk provided ample support for the heavy shoulder that rested against it. He was listening closely to Tariq Ibn Ziyad meticulously going over his plan one last time.

According to Ilyan, their most pressing threat at the moment was Count Theodomir. His force was by far the biggest force they would meet in the South, especially as he had been left behind by Roderick as its protector. Tariq had no doubt. As soon as the news reached his ears, Count Theodomir was sure to send a battalion out to meet them. So, Tariq's plan was simple. He would lead the main body of his troops inland to drive them back, leaving Tarif Ibn Malik and his troops free to subdue the smaller towns of Julia Loza, White Port and Gaddes. The more territory that came under their control, the stronger their hold would become.

Hisham, Qasim and Ya'qub were close by, also busy preparing to leave. Hisham sat on the hard-packed sand, his fingers busy with nimbly stringing his bow, while Qasim was rubbing down Warda with straw. So, it was left to Ya'qub to notice a lonely figure quietly lingering in the shadows of a nearby copse. Sensing the presence, Ya'qub suddenly looked up and stiffened, stock-still. Seeing Ya'qub, the figure hastily stepped into the sunlight to make herself known.

It was an old woman, hunched over and swaddled in a ragged shawl that she held close about her. Her gaunt face revealed a pale skin heavily lined with gossamer veins surrounding a pair of strange eyes. One eye held his with a steady gaze, while the other was glazed over by a lifeless blue cloud. The old woman's ribs rose and fell from the effort of walking as she continued to hobble her way towards him, until to his surprise, Ya'qub recognised her too. By now both Hisham and Qasim had stopped their chores, having both locked eyes on the old woman too.

"Mother Magda! What are you doing here?" exclaimed Ya'qub, taken aback at the sight of her. He hadn't seen Old Mother Magda in over a year and to see a familiar face after so long gave him a strange feeling, a cold reminder of another life he once knew.

The old woman's breath rasped in her throat before the words came fitfully.

"Jacob – young Jacob?" she asked searching his face. It was the only thing about him that looked familiar, despite his unusual clothes.

"Aye, it *is* you! My good eye didn't fail me – except you have changed I think, but never mind that right now, where is he Jacob?" she faltered between deep breaths before continuing. "I must see him – I must!"

"Who, Mother Magda?" asked Ya'qub looking at the old woman, puzzled. Who among this gathering of strangers could she mean? But then again, it was what one might expect from her, he reflected on second thoughts. Old Mother Magda could be a trifle eccentric at times and the towns-folk did think her 'a little touched in the head.' Still, Ya'qub knew her to be nothing more than a harmless, frail, old woman who wandered from the fields to the thick woods, lonely as she was since the death of her husband.

Having abandoned his bow, Hisham stood up and came to her side. Old Mother Magda was by now parched from the effort of talking in the heat.

She looked at Hisham with curiosity and asked for some water. Hisham disappeared and soon returned carrying a pitcher of water and a wooden beaker.

It was another hot, sweltering day in Iberia. The old woman took the tumbler and gratefully drank down its cool contents, wiping the back of an unsteady hand across her mouth after she finished. She had been watching Tariq's men from afar with a keen eye for some time now. They were beings like she had never seen before, yet they did not frighten her in the least.

"Thank you," she smiled, revealing her pink fleshy toothless gums.

"Now, who is it that you want to see?" Hisham asked good naturedly.

"Your master – take me to him. I must see him!" she pleaded, wringing her old, withered hands before her.

"Tariq Ibn Ziyad?" asked Ya'qub with a startled face. "Why do you want to see Tariq?"

"I must speak with him – I must – I'll not leave until I do," she demanded like a petulant child. "I have something important to tell him that may be of benefit to him!"

Both men looked at each other helplessly, knowing how near impossible a request it was that she was asking of them.

"Why don't you tell me – and I'll make sure he gets the message," offered Hisham kindly, before he was cut short.

"No! Only him, I must speak only to him and see him with my own eyes," she chided.

Hisham caught Ya'qub's eye with unease and the younger man read his worry. Ya'qub quickly moved to his side and in a low voice vouched for her harmless nature. It was enough to satisfy Hisham as to see him nod his head in response.

"I can't promise you anything, but I'll see what I can do," said Hisham, to Old Mother Magda's obvious relief.

"Stay with her Ya'qub," shot Hisham over his shoulder, as he quickly strode a short distance away towards where Tariq and his men sat in serious conversation beneath the cover of the great elm tree. Hisham hesitated to interrupt, but soon managed to catch the attention of Humayun. He was part of the detachment of Tariq's guards, and a less daunting a figure for him to approach in the first instance. Hisham sought permission to speak to Tariq, explaining the old woman's request, and that she had refused to speak to anyone but Tariq Ibn Ziyad himself. Humayun looked sceptical at first but then relented to Hisham's strange request.

"Alright, but only because you tell me Ya'qub knows her!" he said finally. "He's busy, *akhi*, but wait here, I'll see what he says." Humayun steered off in Tariq's direction to speak to him.

Tariq had just finished his briefing when he looked up to find Humayun coughing discreetly at his side. Hisham eagerly watched with bated breath the exchange that passed between the two men until finally he was summoned before Tariq.

"Hisham – you wish to speak to me?" asked Tariq curiously.

"Yes, *Sayyid*, forgive me, *Sayyid* – I know you're

busy, but there is an old woman here from among the local folk who wishes to speak to you. Her name is Old Mother Magda – Ya'qub knows her well."

"An old woman?" asked Tariq with mild interest. "What does she want?"

"I don't know *Sayyid* she wouldn't say – only she insists upon seeing you and refuses to leave," said Hisham earnestly as he looked across and saw the woman in question, looking pathetic and frail.

"She says she has information that may be of use to you *Sayyid*!" If it was a piece of intelligence, Tariq found this intriguing.

"Very well, bring her to me," he said finally.

"Yes, *Sayyid*," replied Hisham, who then hurried away.

"A mystery no less, *subhana'Allah*," said Tarif Ibn Malik as he watched Hisham return to the old woman's side. "But do you really think it's worth speaking to her?"

"I don't know but she's old and so it behoves us to listen to what she has to say," reflected Tariq, as he watched her curiously from afar. After all, he did hope to win as many people over as he could without having to resort to meeting them through resistance. He had already hoped to gain as many supporters as possible amongst the Iberians through young Ben – and especially his father whom he had met only a few hours earlier that very morning. Who knows, he reasoned, perhaps like them the old woman may also have an influence over her people too. He watched her make her way towards him with Hisham and Ya'qub flanked on either side, her gait slow but determined.

As she came before him, he was surprised to see her now at close quarters. She was much older than he had expected, judging her to be close on a hundred years. Heavy lines marked her face, gathered there like a tally of every season she had witnessed. He had never met anyone as old as this, only heard about such people. In fact, Musa Ibn Nusayr had told him how the Prophet Muhammad had once prayed for the wellbeing of his little servant, Anas Ibn Malik when he was a young boy.

The Prophet's supplication was answered, for Anas was blessed with abundance in wealth, children and life. He still lived among them to this day, having reached a ripe old age of more than a hundred years, settled as he had been for a while now in the bustling city of Basra. Of all the companions of the Prophet, only Anas Ibn Malik and Aamir Abu Tufail were left to walk amongst them, still spreading the message of truth.

Beneath the whispering leaves of the elm tree, Tariq Ibn Ziyad now began to appraise the old woman with a degree of fascination. She was dressed in moth-eaten rags, long since faded to an earthy colour. As Old Mother Magda stood before him, she lay a shaky hand over her chest to still her excitement, fixing her one good eye intently on him. Hisham would have introduced her but in her haste to speak, she was the first to break the silence between them.

"No one would believe my husband, but he said you would come one day!" she spoke eagerly, as her jowls hung quivering beneath her chin. Surprised, Tariq looked at her questioningly and she continued to speak.

"Oh stranger, you should know that my husband had a dream you would come," she continued in a wheezy voice, moving a little closer to Tariq, still studying his face closely as her good eye bore into him.

"I heard him say so, over and over again to the people of this land – a foreign general will come to this island and subdue it and subject it to his arms."

By now Tariq was astonished, while a few of the younger officers' lips had begun to tug at their corners until he threw them a warning glance, reminding them of their manners. The gesture brought them swiftly back to attention. He could imagine their young heads whirling with words that would condemn her as '*majnoon*'.

Tariq looked back sympathetically at Old Mother Magda once again, not knowing what to make of her, except that it was the Prophet, blessings and peace be upon him, who taught, "He is not of us who does not have mercy on young children, nor honour the elderly." Tariq didn't have the heart to rebuff her.

"And you think it's me that your husband spoke of?" asked Tariq kindly. "How can you be so sure?"

Old Mother Magda broke into a toothless smile.

"*Ah*, but he described *you* to me," she said pointing a crooked finger at his forehead. "A man with a prominent temple such as I see in thee, but he shall also bear a mark upon him – 'tis a

As Old Mother Magda stood before him she lay a shaky hand over her chest

black mole covered with hair, upon his left shoulder."

Intrigued by Old Mother Magda's words, Tarif Ibn Malik drew near to Tariq to ask if he had seen such a mole on his person. Tariq shook his head, not knowing the answer to this. He had never thought to check for any distinguishing marks on his body – and he certainly wasn't in the habit of looking over his shoulder for any reason to have noticed one either. Tariq discreetly loosened the tunic around his neck and laid bare his left shoulder. To Tariq's and everyone else's surprise, the mole revealed itself. It was just as she had described it, a small dark blemish with hair sprouting out from it.

"There you see – just where I said it would be," pronounced Old Mother Magda with satisfaction, followed by a crack of laughter, a cheerfully rusty noise. "I'd like to see their faces now," she said with glee.

Tariq's cheeks lifted as he smiled, amused by her infectious excitement.

Tariq realised, as was true of many medieval societies, that the locals may be deeply superstitious and could well believe in omens. He himself knew that all matters transpired only by the decree of Allah. Still, if the story were to spread amongst the Iberians it may be to his advantage.

"Then you do not object to our being on your shores?" asked Tariq curiously. Old Mother Magda shook her head.

"No – not when I know you can rid this land of its plague," she said suddenly serious again. Tariq inclined his head.

"I pray that you are right *insha'Allah*. I am only here in this land by Allah's design and decree – and if I do succeed, this too will only happen by His leave," said Tariq. He knew that his destiny and indeed the destinies of all people are written by Allah and within His knowledge alone, recorded in the *Lawh al-Mahfuz*, the Preserved Tablet of Forms. Allah knew before He wrote and wrote before He created – and thus does all creation unfold and proceed in accordance with His knowledge and writing.

"Oh, that I should have lived so long as to finally see this day," exclaimed Old Mother Magda beginning to sob, slow tears of joy washing her grimy face.

"I know you'll prove my husband's naysayers wrong – and I'll rejoice in telling 'em so," she said adamantly.

Tariq turned to look at Hisham.

"Give our guest some food to take away with her and some money before she leaves," instructed Tariq before dismissing them.

"I will, *Sayyid*," said Hisham. Then along with Ya'qub, they guided Old Mother Magda away from Tariq's company.

Once they were out of earshot, Tarif Ibn Malik looked to Tariq eager to know his thoughts on this strangest of encounters.

"If they're a superstitious people," revealed Tariq, "let's hope Old Mother Magda convinces them this time. If they're expecting us, it will make things all the more easy for us if they accept our protection from the Goths, *insha'Allah*."

Tarif nodded and just as he was about to add his own views along the same lines, a loud commotion erupted in the camp. Two spirited riders had stormed into their camp like a whirlwind. Tariq's scouts Mustafa and Abdullah had returned, and both made a bee line for him.

As they drew level to Tariq, their horses puffed and snorted from their strenuous journey. Abdullah's eyes clamped eagerly onto the Umayyad general.

"Theodomir's on the move – he and his men are preparing to march towards us even as we speak, *Sayyid!*"

Tariq nodded his head and motioned his men into immediate action.

"Have everyone ready – we move out in thirty minutes!" ordered Tariq. The news quickly began to spread throughout camp.

Tariq turned his attention back to Tarif Ibn Malik as he still stood quietly beside him, knowing Tariq would have a few final words for him too. Tariq Ibn Ziyad put out his hand to press Tarif's shoulder assuredly.

"You know what you must do, *akhi*. Make haste towards the West whilst we confront Theodomir and his minions," said Tariq Ibn Ziyad with a confident smile that stretched from cheek to cheek.

"We'll catch up with you and your men soon enough, *insha'Allah*."

King Roderick

Basque Country

WITH head bent low over the parchment, King Roderick read it once through, then read it again in disbelief as Count Theodomir's words swam before his eyes.

> *– Sire, this our land has been invaded by people whose name, country and origin are unknown to me. I cannot even tell thee from whence they have come, whether they fell from the skies, or sprang from the earth –*

Roderick felt his pulse quicken as he slowly allowed the parchment to furl back into a roll. His fingers loosened their grip over it, as though all the strength had left them, and he let it slip from between his hands onto the wooden table. Roderick looked questioningly at the dusty, dishevelled messenger who paled under his scrutiny as he stood nervously before him.

They were inside a weather-beaten, grimy command tent that had been Roderick's dwelling these past weeks. Roderick wanted to know more; more than what was briefly recorded on the piece of vellum sent by Count Theodomir from which he had just read.

It had been a long time since any news had reached him from the South through Theodomir, but no news was good news as far as it concerned King Roderick. There had been many long weeks of fighting purging the rebels. All he yearned for was the creature comforts of his palace in Toledo, where its beautiful gardens beckoned and its idle life of amusement called out to him invitingly.

A shroud of despondency settled over him now as he listened with all ears to the messenger relay back all he had seen and discovered of this invading force from across the Straits. The more he heard, the more his heart sank. Somewhere at the back of his mind echoed the notion that he had brought this upon himself. He moved to press the man for more information.

"These men – what are they like?" asked the king, staring fixedly at him, with some disquietude. This attack seemed more than a mere raid in search of spoils of the kind to which the Goths were accustomed.

"Brave men or mad men I cannot say, Sire, but no sooner had they landed than they burnt their boats – or rather Count Julian's!"

"*Julian!*" exclaimed Roderick, his voice ringing strangely in his ears. "So, that's the way the wind blows," he muttered beneath his breath in disbelief. Stunned, he slowly stood up from his seat and began to pace about the confines of his command tent.

Roderick had guessed many months ago that Julian had discovered the truth about Florinda when he had made raids inland, wreaking havoc upon his land. But that was nothing compared to what he had done since. Roderick could overlook the raid if he wanted, but not this. It was now clear to him that Julian was intent on seeking revenge by destroying him in a way he never thought imaginable. Roderick's lips began to feel dry.

"You are certain it was Julian's boats?" asked Roderick after a pause.

"Yes, Sire, there's no doubt," said the man nodding his head adamantly. "It's his boats alright and he's been seen in their company too. I fear Count Julian has betrayed you," added the man hurriedly. Roderick pursed his lips in fury.

"Count Theodomir went to seek 'em out. There was a skirmish to be sure, but he was forced to withdraw. We were outnumbered, outclassed on the field, and their general, Tariq Ibn Ziyad is not one to be trifled with. We need reinforcements, Sire. Count Theodomir begs you to return to the South immediately," implored the messenger, pausing to brace himself before he could reveal the next big blow.

"Sire, there's something else …"

"What?" said Roderick tersely feeling his spirits slip even lower. Surely there couldn't be anything worse than what had already happened. The man stared back at him wondering how best to phrase the awful news.

"Sire … the South has fractured. The enemy's

standards fly over our turrets – they have laid
claim to many of our towns already!"

Roderick froze in his steps. His eyes turned
bloodshot. He listened with mounting dismay as
the messenger described to him how soon after
Theodomir's encounter, the speed at which the
towns surrendered was unprecedented. Most of
the peasants had been won over by an enemy who
offered them security and protection in exchange
for a small tribute.

"*TREASON!* – This is *treason!*" spat Roderick.
By now the veins in his temples were throbbing
menacingly, as the messenger quaked in his boots.

"They'll pay dearly for this treachery!" seethed
King Roderick between clenched teeth, not willing to accept that the collapse of his kingdom
might be the consequence of his own wretched
actions. Roderick had meted out nothing but
cruelty and injustice upon the innocent lives who
now most willingly and gladly had turned against
him.

"*Get out!*" ordered Roderick. The bedraggled
messenger eagerly slipped out through the flap
door of the tent. His legs feeling heavy, Roderick
suddenly collapsed back into his seat. He held his
face in his hands.

"What have I done?" he asked himself in
despair, even now not thinking about the many
thousands of lives on which he had inflicted much
suffering. Instead, he was haunted by the memory of a terrible day soon after he had taken the
throne. It was an ill made decision, which had led
him to the doors of the Palace of Secrets, that now

seemed inescapably to have sealed his fate of doom.

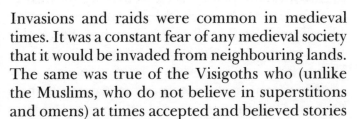

Invasions and raids were common in medieval times. It was a constant fear of any medieval society that it would be invaded from neighbouring lands. The same was true of the Visigoths who (unlike the Muslims, who do not believe in superstitions and omens) at times accepted and believed stories and superstitions spun out of their own worst fears and worries ...

In the desolate foothills of the old city of Toledo stood the Palace of Secrets. Now it was a curious thing that the last twenty-seven Visigoth kings of Iberia had faithfully taken to practising a tradition of placing a lock upon its strong gates. It was said that within the walls of the sacred palace lay secrets in need of being protected. So it was, that succession after succession of superstitious Visigoth kings had chosen to follow this custom.

By the time Roderick had claimed the throne for himself, twenty-seven padlocks barred the gate of the Palace of Secrets, placed there by the twenty-seven Visigoth kings who had ruled before him. Yet Roderick was unlike any of the other kings. For he, on the other hand, looked upon the locks with derision and the hidden secrets it guarded with greed. Surely such protection could only mean one thing: that what lay within in its walls was precious. So, his mind toiled to unearth the only mystery he could see and one he sought to solve, 'exactly how precious?'

It was with a pale, stricken look that his first minister had come to him one morning, after he had discovered that it was Roderick's plan to break open the padlocks fixed to the palace gate. In vain did he beseech the king to come to his senses and not break with what had become a long-standing tradition of all the sovereigns before him.

"I beg you would not, Sire," exclaimed Bishop Oppas, desperate as he was with worry. His long silvery head of hair shook over his shoulders and his eyes were large, full of concern.

"Surely it cannot be important to you, with all that you have acquired already?" said Oppas, the merest trace of sullenness in his voice. For if the truth be known, Oppas despised him from the very depths of his heart. Roderick had usurped the throne from his nephew, his very own beloved brother, Wittiza's son, along with most of their wealth and that of the kingdom.

Roderick, who was sat down to breakfast, gave an indifferent shrug.

"Come now, I simply wish to open the gate and know what lies within," he replied nonchalantly, as he carelessly popped a succulent grape from a nearby platter of fruit into his mouth.

"Am I not the king, and is this not my realm?" shot Roderick at his minister, with a haughty wave of his hand in the air.

A slight pause followed, and Oppas held his gaze for a moment.

"Yes, Sire," replied Oppas quietly.

"Then do I not have the right to see what my

hands possess?" asked the king, his expression confident and exultant.

"Yes ... but Sire, consider if the gates have been locked for as long as they have, then one can only presume it has been for a good reason. Surely it would be better to let sleeping dogs lie? Please Sire, place a padlock like your predecessors and be done with it!" replied Oppas, desperately appealing to Roderick's better judgment.

In truth, he was petrified. No king before had meddled with tradition nor sought to unearth its mystery. Oppas was fearful of what lay behind the strange palace walls and of the consequences of what might befall them all if the king followed his whim. Roderick on the other hand was poised to think otherwise. He could not resist the temptation of its mystery and *he* was a determined man.

"I have a mind to open the Palace gate," said Roderick with a stubborn light in his eye. "And nothing you say will convince me otherwise. I myself believe it to be a hoax and I'm not the kind of king who shall yield to anything, least of all a jest."

"It may indeed be a mere jest as you say, Sire, but prudence and caution dictate that we should not delve into its mystery," urged Oppas, now wringing his bony hands together in despair. Suddenly a thought came to him on an impulse, pushed as he was to the point of desperation.

"Tell me, Sire, if you think there is treasure to be found inside the Palace, how much do you believe it's value to be? Your other ministers and I shall collect the same sum amongst ourselves and present it to you for your royal treasury."

Roderick threw his head back and roared with laughter.

"If I were you, I should not pledge as you do for it would take everyone's entire wealth to stall me!" said Roderick mercilessly, wiping his eyes. Oppas couldn't think of a reply to this, stunned as he was into silence.

"I leave in an hour for the Palace of Secrets – join me if you wish, or else step aside!" ordered Roderick rising from his table. He swept past his minister as he stood silently by, his mouth agape and his back hunched over with disappointment.

Roderick made good his intentions. An hour later he and his entourage, including Oppas, the rest of his ministers and his guards, left for the Palace.

The Palace of Secrets stood bleakly on a hill looking down over the ancient city of Toledo. Creeping ivy spread unchecked over its old damp, thick, stone walls. Even the patch of sky above it lacked the usual lustre and warmth of the Mediterranean clime. Instead, it seemed to watch coldly from above, brooding. Toledans knew better than to go anywhere near the place, which stood lifeless and empty and seemed to warn them away. Over time, such stories had been spun as to leave them shuddering, suspicious and scared out of their wits. They scuttled past it if ever necessity brought them anywhere close to its walls.

Undeterred and insolent, Roderick stood before the gate which was flanked by tall stone newels on either side. His eyes eagerly latched on to the twenty-seven rusty padlocks tethered together by a noose of chains. He summoned his guards forward and gave orders to break them open. Oppas and the other ministers stood by helplessly, watching and praying. Finally, the chains clanked and clamoured as they fell to the ground.

Smiling in a self-satisfied way, Roderick stepped forward and placed his hand on the ambient metal for a moment. Then with a push the rusty gate swung wide open, protesting noisily. The ministers, who had held their breath as though they expected to be struck by lightning at any moment for attempting such a sacrilegious trespass, finally heaved a sigh of relief. They cautiously stepped through the gateway, following in Roderick's footsteps who by then had already entered into the Palace.

Inside was a great cavernous hall, unpleasantly cold. The air smelt distinctly musty. The walls around them were plastered with dust and hung with cobwebs that occasionally caught at their heads. As their eyes widened and accustomed themselves to the dim light, a curious object slowly began to materialise out of the semi-darkness before their eyes. Roderick gravitated towards the far corner where it sat and gasped in feverish delight.

"What is it, Sire?" asked Oppas curiously craning his neck over the tall, burly figure of Roderick, trying his best to get a view of the object for himself.

"It's a table," replied Roderick. Never had he seen anything so exquisite, made as it was of intricately carved, aromatic wood. It was set with gold and precious stones like emeralds for beading. Even its slender legs were decoratively embellished with gemstones. As his hand roved over its smooth, shiny surface, his fingers ran over an inscription in Greek.

"Wait, it says something here: '*This is the table of Solomon, son of David, upon whom be peace*,'" said Roderick reading aloud the inscribed words. An excited babble rose amongst the ministers.

"It cannot be... but this is incredible!" exclaimed Oppas as he stared in wonder and awe at the old relic.

"Sire, we've found another locked door!" came another voice with urgency, interrupting them from behind. Roderick spun on his heels. It was one of Roderick's guards who appeared from the shadows, hastening towards him.

"Show me!" he ordered. The eager young guard led Roderick only a short distance away, his ministers following close behind. They soon stopped before a small, heavy door sealed by a strong padlock.

"Break it open!" commanded Roderick. His men promptly complied. Within moments the lock was snapped, and the door opened on its hinges, creaking resentfully. Roderick and his ministers filed through the opening, to find themselves inside a small chamber. It was completely empty except for a curious, solitary object that sat in the center of the room.

Roderick moved towards it and soon found himself looking at a beautiful marble urn with an ornate lid.

"Sire, maybe we should leave it be, you have Solomon's fabled table – surely it's enough for you?" ventured Oppas as he eyed the urn uneasily. He could sense there was something strange about this place, but Roderick had come too far to turn back now. Ignoring Oppas' plea, Roderick lifted off the heavy lid of the urn and slipped his hand inside. His fingers soon curled around an object. He pulled it out to discover it was an old, rolled parchment, which he carefully began to unfurl.

One of the guards hurried to his aid, bringing a torch closer into the otherwise darkened room. The flickering light soon illuminated the parchment to reveal a mysterious drawing of rich, vibrant colours. There were figures of men, neither Visigoth nor Roman nor Greek in appearance, but foreign. They were turbaned and dressed unlike any people he had ever seen before, riding horses and armed with swords, spears and bows. Then Roderick's eyes were drawn to an inscription that he slowly began to read.

"*Oh ye be warned, should this sanctuary be violated, the people depicted in this parchment shall invade this land, overturn the throne of its kings – and subdue – the whole country…*" read Roderick, his voice faltering and fading away into silence. At first a deathly quiet filled the room until finally a low moan broke its stillness.

"We're ruined!" exclaimed Oppas and the ministers woefully as they began to weep for fear. Roderick stared blindly down at the parchment, petrified and filled with sudden remorse. '*What have I done?*' he wondered, as a wave of panic and fear swept over his mind and soul. He shuddered. Could this be true? If the Palace of Secrets housed something as sacred as the table that once belonged to a Prophet of God, then what did the violation of this sanctuary and words of the scroll mean for him?

The Palace of Secrets was sealed at once. Roderick spent the days that followed feeling penitent for a time. As the weeks went by however, and nothing happened, he soon returned to his old arrogant ways and life moved along blissfully for him, as before.

When the Basque rebellion had broken out, his mind had soon become diverted solely towards dealing with the insurrection in the North, having convinced himself by then to believe that there was no substance to the prophecy contained in the parchment, especially when no foreign force had appeared. Roderick had soon forgotten that fateful day at the Palace of Secrets – until now.

A firm breeze rose outside and the sides of his dusty command tent flapped. King Roderick's hand tightened on his goblet as he began to twist it on its spot. His eyes kept returning to Count Theodomir's vellum as it lay open on the table, his mind lingering over the words,

"Sire, this our land has been invaded by people whose name, country and origin are unknown to me ..."

Roderick could not shake off the sickening feeling rising in his stomach. It appeared that the prophecy in the urn from the Palace of Secrets now had a ring of truth and may have confirmed with its words of finality, the eventual means of his undoing – and yet a hope persisted in him. Roderick's mind worked hard to formulate a plan, for he would not be defeated – he *must not* be defeated. Then after a time pacing, he called out to his guard and the man soon appeared from behind the flap door.

"Assemble the men! We leave tomorrow for Cordova!" ordered Roderick harshly. Quailing under his icy glare, the guard quickly nodded his head and disappeared back through the flap once more. Roderick picked up his goblet and threw it forcefully across at the wall of the tent, splattering its contents. He would go to his castle at Cordova and put together the largest army this land had ever seen and go out and meet Tariq's force.

18

HEIRS OF WITTIZA

TWO lone figures on horseback watched from afar on a gentle rise that overlooked the grassy banks of the Guadalete river. On the other side of its waters, in the far distance about half a mile away, they could make out the ghostly shapes of hundreds upon hundreds of tents, that went back and beyond as far as the dark tree line on the horizon. The young Visigoth princes, for they were of royal blood from the blood line of King Wittiza, silently studied the landscape before them. The older, fairer haired of the two princes turned now on his saddle to address the younger prince.

"He's clever. He's chosen his ground well, this Tariq."

"I agree, brother. He has everything he needs here. There's water, the hills, access to the woods and the flat plains – all can be put to good use in or out of battle," said the younger prince thoughtfully, as his full head of dark curling hair ruffled in the breeze.

"I'm told by our spies that Tariq Ibn Ziyad has

won over the peasants – they've accepted their
security and protection in exchange for a tribute.
What do you think of that?" asked the fair-haired
prince, seeking his younger brother's opinion.

"So, it's true then – we've lost White Port and
all the other towns in the South to them?" asked
the younger prince.

"We have," came the firm reply from his older
brother who was staring ahead once more at the
tents and their pennants fluttering in the distance
under the bright sunshine. He knew the spark of
rebellion lit by the Goths' own oppressive ways,
had been fanned by a resentment that had grown
over time.

"Do you think this army will leave?" asked the
younger prince, studying his older brother's profile
impatiently, as if seeking the answer in his expression.

The fair-haired prince considered the question
for a moment.

"No," he said flatly.

"And our brother-in law – has Julian *really*
joined their side?" asked the younger prince
curiously.

"Yes," he said, "I have no doubt of it."

The younger prince for a moment quietly
digested all that he had heard.

"Maybe we ought to negotiate our own position, our security, before anyone else's," said the
younger prince finally. "We've lost so much
already to Roderick. I'd hate to lose all that we
have left," he sighed, staring at Tariq's encampment. From where he stood, they looked formidable, ordered and disciplined.

"I agree," said the fair-haired prince, with an unfathomable light in his eyes, "but I have a better plan, brother."

Upon hearing the strange note in his older brother's voice, it was the younger prince who turned in his saddle this time, to look at him squarely in surprise.

"What do you have in mind, brother?"

"I think Olmund, it's time we avenged our father, don't you?" said the fair-haired prince.

Olmund's eyes grew wide in surprise.

"I have no intention of riding beside Roderick if I can help it," said the fair-haired prince, curling his lip in disdain with the pride and arrogance of a young warrior who had been wronged. "Send a messenger to parley between us and Tariq. I will endeavour to reach an agreement with him that all our father's possessions, his lands, his farms and our royal inheritance be returned to us after the battle. All this will be in exchange for our switching sides and fighting with Tariq," added the fair-haired prince.

The younger prince stared back at his brother, Prince Achila, in awe. From cheek to cheek, a wide grin slowly spread across Olmund's face. It was something that Achila had not seen his younger brother, Prince Olmund, do in a long time – at least not since Roderick had destroyed their lives. He had usurped what ought to have been Achila's throne, right from under his very nose, once their father had died – or rather, as he suspected, had been murdered.

Roderick had pushed Achila aside to take the

"What do you have in mind, brother?"

throne for himself. He had protested that the prince was too young and inexperienced to rule, whilst he on the other hand was older and wiser. Yet now, perversely, Roderick had summoned them in the expectation that they, the sons of Wittiza, should ride beside him into battle in solidarity with him, to defend *his* throne. Both he and his brother Olmund had been given command of the right and left wings of Roderick's army. It was about the only thing Roderick had ever done right and Prince Achila would soon show him why.

It was with a conspiratorial smile upon his lips that Prince Achila took one last look at Tariq's encampment. Then he drew his beautiful, white stallion round on its haunches and both the young princes kicked into a brisk canter and rode away.

------>

27th Ramadan, 92 AH, July 711 CE

"*Subhana'Allah*, he's a slippery one," said Qasim irritably under his breath, as he stood shin deep in the river. It was a beautiful summer's day in July and the warm season made for perfect conditions out on the river of Guadalete. The waters that glistened under the bright sunlight were wide, but their depths shallow. It was also deliciously cool, a most welcoming relief from the heat of the day.

Qasim was standing in a part of the river where

the water was at its shallowest and ran slowly. Still, the river bubbled with froth mostly because of Qasim's poor efforts at fishing that marred the otherwise clear, beautiful waters of the Guadalete. It was his fifth attempt and he had already lost two plump trout, that had narrowly escaped from his clutches.

He stood still in the water at that moment, focusing hard, his brows knit together in concentration as always. Bent over, he watched with a keen eye the silvery, scaly armour of his prey, shimmering as it swam beneath the water's surface, toying with him. The spear in his right hand hovered in the air above the water, waiting for the precise moment to strike.

Qasim held his breath, *'Bismillah,'* and then *whoosh!* He plunged the spear into the river and struck its bed. He was too late – the fish had flexed its body in time and made its escape. Qasim kicked at the water in his frustration. A hearty laugh soon rose from the riverbank. It was Hisham as he lay resting on the lush green grass beside the river. He had been watching Qasim's efforts with great interest.

"*Akhi*, there goes my *iftar* again! By the time you catch it the campfire will have burned out," teased Hisham.

Qasim scooped the water in his hands and splashed Hisham with it, grinning mischievously. Blissfully grazing on the grass nearby, Warda paused to look disapprovingly at the pair. She tossed her head and nickered at them in a show of protest for disturbing her peace. The men were all as eager as each other to prepare for *iftar*, especially after having spent a long day at drill practice, with Humayun putting them through their paces, as always.

The food reserves which they had brought over from Tangiers had all but almost gone. Even the generous gifts of vegetables and fruit given to them by the peasants from the towns they had taken over in the South had been exhausted.

So, it was a blessing for them that the Guadalete river was rich in trout and salmon, if only one could catch them. Qasim had only managed to catch two so far. It didn't help that his arms already ached so much from hours spent being wrenched. He had been practising hard, trying to mount Warda on the move again. He still hadn't mastered the art of vaulting and had failed miserably at it again today, so he wasn't in a particularly good mood anyway.

Just at that very moment, Ya'qub, who was a little further along down the river, exploded in a hoot of laughter.

"Got another one! That's five now, *alhamdulillah*," he shouted, adding to Qasim's own frustration. Feeling a little piqued and exhausted, Qasim gave up and waded back towards the bank.

"Never mind *akhi*, you'll do it next time, *insha'Allah*," said Hisham, offering his hand to pull him out of the river. "You just need more practice, that's all. It's not easy, I know. The water casts an illusion – you think the fish is closer to the water's surface and further away than it really is. That's why a fisherman aims ahead of the fish as it approaches – you see, it's a different skill to the one you need in battle." Then Hisham's eyes fell on Qasim's meagre basket.

"*Subhana'Allah*, His word is true," marvelled Hisham shaking his head.

"Whose word?" asked Qasim as his feet clambered up the soft spongy grass.

"Allah's – He says so in the Qur'an: '*Oh you who believe! Allah will test you with game animals which come within the reach of your hands and spears, so that Allah will know those who fear Him in the Unseen.*' "

Qasim smiled. Suddenly, he didn't feel half as bad as he had a few moments ago. It dawned on him that he could only have caught what Allah had apportioned for him. He looked at the two big fish in his basket with a fresh pair of eyes. At least he had two, *alhamdulillah*. It would have been all the more embarrassing to have come back from the river with nothing. With his modest catch he would still be granted some reward for feeding the fasting, *insha'Allah*.

"Are you alright now, *akhi*?" asked Hisham as he clapped his back warmly. Qasim nodded. Hisham had a knack of always saying the right thing to make him feel better. He looked upon Hisham as a big brother. He was as dear to him now as his own flesh and blood, his siblings whom he had left behind back home in Tlemcen. Ya'qub had caught up with them by now as he made his way noisily out of the water, clutching a basket full of fish.

"Hope the fire's hot!" he said, his eyes bright from all the excitement and exercise. It was

Ya'qub's first Ramadan and he was taking joy in everything he did, especially knowing that it brought him closer to Allah. Fasting wasn't proving to be as difficult as he had thought it might be. Instead, it seemed to nourish him and uplift his soul in a way he had never expected.

Just then, they heard the sound of a gentle whinnying. Hisham and the others looked up and froze. Out of the blue, on the other side of the river, a Goth horseman appeared, bearing a white flag of truce. He slowly entered the river which his horse forded with ease, barely giving Hisham and the others a passing glance. His eyes were busy fixed elsewhere, staring nervously ahead at the other side of the riverbank. His arrival had caused a stir on their side amongst the posted guards. By the time the Goth reached their side of the river Tariq's scouts, Abdullah and Mustafa, had appeared alongside the sentries.

The lone rider dismounted, eager to make his intentions known. He had been sent here to parley between Tariq and Prince Achila. After he had been relieved of his weapon, Prince Achila's envoy was escorted by Abdullah and Mustafa towards their camp which lay just half a mile away on the broad plain beyond the river. Once at the camp they walked straight towards Tariq's command tent. All this was under the keen and watchful gaze of Tariq's men, as they sat beside their tents. Curious as to what was afoot, Hisham, Qasim and Ya'qub followed close behind them.

"What do you think?" whispered Qasim.

"Let's hope it's good news for us, *insha'Allah*,"

said Hisham as he took Ya'qub's basket of fish from him.

"If Prince Achila sent him, it's sure to be good news, *insha'Allah*. Achila hates Roderick," revealed Ya'qub. By now they had arrived outside their own tent just as they saw the envoy disappear into Tariq's tent, away from everyone's scrutiny.

With nothing else left to do, Qasim and Ya'qub sat round the campfire and watched Hisham as he first cleaned the fish, then filleted them with skill, cutting the portions into wide strips. These he rubbed with salt before hanging them above a low smoky fire made from the burning branches of oak gathered from the nearby woods. They would be cooked perfectly in time for *iftar*. In the meantime, Ya'qub told them all about the feuds between the heirs of Wittiza and Roderick, and many other princes of the realm.

It was almost an hour or so later, as they all sat supplicating and reciting the Qur'an, waiting to perform the *maghrib* prayer just after sunset. Nearby, one of Tariq's men could be heard reciting softly verses from *Surah An-Nahl*, The Bees, "*Surely Allah commands justice and doing good and giving to relatives. And He forbids indecency and doing wrong and tyranny …*"

As he finished, Achila's envoy emerged from Tariq's command tent, ready to leave. It was hard to read his face, but, judging by Abdullah's and Mustafa's expressions, the parley must have been a success, for them at least. After he was reunited with his weapons, the Goth mounted his steed and took himself off, riding over the broad plain once more. He crossed the river and then soon disappeared into the dark woods from where he had come. The negotiations had been a success.

Back in the command tent, as Tariq Ibn Ziyad finally sat down for *iftar,* he broke his fast with the customary prayer, lifting his hands palms up.

"O Allah, for You have I fasted and with Your sustenance I break my fast," said Tariq. He then eagerly put a sweet date in his mouth and chewed it, sipping on some milk from time to time, savouring the textures and tastes on his palate – it was simply delicious. He was reminded of the Prophet's words, how there are two joys for the fasting person; the joy when he breaks his fast and the joy when he meets his Lord. Tariq relished the sweet flavours, but his mind soon became preoccupied once again by his mission and by his most recent visitor.

Tariq had agreed to the two princes' request, with his own conditions applied, which included the princes agreeing to pay a small tribute. All that remained now was for the heirs of Wittiza to desert Roderick's ranks. If they did, this would be sure to further reduce the enemy's numbers, which he now knew to be as large as one hundred thousand men.

Tariq's scouts had already travelled to Cordova and back, after a rumour had reached him a week ago, regarding troop movements. Roderick had left the north of Andalus, as was to be expected, and had marched to his castle in Cordova rather than to his usual residence in the capital of Toledo.

Roderick had chosen his castle in Cordova since

it was more centrally situated in Andalus. From there he was raising his army, drafting both soldiers and peasants from far and wide, leaving out no corner of his kingdom. Abdullah and Mustafa had come back with such intelligence that it left Tariq with no other recourse than to write to Musa Ibn Nusayr, requesting more men as reinforcements. So it was with relief that he received word from Musa of the encouraging news he had hoped for.

Hani the seafarer from Alexandria had come through with the boats as he had promised. Musa's new vessels were ready and quickly put to their use of transporting five thousand men; all that Musa Ibn Nusayr could spare. Tariq's numbers had now swelled to twelve thousand men. This was still nowhere near the numbers which Roderick had amassed. Still, Tariq was satisfied. Even if the heirs of Wittiza were to fall short in their promise to abandon Roderick's ranks, it still would not matter to him.

Tariq Ibn Ziyad was grateful and quietly confident. If he had learned anything from the stories of the Battle of Badr, it was simple. Numbers were meaningless when under the protection of Allah. This, and the fact that they were in the holy month of Ramadan, all bolstered his conviction. Tonight was even more special being an odd night, the twenty-seventh night of Ramadan, one of the nights most likely to be *Lailat'al-Qadr*, the Night of Power. It was described in the Qur'an as a night 'better than a thousand months.' So the Prophet encouraged to seek out this special night; one on which the Qur'an too had first been revealed to him by the Angel Jibril.

As Tariq walked through the camp after *iftar* to pray *taraweeh* with his men, he looked curiously up at the cloudless, rainless sky. It was a clear evening, the air on his skin neither too hot nor too cold. He and most of his men were almost certain this night was the sought-after night of *Lailat'al-Qadr*. They planned to busy themselves in worship, for it was a night in which supplications are answered and for those who spent their night doing so, full of faith, all past wrongs would be forgiven.

So, on this special of nights, Tariq was filled with hope and faith – that and the memory of his dream of the Prophet as he sailed across the Straits. Not a day went by since, in which he did not think about that dream. It sustained him and assured him of their victory, God willing.

Not even did he flinch when finally, the next day in the afternoon there was a simmering sound like a storm brewing in the far-off distance. It began as the faintest of murmurs, then a rumble that grew louder and louder. As it drew closer, cumulus like clouds of dust visibly hung over the land, obliterating the horizon. Even the ground beneath them soon vibrated to a colossal weight on the move.

Tariq Ibn Ziyad emerged from his command tent to join his men in a display of discipline and strength. They stood there, both stalwart infantry and vast cavalry, born to the saddle, staring out and across at the other side of the river Guadalete.

Tariq and his men were serried in rows waiting,

watching resolutely as their enemy materialised out of the cloud of dust which was slowly advancing towards them. Roderick had finally arrived with his vanguard, at the head of one hundred thousand men.

19

ON THE BANKS OF THE GUADALETE

July 711 CE, 28ᵗʰ Ramadan, 92 AH

IT was almost the end of Ramadan. Night had fallen over the Guadalete. Tents on both sides of the river glowed brightly from the burning lamps and campfires lit outside their entrances. Roderick's army had pitched their city of tents opposite Tariq's encampment, on the other side of the river. It stretched back as far as the eye could see. They intended to rest for the next few days, waiting for the remainder of the army to catch up before they engaged in battle.

Tariq knew there were bound to be smaller encounters with the enemy until then. Seizing the opportunity, he sent an emissary, as was the custom. He would offer Roderick the chance to voluntarily surrender and spare the countless lives of innocent men.

Roderick was in his command tent with his counsel of allies when they received Tariq's messenger. They included the sons of Wittiza and a few of his ministers including Count Sisibert and Bishop Oppas. Roderick listened impatiently.

Then in no uncertain terms, he rejected Tariq's conditions, turning the messenger away with contempt. He had placed far too much confidence in the size and strength of his own army.

Yet, if he had not been so sure of himself, perhaps he might have noticed the knowing look that passed between the sons of Wittiza at that moment – and stranger still, the curious look which followed soon after between them and their uncle Oppas. Instead, Roderick believed he had convinced his rivals to set aside old feuds and differences for a greater cause – albeit *his* cause. The young princes soon left along with Oppas and the ministers. They were all eager to turn in for the night.

As they left, Roderick switched his attention impatiently elsewhere. He was far from done. Only one man was left half-shrouded in the shadows of his command tent. Sensing his cue to come out, a thin, unassuming man stepped forward into the soft light of the glowing lamp.

"What news do you have for me?" asked Roderick of his best spy. "Did you get a good look at them – what are they like?"

The man's brow furrowed deeply.

"I have news, but none that will please you, Sire," said the man fearfully, his eyes so large that they filled his grimy face.

"They're not like any people I've ever seen – they sharpen their teeth on sticks and from all their talk, it seems they plan to feast upon the flesh of our slain!" he said grimacing. Roderick's mouth fell open. For the next few minutes, he listened in consternation to every detail. The spy began to describe Tariq's men. Their description eerily matched the painting which had been hidden in the urn he had found at the Palace of Secrets. Still, once the spy had left, Roderick banished all such thoughts from his head. As far as he was concerned, he had an army the size of which was bound to crush them all, and no ill omen haunting his heart was going to convince him otherwise.

"Well – did he accept?" asked Tariq Ibn Ziyad although he had an inkling just by the look on Humayun's face. Humayun shook his head gravely.

"He refused, *Sayyid*," replied Humayun. Tariq had expected as much.

"Tell me, what is he like?" he asked curiously. Humayun smiled. He had taken note of every detail in the brief moments he was allowed to meet with Roderick.

"He is tall, well-built, but perhaps a little too proud and overly confident I believe," reflected Humayun, as he recalled his first impressions of the king, sensing a blustering arrogance in him. Roderick had sat on a temporary throne-like chair. On his chest was a shiny, ornate breastplate, both bulky and heavy.

"*Subhana'Allah*, he obviously is, if he turned down our terms," said Tarif Ibn Malik bluntly, as he stood to one side listening curiously.

"Still, he might change his mind after Abdullah

and Mustafa's performance earlier," he continued, grinning with a sudden flash of white teeth.

"I take it they were successful?" asked Tariq Ibn Ziyad over an amused smile. Early in the evening he had been informed that a spy from Roderick's camp had been seen snooping around, thinking he was incognito. Tariq had seized the opportunity to play out a strategy aimed at stirring fear in the hearts of Roderick's men.

"It was more than successful," revealed Tarif Ibn Malik. He took pleasure now in recounting what had happened. Abdullah and Mustafa had sat around a huge bubbling pot while cleaning their teeth with *miswak*s. Their loud words planning their victory feast had painted a disturbing picture for their intruder, who appeared to have fallen for the bait.

"Let's just say Abdullah's and Mustafa's *interesting* conversation was enough to make the man put two and two together and flee in fright," laughed Tarif Ibn Malik, as he remembered the rapid pace of the spy's retreat. He had practically thrown himself into the river. Tarif Ibn Malik had not seen a man leave in such a panicked haste in a long time. Tariq Ibn Ziyad smiled, shaking his head.

Later that night, after *taraweeh* prayers, Tariq walked through the camp to take one last look at Roderick's encampment. They had pitched their tents half a mile away from the river on the other side. Sentries were posted along the river on Tariq's side. They stood quietly to attention, ready to pass the night watching the enemy. Tomorrow Tariq and a few of his men would test the waters by means of a light skirmish, each side determined to study the other. Tariq made *du'a* for success, however long it took, whether a day or more. The quicker this battle ended, the better it would be for everyone. Under a beautiful starry night, he continued to look across the moonlit river between the two camps, with an evening *dhikr* flowing from his heart and past his lips.

The next morning, and for the following few days after, the opposing sides met over light skirmishes. Tension hung on the air, as intangible as the particles of the morning mist. Their clashes brought home to Tariq the fact that they were at a disadvantage, but only in numbers. Each encounter taught him a lot about his enemy's tactics. They were just as Count Ilyan had said they would be. Even Tarif Ibn Malik's descriptions from his own encounter with the Goths the year before also proved to be accurate. Tariq was confident that when they met in the full-scale battle, he would gain the upper hand, God willing.

It was on one of these days that Ramadan finally drew to an end, marked by the sighting of the new moon of *Shawwal* that heralded the celebration of Eid for Tariq's men. During those last sacred days of Ramadan they had been eagerly scouring the evening sky for the new moon. Firstly, on the twenty ninth day to no joy, then finally on the thirtieth day of Ramadan, they saw it etched visibly clear as it lay low in the western sky. The thin silvery-white arc of light had appeared through the sky not long after sunset, signalling the first day of *Shawwal*, ninety two years after the Hijra.

The next morning, on the day of Eid, soon after the sun had risen, the men gathered together serried in rows for the Eid prayer led by Tariq Ibn Ziyad. For those on the other side of the river in Roderick's camp, it was a mighty spectacle that did not go unnoticed. The Goths watched curiously from afar the motions of prayer as thousands of Muslims fell down in prostration, their foreheads placed on the ground in humilty, glorifying their Lord Most High.

After the prayer had finished Tariq's men sat quietly listening to the customary talks that followed. They were short speeches in which he praised and thanked Allah for the many blessings of the Ramadan that had just passed them by to finally ending with an earnest prayer on his lips for victory in the battle ahead against the army of Roderick.

It had not been the kind of day of celebration they were all used to. Many of the men's thoughts were with their families, wondering about what they might be doing back home at that very moment. It had been many moons ago when they had last seen each other. Most of them (except for those like Ya'qub for whom it was their first Eid) fondly recalled past Eids they had celebrated with their families in times of peace. Their thoughts lingered on those precious memories of gatherings with cherished family, friends and neighbours. They reminisced over the exchange of gifts, the warm greetings, and the strange experience of once again sharing delicious food and drink with their nearest and dearest, during daylight hours.

But there was none of this on the banks of the Guadelete that day – and yet it was still a joyful day with its own modest Eid feast and a unique *barakah*, coloured with the mindfulness of the decisive battle soon to come.

When that day finally came, Tariq and his men called on their Lord like never before. Like early birds as usual, Tariq's men awoke first for the night prayer in the last third of the night, rising again for the *fajr* prayer before dawn. Only as daybreak appeared, with its warm yellow light splitting the horizon in half, did a stirring of sound rise from the other side in Roderick's camp. Then, as the sky slowly began to lighten from an inky blackness to a deep blue, the ranks of men materialised on both sides, like the sea when the fog lifts.

Over the morning mist that hung above the river Guadalete, Tariq Ibn Ziyad finally surveilled Roderick's full force of one hundred thousand men. The sons of Wittiza and their men had only now come out, having not played any role in the light skirmishes during the days before. Both sides had initially held back from committing their entire armies in battle as they tested each other's mettle.

Now they stood with their flying pennons and fluttering standards, every man at the ready, with their horses and weapons. The Visigoth cavalry, mostly noblemen, were easy to pick out by their distinctive dress. They wore decorative breast plates, that glinted in the early morning light, their lances readied and horses raring to go. The foot soldiers were gruesome groups of Goths, holding spears and shields. Some held swords pointing forwards and downwards, ready to lunge, while others hammered them noisily against their shields, baring their teeth.

Among them also were peasants, clutching pitch-forks, sickles and scythes as little more than crude weapons. For anyone who could see their pale, frightened faces, it was more than likely that they had been conscripted by force. From Tariq's inspection, only Roderick was yet to arrive on the scene.

Standing face to face with their adversaries, it was clear to everyone that Tariq's men were greatly outnumbered. Now that Tariq could see the entirety of those who had come out to meet his army, he judged that even were the heirs of Wittiza to join his forces, along with all of their men, this was still unlikely to tip the scales towards an evenly sided fight.

Still, regardless of what the final numbers would be, Tariq had no doubt that his army would quash their opponents. If they stood with firm faith, they would vanquish the enemy, just as David overcame Goliath, whose forces far outnumbered those of Saul and David, so that some of Saul's followers had said, "*'We do not have the strength to face Goliath and his troops today.' But those who were sure that they were going to meet Allah said, 'How many a small force has triumphed over a much greater one by Allah's permission! Allah is with the steadfast.'*"

Qasim, Hisham, Ya'qub and Humayun, together with the scouts, were stood with the archers, watching the parade of the enemy. Tariq could sense a restlessness amongst his men, exposed as they were now in full sight of their enemies. He closed his eyes for a moment and recalled the dream of the blessed Prophet. Then he moved off ahead of his men and was soon seen turning his beautiful sorrel round on her haunches to face them.

A whispering broke out as all eyes converged on Tariq. The troops were lined along the length of the river, though some distance back from its bank. They stood a span behind, ranging back rows upon rows. The dew was still in the ground, curling upwards and around their legs in faint tendrils as the sun dispersed it. Above them in the sky a honey buzzard circled overhead and suddenly swooped down towards the river. With its claws clamped around its prey now, it rose up and fled from the scene, quickly and quietly.

Tarif Ibn Malik caught Tariq's eye in a wordless show of support. Tariq smiled and nodded. He looked at his men waiting for a precise moment. There was that expectant silence that comes just before an orator begins his speech. His men leant forward slightly, waiting eagerly, straining their ears, not wishing to miss a single word of what was to come. Then as the heat of the sun beat down upon them, Tariq began to speak:

"Where will you run?" asked Tariq, his voice cutting through the silence as his dark eyes swept over his soldiers. He could feel their concentrated gaze upon him.

"Behind you is the sea..." he said, raising his sword and pointing it straight towards the distant horizon to their rear.

"...and the enemy is before you!" Tariq continued, only this time turning in his saddle to look towards the gathered enemy awaiting in the distance beyond the river. His sword arm held out before him, Tariq pointed the sharp edge of his blade at Roderick's army, then swept it along the full length of its solid square column.

"Nothing can save you but the help of Allah, your courage and perseverance..." he exhorted, in a bid to rally his men's strength and determination.

"You will soon be met by a powerful army whose number is innumerable and armed to the hilt. They will engulf you from all sides like a tempestuous sea. You have no other weapons than your swords, no food to eat except that which you snatch from the hands of your enemies. We must attack now, for the longer we continue in our state of privation we will soon lose our strength and energy – and then the fear that lurks in the hearts of our enemy may well change to one of indomitable courage.

"My brothers, banish all fear from your hearts, trust that victory shall be ours, and be certain that this tyrant will not be able to withstand the shock of our arms. He has come to make us masters of his cities and castles, to deliver into our hands his countless treasures. Here is a splendid opportunity to defeat him now, if you will but stand bravely in the face of death!"

Tariq paused to look at his men in earnest, noting their resolute faces staring back at him and then he continued:

"Do not suppose for one minute that I impose upon you a task from which I shrink myself. I have not concealed from you the reality of what we are about to face. Indeed, we have a great task ahead of us. If you suffer, it will be only for a while, but in the end our worldly gains will be in abundance – and the rewards of Allah await you if you are resolved to uphold His words and proclaim and establish His *deen* in this land.

"In telling you all this, know that I speak to myself before any of you. I will fight alongside you and do what I have advised you to do – and in the midst of the meeting of the two armies in battle, know that I intend to seek out this tyrant Roderick and slay him with my own hands, *insha'Allah*.

"If I kill him, the victory shall be ours; If I die before I reach him, do not trouble yourselves over me. You will have no difficulty in finding a brave man to replace me. Continue to fight as though I was still alive and among you and complete my intention. If you attend to my instructions, we are sure of the victory!" promised Tariq, bringing his speech to a close.

There followed a sublime silence for several seconds; a profound tribute to an orator that had moved their souls. Then from somewhere amongst his men came a cry that began as solitary praise. Soon, it was joined by others until it rose to an overwhelming crescendo that overcame the land like an unstoppable wave, a giant *takbir* which drowned out every other sound, including the harsh beating of the Goths' swords on their shields. Tariq raised his sword in salute to his men.

At that most timely of moments, on the other side of the river a commotion struck up. Roderick's men parted down the middle – and now Tariq and his men caught their first glimpse of the tyrant king making his grand entrance. He came riding upon a strange contraption. It was a chariot pulled by two magnificent white horses. Yet what drew everyone's eyes was the ornate throne which to their astonishment was fixed upon the chariot that bore Roderick.

Shading him from the full glare of the sun was an awning made of fine, colourful silk that canopied high above his head. The rich fabric had been stitched with all manner of precious stones – pearls, rubies and emeralds which caught the sunlight and winked at them from afar. Behind Roderick's chariot trundled a curious litter of carts, carrying what could have been anything from more treasure to military stores and goodness knows what else.

As he beheld the spectacle, Abdullah the scout broke into a choking laughter.

"That's *their* king? *Subhana'Allah!*" he said shaking his head. "He fancies himself as something, that one!" he continued with contempt, turning to look at Mustafa beside him, who sat on his horse with his mouth agape.

"*Akhi*, he's just made it all the easier for me to find him!" said Abdullah with relish. "What do you think?"

"Well, I don't mind, if *he* wants to play at being a sitting duck!" grinned Mustafa.

Tariq was just riding past them when he caught their banter, prompting him to swiftly interject.

"*Ikhwan*, charge along beside me by all means – but mind you leave Roderick to me!" smiled Tariq with a determined light in his eyes.

"As you wish, *Sayyid*," replied the scouts quickly in raised spirits. Morale was running high, including in Hisham, Qasim and Ya'qub. They were dressed in light chainmail that blinked with every fall of light. Their scintillating swords were held to the ready, their horses just as raring to go. Tariq's speech had leant them courage. Qasim shifted forward in his saddle to smooth Warda's soft muzzle and whispered words of encouragement in her ear.

"He's spared no man in the kingdom," said Ya'qub beside him as he studied the Goths intently. He could see the peasants clutching their farming implements, their eyes large, no doubt filled with terror and fear. With a sinking heart he wondered if his brother David was out there among them.

Hisham, who was alongside him too, was staring off beyond the horizon, obscured by Roderick's army, at some distant place in time when he heard Ya'qub's words.

"You know it was on the seventeenth day of Ramadan, in the second year after the Hijra that the Battle of Badr was fought and Allah in His mercy sent three thousand angels to help," said Hisham, attracting Qasim and Ya'qub's attention now.

"Allah called it *Yawm-al Furqan* – the day of distinguishing, because it was a decisive moment in history between good and evil – a turning point," continued Hisham proudly.

"Despite their meagre resources, the Muslims overcame the tribe of Quraysh. I hope that our moment in this time of history brings similar blessings and a prosperity of its own in some way for the future, *insha'Allah*. Now wouldn't that be something?" smiled Hisham.

"It would," agreed Qasim, "but right now let's just get through them first, *insha'Allah*," jerking his head towards Roderick's fierce ranks, "before we worry about the more distant future!"

"I'll do my best to watch your backs as you will mine," said Ya'qub, "but it'll be hard out there to keep track of each other – we may get separated."

"Don't worry *akhi*, we're friends – we'll find our way back to each other, if not today then in the next life *insha'Allah*," said Hisham, but before anyone could reply just then the sound of a war-horn blasted through the air. It came from the Visigoth's side of the river, along with a continuous roar. Roderick's vanguard was on the move.

On Roderick's side of the field a different story was playing out. Despite Roderick's superior might, he didn't like the cry of confidence or the sound of swords beating down on their shields as he had just heard moments ago rising out from Tariq's coalesced ranks. It annoyed him in fact, as he clenched his teeth in irritation; that they should even now be standing there, as still as statues, staring back at his army, fierce, ready and not giving an inch or fleeing out of fright.

Roderick slowly advanced, jaw jutted forward, as his horses inched their way closer towards Tariq's front line. On either side of him flanked to the left and right of his troops, he could see the young princes riding their horses slightly ahead of them, encased in their iron breastplates.

Sisibert and Oppas were among them too, as was a small cavalry headed mostly by noblemen. The bulk of Roderick's grisly men were infantry, fully armed with their heavy long swords and coffin shaped shields, moving ponderously on foot towards their enemy. Then over the heads of his men, Roderick's eye fell on the frontmost ranks of Tariq's army, who were waiting resolutely. He gasped. He had never led his men out in the days before, during the skirmishes. Today was the first time he beheld Tariq's troops for himself.

The vision of the painted men in the scrolls he had found in the urn at the Palace of Secrets rose before his eyes. Like the men in the scroll, Tariq's soldiers wore the same cloaks, the same strange white turbans wrapped about their heads, and were wielding the same weapons just as he had seen that day at the Palace. They stood now before him in the flesh, watching their advance, fearless and steady.

"By the faith of the Messiah, it *is* them!" said Roderick beneath his breath, as a sudden coldness clutched at his heart. Was Tariq to be his doom?

"Did you say something, Sire?" asked his

lieutenant beside him, fearful he had missed an instruction.

"Nothing – *no wait,* remind the men to hold their positions and stay in formation. We'll move together and crush 'em," ordered Roderick.

The Visigoth's great column of men continued to close the distance between them. Tariq's infantry, who were standing abreast in lines several ranks deep, were waiting for just the right moment. When it came, they made their first move. Archers fired fierce volleys of arrows that pierced high into the air, flying in deadly arcs until they rained down hard upon the enemy, felling as many of the Goths across the centre column as they could. Heads disappeared amongst Roderick's marching ranks, as bodies dropped to the ground, soon to be trampled and forgotten.

Then there came a terrible sound, the thud and thunder of thousands of galloping horses that shook the earth beneath them. A dense cloud of dust rose into the air, roiling and raging, as Tariq's cavalry stormed out towards the Visigoths like a breaking wave, with nothing but the river between them. Once they reached the waters, they would be shallow enough for the horses to plunge in and ford with ease.

Roderick had never seen so many riders on horseback. The clamour of horses' hooves made a deafening din. Then, out of the corner of his eye, he perceived something strange. Fear suddenly squeezed his throat. The flank to his right led by Prince Achila pulled away. Moments later, he saw

Achila's brother, Prince Olmund do the same on the left flank, leaving gaping gaps in the Goth's defences. Closely following in their suit were Oppas and Sisibert, leading their own bands of men away and exposing the main body of Roderick's men still further.

The peasants too suddenly dropped their sickles and scythes and fled for their lives. Only Roderick's centre square of soldiers was left standing, looking altogether weak, more from the terror and confusion of witnessing so many of the Goths abandoning their ranks, than anything else. Still, all this was nothing compared to what was to come next. To the remaining Goths' consternation and dismay the defectors, apart from the peasants, were now manoeuvring into place and ready to join Tariq and his men who had almost reached the river.

The front of Roderick's column, now running hard, had arrived at the edge of the river and as they entered the shoal waters the collision between the two armies soon began, both sides bracing themselves. Like two mountains, rocks dashing against rocks, they met with the force of an earthquake. There was fighting everywhere; in the water to both sides of the riverbank and beyond. Hisham, Qasim and Ya'qub were fighting on the banks. They were surrounded by Goths all around thrusting spears and swords, whilst they sat on their horses thwarting the assaults with their own weapons.

Qasim could feel his legs tighten around Warda as Goth after Goth came at him, but he managed to keep his balance. He was just fending off a Goth when he felt a sharp blow between his shoulder blades. Warda suddenly reared upwards, throwing Qasim from his seat, then she bolted in fright.

Sickness threatened to overwhelm him, and his legs felt numb. The world spun in silence for a moment and then Qasim came crashing head first to the ground, stunned and dazed. He lay flat on his face, breaths coming hard and fast between his lips. All around him, he sensed only a deathly silence and then slowly a ringing began. It was somewhere far off at first, but it grew louder and louder, until the screams and guttural cries of men, with the clamouring, clanking and clanging of weapons returned all around him with full force.

Spitting red from a badly cut lip, Qasim staggered to his feet. He'd been thrown to the edge of the mêlée. For a moment he took in the terror of the bloody scene before him, until his eyes rooted to a spot. He saw Warda. She was standing some way away, her reins hanging loose beside her. He whistled to her with a high-pitched summons which she had come to know and respond to, ever since she was a youngling.

Warda's ears pricked up. She obeyed instantly, galloping towards her master. Just then a Goth appeared charging head on towards Qasim from the same direction, sword pulled back menacingly over his head. Qasim's heart hammered in his rib cage. He knew what he must do. Warda would soon overtake the Goth but he had to mount her on the run if he was going to evade his attack. Qasim was petrified. His eyes fixed on to Warda's flaming withers and the prayer of Prophet Musa, peace be upon him, came to his lips; the very same he made when he fled from the clutches of Pharaoh to the land of Madyan, "*O my Lord, I am truly in need of any good You have in store for me.*"

Then as Warda came alongside him, his hands reached out for her withers and mane and for one terrifying instant he thought he had missed her. In the next moment Qasim felt his feet fly off the ground, as he tried to ignore the pain that suddenly seared through his arms and shoulders. He landed his saddle just as the Goth reached his side, in time for Qasim to plant a boot squarely into his attacker's ferocious, grubby face, sending him flying into the river with a resounding splash.

It was then that he caught the sound of Hisham's laughter in the near distance.

"Good work, *akhi – masha'Allah!*" he shouted across as he finished clobbering a Goth over the head with the hilt of his sword. "I knew you could do it!"

Although Qasim's face bore both his relief and a giddy delight, there was no time to reply. Within seconds, Qasim and Hisham were assailed once again by more furious Goths, out for their blood.

As he fought on, Qasim suddenly became aware of Tariq Ibn Ziyad. It had seemed to Qasim that in the mêlée of the fight Tariq was everywhere. He had promised his men he would be beside them in the thick of the battle – and he was true to his word!

Tariq was busy cleaving his way through the

mass of Goths, still searching for King Roderick as he fought when there came an excited cry. It was one of the scouts, Abdullah. Both the scouts and a few other men were fighting nearby, sticking close to Tariq.

"*Sayyid*, I see the king," shouted Abdullah. "He's there by the river – his men surround him!"

Tariq followed the line of Abdullah's pointing finger. With a squeeze of his knees, he urged his horse forward, plunging into the river and making a beeline straight for the king. Roderick and Tariq were soon in the throes of mortal combat, with the men that had surrounded Roderick falling away fast. Swords and shields collided as they parried each other's blows.

Before long Tariq had gained the advantage over his foe.

"Do you yield?" shouted Tariq over the noise and clamour of the mêlée.

"*Never!* This is *my* kingdom!" roared Roderick, eyes flaring with rage, clutching his blade and bringing it down towards Tariq's head with all the might he could muster. Tariq deflected the strike with his shield in a split-second.

"You're wrong – this is the kingdom of Allah – Lord of the Creation – *Al-Malik al-Mulk*," thundered Tariq defiantly, wielding his sword and dealing deathly blow after blow upon Roderick's shield, leaving him cowering behind it.

"We are only His care-takers, and you shall no longer inflict your tyranny upon His creatures!" shouted Tariq. Roderick glowered back, his breath coming in fits.

"Do you yield?" asked Tariq again.

"Never!" spat Roderick, his face an ugly shade of puce. He could feel Tariq's eyes burning into him with every blow. They fought hard. Tariq then saw an opening and took his advantage. He struck low at the king's leg and Roderick momentarily lost his footing from the full force of the blow, swaying on his chariot. His hand fell forward as Roderick tried to regain his balance, but with a deft swoop, Tariq's sword came crashing down through his helmet. The king dropped to his knees. His eyes flashed for a moment and then the light in them slowly dimmed. Roderick toppled from his chariot into the river like a felled tree.

At that very moment a line of riderless horses broke through from the opposite bank. They entered the river and were soon a blur streaming wildly past Tariq, coming between him and Roderick's chariot, temporarily stalling him from pursuing Roderick's body. Tariq shouted out urgently to his men on the other side to find and retrieve it. Around them, chaos suddenly erupted amongst Roderick's ranks.

"The king is dead – the king is *dead*!" Voices rang out and the word quickly began to spread on both sides of the river.

Qasim spun his head as he heard these words in surprise. His eyes flew to the place where he had last seen Tariq fighting Roderick, only to be distracted by the sight of Hisham. He was fighting furiously with a Goth when suddenly he slumped forward in his saddle and disappeared over the side of Laylah, falling to the ground. Stunned,

Roderick and Tariq were soon in the throes of mortal combat

Qasim pushed Warda into a wild gallop, at once desperate and terrified. When he reached him, he found Hisham lying on the ground, still. A crimson pool was slowly collecting beneath him.

"*Hisham*! *Hisham*, can you hear me? *Akhi*, *please* get up!" Qasim's voice cracked under a strain, but Hisham lay quiet and motionless.

It was a mistake – Qasim knew it, but he had to do it. He had to get down to help Hisham. After the briefest look around, with his heart in his mouth, Qasim quickly dismounted. No sooner had his foot landed on the grass than he felt a sharp blow to the back of his head and a painful swipe to his ankles. As he crashed to the ground, a black fog began to engulf him. The last thing he saw was Hisham's pale face swimming before his eyes, then a darkness claimed him.

A while later the ground moved beneath him. Rough fingers grabbed hold of him, gripping tightly under his arms. He was being dragged over the earth. Then for a moment he heard familiar, melodious sounds around him. It was the call to the faithful for prayer. Was it time to pray? He must pray now he thought. As he attempted to move, he winced as he felt a red-hot burning pain in his ankle… then there was only darkness and silence once more.

20

THE FALL

10th of Shawwal, 92 AH, July 711 CE

A LONG time passed before the hushed voices were back again. He could hear them, like the night before. It was pitch black where he was, except for when the moonlight sometimes peeped through a small window at the top corner of the strange room in which he slept. He could hear those same voices now, talking in low urgent whispers just on the other side of the door. Qasim closed his eyes slowly and tried to gather his thoughts. A dull ache pulsated at the back of his head and shoulders – then everything came flooding back to him.

"Hisham!" he said with a sickening feeling. Qasim pushed the blanket away from him and tried in vain to lift himself up off his pallet of straw bed. Suddenly, he heard the creak of a door open, then light flooded blindingly into the room. His eyes strained to see the intruder, but he soon relaxed as he accustomed to the light and saw a familiar, friendly face poking around the door.

"Ya'qub! Oh subhana'Allah, it's you – *Alhamdulil-*

lah, you're alright!" exclaimed Qasim. His voice croaked with a dryness in his mouth and throat, but there was no mistaking the mixture of relief and joy behind his words.

Ya'qub smiled as he entered the room carrying a tallow lantern and a pitcher of water. He sat down beside Qasim, glad to see him awake.

"Here, drink this," ordered Ya'qub, pouring the water into a tumbler on a small table beside the bed, then delivering it into Qasim's slightly shaky hand. Qasim managed to hold on to the tumbler tightly. Mindful of his scabbed lip that felt stiff and wooden, he gratefully drank down its contents, relishing the cool liquid as it slipped down his throat.

"You look better than before, *akhi, alhamdulillah*," continued Ya'qub searching his face but noting he still appeared to be a little pale under the skin. "I was worried about you. You've been sleeping for five days now, with a high fever too." Qasim looked surprised, shaking his head wearily with confusion. For him, it felt like only yesterday that they were in the battlefield, in the thick of the fight.

"What happened? Did we win?" asked Qasim anxiously.

"Yes. Roderick is dead. He died that same day, the fifth of *Shawwal*," said Ya'qub firmly with a determined nod.

"Where am I?" asked Qasim after a moment, with a bewildered expression. He looked curiously about him at his new, alien surroundings.

"This is Ben's home," said Ya'qub, taking Qasim completely by surprise. "After the battle, the townsfolk came out to find us."

Ya'qub then brought him up to speed on everything that had happened since the battle; of how he had finally found Qasim after searching for hours – and he couldn't have done it without help either.

"I found my brother David," said Ya'qub joyfully. "He was among the peasants that fled from the fighting. I found him just when I was beginning to think I would never see him again." It was a reunion Ya'qub wasn't expecting, but it had happened all the same.

Like many others who had fled from the battle and refused to fight, David had gathered at a distance from all the action. They had stayed on to watch with bated breath until the final outcome was clear and the victors revealed. Tariq's men were re-grouping after the remainder of Roderick's men had been captured. In blind panic, a few had managed to flee into the nearby hills and woods once they heard Roderick was dead. There were also plenty of rich pickings from the spoils left behind that they had collected.

David and a few peasants had ventured out to meet the victors. Rumours had reached them long before that the Muslims were chivalrous and compassionate people. When Ya'qub, by some miracle, clapped eyes on his brother, it was an emotional scene between the two siblings.

"Brother, is it really you?" asked David in disbelief, his voice cracking suddenly. "Yes, it really *is* you! Oh, thank God you're alive. What... what happened to you?" he continued, as tears gathered in his eyes, blurring his vision momentarily. Still, it had not escaped David that Ya'qub looked very different standing before him now, than the last time he had seen him.

"Yes, it's me, brother!" said Ya'qub, his voice ringing with joy. Ya'qub could see the conflicting emotions in his brother's face. They were tears of joy and of pain. David wrapped his arms around him in a tight embrace, now sobbing.

"Forgive me, Jacob," he pleaded. "Please forgive me for leaving you that day." Ya'qub smiled and returned his brother's embrace with an even stronger hug to reassure him.

"I would rather be dead than to have left you. When they chased us in the fields, I swear to you, I thought you were right behind me. But we got separated. After, I went back and searched and searched for you everywhere but .,." he paused, overcome with emotion.

"It's alright," consoled Ya'qub. "Brother, there is nothing to forgive!" soothed Ya'qub, still beaming with joy at having been re-united with his nearest kin. "Look! You see, I'm fine..." he continued, raising his arms up to the sides.

Allah had set his life upon a different course. For Ya'qub, his capture was the best thing that could have happened to him, although it would take David some time to see it that way.

With David's help, they had scoured around the river and the lush, green grass that had become buried under a tangled mass of fallen men. Eventually they had found Qasim and Hisham and their horses nearby.

They found Hisham first. He lay peacefully with the fallen.

A short distance away Qasim was slumped on the ground. He was unconscious but breathing shallowly, yet evenly. They brought him back to the camp and tended to his wounds as best they could. It was only when Ben and his father had made themselves known a day later, that Qasim was relocated to their home (at their insistence) to recuperate. Like many of the cautious peasants from the surrounding towns, they had waited a short time before venturing out to the battlefield. In fact, most of Tariq's men had moved back towards the towns to recover from their battle fatigue.

After this, Qasim healed fast and grew better day by day. For Ya'qub there were still more surprises to come, for when David met Ben's father in Tariq's camp, he immediately recognised the old man as his maternal uncle. That Ya'qub should overnight go from being an orphan to having found his brother, a cousin in Ben and now an uncle, all in the space of a few days, was beyond anything that he could have imagined or hoped for. Their lives had already begun to change so much for the better.

Qasim sat listening, overwhelmed with a mixture of emotions. Happiness on the one hand for Ya'qub, but an aching pain in his chest at the loss of Hisham. His eyes welled up, a trembling hand pressing over them, but he did his best to endure it with fortitude just as the Prophet did when his own son died. His infant son Ibrahim was drawing his last breaths when the eyes of the Prophet flowed with tears and he said;

"The eyes are shedding tears and the heart is grieved, and we will not say except what pleases our Lord. O Ibrahim! Indeed, we are grieved by your passing."

Qasim knew this is what Hisham would have wanted him to do. He also remembered with much comfort Hisham's words just before the battle – that they were friends and they would find their way back to each other, if not today, then in the next life *insha'Allah*.

All who had fallen in battle were buried in the places they had been found. It was done quickly, with no washing of bodies or *janaza* prayer made upon them, as was the Muslim tradition, for those who were considered to be alive with their Lord.

The days passed peacefully and Qasim's health improved with each one and soon the colour returned to his cheeks. Ben looked after Laylah and Warda while Qasim was laid up in bed, restless and impatient to join Tariq's men. Roderick's body was never found. Though they hunted through the river, the woods and the hillsides, it was to no avail.

Most were convinced he couldn't have survived Tariq's onslaught, but there were those few among the Goths, loyal supporters, that would say he had escaped. If that were true, then Roderick must have fled for his life to some obscure monastery in a far-off distant land by now. The only thing that Tariq's men could find that remained of him, was one of his sandals.

It was encrusted with pearls and rubies. Its laces, that must have come undone as he had fallen off his chariot and toppled into the river, were still attached. The sandals were valued at one hundred thousand golden dinars, much to Mustafa the scout's amusement. As soon as he heard this, Mustafa belted out in laughter over the most 'expensive duck' they had ever caught. The spoils from the battle had been distributed by Tariq amongst the men, after making sure that a fifth was set aside for the treasury, which would go back to Damascus. Tariq was already busy with his plans to advance on the capital of Andalus, Toledo. He was eager to take command of the capital and thereby maintain the upper hand in the region.

"When do they go?" asked Qasim anxiously one morning over his breakfast. He only prayed he would be well enough to leave with them.

"In a week or so, *insha'Allah*," said Ya'qub. "Tariq wants everyone rested and recovered before we move on – but don't worry so much. Get better first. I spoke to Humayun and he said we could catch up. Personally, he doesn't think there will be any opposition going forward. Everyone's hoping the Goths will throw the gates of the city wide open for us as soon as we arrive, for the news of our victory would have reached them by now."

"Well, if they do, be sure to go straight to the church beyond the city," grinned Ben.

"They say that Roderick's hidden the Table of Solomon there, along with all other kinds of precious treasures."

"What's the Table of Solomon?" asked Ya'qub, intrigued.

The next half hour was spent by Ben describing

the priceless relic, rumoured to have been removed from the Palace of Secrets by Roderick.

"It has the finest emeralds and jewels you'll ever lay your eyes upon, if you can find it!" laughed Ben. "It's sure to be worth a king's ransom. It would set anyone up for life."

The next morning Qasim was strong enough to step out and go to the orchards with Ben to get some fresh air and exercise. His ankle didn't hurt so much now and the headaches that had been his constant companion since he had been injured had begun to abate. He also went to visit Warda who was enjoying the rich green pastures of Andalus. At the first sight of her master, she trotted up to him and nuzzled him warmly. Ben was obviously doing a good job of taking care of her. Her chestnut coat was glossy and looking as healthy as ever.

Ya'qub soon trotted up beside them on his own horse, Laylah, having taken her out for a gallop. Laylah belonged to Ya'qub now. Hisham had no living family and he had left her to him, while Qasim had inherited Hisham's bow. He had also left Qasim his collection of pearls that he had recovered from the bay in the first weeks of their arrival in Andalus.

Hisham had been a strong swimmer. Despite his coaxing and reminders that it was part of the *sunnah* to know how to swim, Qasim had never ventured very far with him into the deeper waters in the bay that was overlooked by Tariq's Mountain. Instead, he had watched Hisham ducking and diving in and out of the deep blue waters which lay beyond the shallows. The pearls Hisham

had found during his deep dives were now a
keepsake for Qasim, full of memories.

It wasn't long before news arrived of Tariq's
planned departure the day after the *jumu'ah*. They
were going to take the capital, Toledo. Before
Tariq left, he had one important message to
deliver. After the *jumu'ah* prayers, he summoned
the townsfolk to address them. It was an address
that his envoys would later repeat to the inhabitants of all the other towns which the Muslims had
so far taken.

They gathered in the thronging town square,
where curious crowds of peasants had come out
to see Tariq and the victors. They were all eager
to catch a glimpse of the young general who had
thwarted Roderick. Qasim and Ya'qub were there
along with many of the Umayyad soldiers, as were
Ben and his family. The townspeople were
wreathed in smiles, as was Count Ilyan, who was
finally at peace. He stood now looking curiously
out at the crowds that had come out to meet Tariq.
Never had he seen such warmth and happiness
among the people of Iberia.

Tariq stood, a commanding and dignified
figure, and addressed the gathering. He began by
praising Allah and asking for blessings and peace
upon the Prophet, his family and his companions.
From there, he went on to explain to those present
that Islam teaches mercy and compassion that
encompass even those of different faiths. Tariq
spoke such inspiring words of tolerance, that it
evoked gasps of amazement from the crowds who
filled the square.

"The Christians may keep their churches and monasteries and the Jewish people their synagogues. All of you may retain your own religious practices, and we will protect your right to do so," proclaimed Tariq.

"You may keep your possessions," continued Tariq watching the Iberians thoughtfully, conscious of the sea of eyes eagerly gazing back at him.

"And fear not – your communities may manage their private affairs and resolve disputes in accordance with your own customs, so long as they do not involve the rights of Muslim subjects. If you come under attack, we will defend your families, your lives and your property – all we ask of you in return is that you accept our authority and pay the tribute – a tribute of three gold dinars to be paid by all able-bodied men, but not by women and children and the old and infirm or those who have withdrawn from the world to glorify God – and that you do not betray us to our enemies," concluded Tariq.

It was a momentous speech that won their hearts and earned the sincere pledge from the people of Iberia, ushering them into a new era, with the promise of peace and prosperity under the Muslims. This was so different to the hard life that they had known under the Goths.

Bella, who had been holding her breath in the crowd, burst into tears of joy and relief. After having suffered for so long under the Goths, hearing Tariq's speech was a soothing balm to her tortured soul. She was finally free to marry whomever she pleased and in accordance with her own religious laws which she no longer had to hide. Leander had no claim over her now. Ben put a comforting arm around his sister, which she returned with a blinding smile.

At that very moment, shouldering his way through the crowd, came Leander, and following close at his heels, Father Martin. Ben and his father instinctively stepped in front of Bella before Leander had reached their side. His steely eyes glinted with a determination in their depths.

"Leander, I trust you are well?" said Ben's father curtly with the briefest of smiles.

"I am, sir," replied Leander tersely. "I wanted to speak to you about the betrothal – we didn't quite finish the last time I visited."

Ben caught his father's eye. On that day, when Leander had come to visit, Bella's father had refrained from breaking off the engagement. He had decided not to do so, not until after the battle.

"As to that, I'm afraid Bella cannot marry you," said Ben's father politely, but there was no disguising the relief in his voice. Father Martin's eyes narrowed, as he listened beside Leander, whose face was growing redder by the minute, anger flashing in his eyes.

"But you promised …" said Leander calmly despite himself, between gritted teeth.

"Why the change of heart?" shot the priest fiercely.

"She is honoured, of course, but I think you know why Bilha has refused," said Ben's father holding the priest's gaze.

"*Bilha?*" The priest's eyes darted over his

shoulder to rest on Bella. Bilha's chin lifted in defiance.

"You heard Tariq Ibn Ziyad," said Ben's father looking squarely at the priest. "We are free to manage our own private affairs. *Bilha* will marry from within *our* community."

The priest gasped, but before he could retort, Leander turned on his heels and walked away, back into the crowd that swallowed him up. Father Martin, his lips pressed into a thin line, was forced to follow after him. Bilha caught her brother's eye in relief and broke into peals of laughter.

The next day, Tariq's men were moving out. A small garrison of men was left behind in the towns, like once before, and in their absence men like Ben's father would hold the fort for them in safekeeping. Qasim, now sufficiently recovered, and Ya'qub were riding their horses on the dusty road to Toledo. A half a mile ahead they could see the great column of the Umayyad army marching or on their horses, kicking up the usual cloud of dust in their wake.

They had left a bit later than everyone else, but Humayun had advised Qasim that he could take his time and leave when he was good and ready. They had taken longer to get their things together, but mostly because Ya'qub thought it best they stayed at the back of the march, away from all the dust and dirt. He didn't think this would be good for Qasim, and the more fresh air he breathed, the better it would be for his head.

Qasim, on the other hand, couldn't see what all the fuss was about. As far as he was concerned, he was well on the mend and feeling stronger and healthier by the minute.

Both Warda and Laylah trotted happily along the road. From time to time their heads turned to the side looking longingly at the blades of lush, green grass on either side of the road that quivered in the cool breeze.

They were making good progress when the sound of hoofbeats travelling swiftly up behind them suddenly roused their attention. Both young men turned around in their saddles in surprise, to find a lonely rider galloping fast, closing the distance between them.

In the next few moments, they recognised who it was.

Ben came riding up beside them, his cheeks flushed from the fresh air and exercise, his eyes bright with excitement.

"Ben, what do you think you're doing?" demanded Ya'qub, looking over at his young cousin critically.

"Please, take me with you!" said Ben his eyes pleading piteously.

"No! It's impossible – besides, what about the family, don't they need you?" snapped Ya'qub, shaking his head adamantly.

"Father's given his blessings and said I can go," revealed Ben with a big smile spreading from cheek to cheek. "They don't need me so much now. Bilha and David are betrothed – and you know what David's like … well, he's practically taken over the farm already."

Ya'qub smiled, shaking his head. He knew this much was true – his uncle had hinted to him that Ben would have more time on his hands now that David was around, and the old feudal restrictions gone.

"It might finally be the time for him to spread his wings, if he likes," his uncle had said good humouredly just the night before.

"But we don't need any help," said Qasim looking at him and feeling a little sorry for him. "You should go back home and enjoy yourself now. You can do what you want."

"This *is* what I want – to travel, see places and do something different," exclaimed Ben, his voice bursting with excitement. "I won't get in the way, I promise! I can take care of the horses for you like a squire! I have been doing that well already, haven't I?"

Ya'qub and Qasim looked at each other thoughtfully.

"I suppose you *did* do a good job with the horses," said Ya'qub looking at his young cousin reflectively, suddenly feeling that he didn't have the heart to turn him away.

"Alright, but you have to do as we say," continued Ya'qub sternly. Ben nodded his head.

"I promise – you won't regret it," he said falling comfortably in pace beside his companions. "I'm so glad David's taking good care of the farm. He's already mending fences and digging the ditches. I would have been left to look after the sheep!"

At this Qasim burst into so much laughter that both Ya'qub and Ben looked at him in astonishment.

"So, you think that's bad, do you?" said Qasim, finally wiping his eyes. "I could tell you a thing or two to change your mind."

"I doubt it," said Ben shaking his head adamantly.

"Well, let me tell you what Hisham told me once," said Qasim with a fond smile, looking up at the beautiful blue sky above, as a solitary sparrow circled high in the air.

"You've not heard about the Prophet Muhammad, blessings and peace be upon him – yet," continued Qasim, "but you do know of the Prophets who came before him like, Abraham, David and Moses. Well, there's not a Prophet that Allah sent who wasn't a shepherd!"

As they travelled along the road to Toledo, they listened to Qasim as he passed on Hisham's words of wisdom. Finally, they caught up with Tariq's column of men and fell in line behind them on the long march ahead.

'Ramadan is the chief of all months and Friday is the chief of all days'

Prophet Muhammad (pbuh)

EPILOGUE

ANDALUS ASCENDING

Yawm Al Jumu'ah, 261 AH, Friday the Day of Gathering, 875 CE
The City of Cordoba, 164 years later...

THE city turned to a rose gold as the sun moved up through the sky from the east. From a hill where the vantage point was at its best, stood an old woman gazing out at the great city of Cordoba. She was tired and had not slept a wink. Instead, she had stayed awake throughout the night, tending to her patient in the throes of a fever. Maryam had been a handful, but her fever finally broke in the early hours of the morning, *alhamdulillah*. Sumayya, a lady physician, was used to night calls, highly skilled and sought after as she was.

After passing a difficult night with a patient, it was her habit to walk to this hilltop on the way back home. It was her favourite spot to look out upon the city as dawn broke over it. No one could deny that the city had been built with such beauty and flair for design that it was sure to delight the eye of any onlooker. Even now, after so many years, her heart warmed at the sight of it, and she smiled.

Cordoba was a fortified city protected by strong,

lofty walls within which lay a maze of cobbled streets. At night, they were lit by fashionable streetlights, oil burners and lanterns, to the awe and admiration of all other cities in Europe. They glowed softly as they waited their turn to be extinguished, now that the sun had flown its nest, rising into the sky, spreading her golden wings.

A bridge, itself a feat of engineering made from a sturdy row of arches, spanned over the river Guadalquivir whose glistening waters meandered peacefully through the city. Its banks on either side were home to marble houses and cultivated gardens with lush flora, fauna and trees. Brought over from distant lands, they would be the pride and joy of any horticulturist or botanist's study.

It was *yawm al-jumu'ah*, Friday – the day of gathering. The *hammams* were already beginning to throng with bathers eager to perform their *ghusl* before the Friday *jumu'ah* prayer began at the Great Mosque of Cordoba. Schools were closed today and in a few hours the streets would come alive with the sound of children laughing and playing. Sumayya's fingers played idly with a pendant that hung down on a long chain obscured by her hijab. It had been in the family for generations, commissioned by one of her forefathers.

He had come from across the Straits with Tariq Ibn Ziyad and had fought bravely to bring peace to this once turbulent and oppressed land. He had been there when Tariq's army marched into Toledo and took it along with nearly the whole of the Iberian Peninsula, all save for its rough and mountainous north-western corner. He had also been there when they finally marched into the city of Cordoba, where they were met by Musa Ibn Nusayr.

When Musa had heard of Tariq's victory, he had immediately sent an emissary to the city of Damascus, bearing the glad tidings of their success to the Caliph Al-Walid. Musa had then crossed over to Andalus on his new boats with a large army, conquering major cities on his way that included Malaga and Seville.

He had finally caught up with Tariq Ibn Ziyad in the city of Cordoba, to where the new capital of the Muslim region of Andalus had been transferred. Together they had remained there for three years, working tirelessly to establish Islam and making peace amongst the people by means of treaties which were destined to last for centuries. They had left only upon the summons of an ailing Caliph. Leaving his able, eldest son Abd al-Aziz to command in his absence, Musa Ibn Nusayr, along with Tariq Ibn Ziyad had left Andalus and returned to the city of Damascus.

They arrived, bringing with them prisoners and spoils from Andalus that included skins of gold and silver coins, along with priceless jewellery of pearls, rubies, topazes and emeralds. Perhaps the most prized possessions of all were the Table of Solomon, copies of the Torah, the Gospel and the Psalms along with a collection of royal diadems. There was one for every king who had ever ruled over Iberia. The crowns were encrusted with precious stones and engraved with their names, a short description about who they were, the durations of their reigns and the names of their children.

Neither Tariq nor Musa ever again returned to Andalus. Musa was said to have fallen ill and died shortly after on his way to Hajj in the company of the new Caliph. As for Tariq Ibn Ziyad, he lived out his life quietly and in obscurity, disappearing somewhere within the bustling streets of Damascus. Only his name and courage continued to be carried on the wind through the annals of history and time.

Sumayya smiled to herself as she drew the pendent out from beneath the folds of her hijab that covered her hair and came draping down over her shoulders and chest. She looked fondly down at it, nimbly turning the precious piece of jewellery over in her fingers. She was nearly two and seventy years old and had possessed it for most of her life. The story as it goes was that it had been passed down through the family. It had belonged to the same said forefather who had commissioned the pendent to be made from his share of the spoils of Andalus, and pearls that had been left to him by a dear friend who had fallen at the battle of Guadalete.

It was made of gold, crafted by a skilled artisan into the shape of a crescent moon encrusted with milky white pearls. On its back, the pendent bore the initials of a bride and groom:

'A & Q'

Qasim, for that was his name, had presented

the pendent as *mahr* to his Andalusian bride, Aisha. They had settled in Cordoba (like most of Tariq's men), where he had raised his family on a farm tending to sheep, living out his life peacefully.

Sumayya sighed and turned away now from the beautiful view of the city. She had much to do for *yawm al-jumu'ah*, which meant that her return home would be delayed more than usual. By the time she had visited the *hammam* and the Great Mosque for the *jumu'ah* prayer, it was afternoon. She finally arrived back home to find a quiet, empty house. She had thought to find her young grandson, Uwais, back from the *jumu'ah* prayer before she was, but he must have been detained.

She looked around her work room fondly. It could easily have rivalled those of the best apothecaries in town. It was just as she had left it. A distinct mixture of smells of vellum, flowers and herbs hung in the air. On the table were strewn parchments with beautiful drawings she had made in her study of the physiology of plants, flowers and herbs. A colourful array of medicinal bottles lined the shelved walls, distilled by her own hand.

On her worktable lay her latest specimen. Reaching for it, she lifted the sprig of myrtle to her nose to breathe in its delicate, sweet fragrance. It could soothe a hot head and had done wonders for Maryam, her poorly, fever-stricken patient from the night before.

It was one of the companions of the Prophet, Ibn Abbas, who had said, "When the Prophet Nuh left the Ark, the first shrub he planted was myrtle." And when the Prophet Adam departed from the

Garden, he took three things: myrtle – the queen of all sweet-smelling shrubs in the world; compressed dates – the queen of all dates in the world; and a stalk of corn – which is the queen of all the food in the world.

As she gently laid the sprig of myrtle back on the worktable, she heard a familiar voice ringing out from the other side of the door along with hurried footsteps. There was a great deal of commotion upon which Sumayya broke into a smile – no doubt it was her tardy grandson. Then, in the next moment he burst into the room with a youthful exuberance.

"*As-salamu alaikum jadati – alhamdulillah*, you're here!" exclaimed a handsome boy of sixteen summers, a look of relief spreading across his face at finding her there. Waves of dark hair fell carelessly about his flushed cheeks, to frame a pair of bright, intelligent eyes that now fixed on her own, accusingly.

"You were supposed to meet me at *jabal al-arus* after *jumu'ah* prayers!" said Uwais, looking aggrieved and disappointed with his grandmother. "Did you forget?"

At her age, Sumayya was prone to forgetfulness about mundane arrangements (especially when she was busy). Reminded by her grandson, she tilted her head to one side bemused and then with a start suddenly remembered her appointment with him.

"Oh, *Subhana'Allah!* – the big day…" said Sumayya, her face quickly switching from surprise to her usual scepticism.

"*Yes,* we need to leave now – the crowd's already getting big around the hill, and we need to find a good spot," said Uwais eagerly gathering her things together for her. "We must make haste – Abbas Ibn Firnas means to do the test flight from the hill in less than an hour's time!"

Sumayya rolled her eyes.

"Well, I still think he's an old fool – you'd be better off apprenticed elsewhere. Oh, why can't you be a physician like your father, and grandfather... and great grandfather before him. It was good enough for all of them! *Or* you could even go to the university and become a scholar, an *'alim*, like your uncle, *Shaykh* Yasir. Where is a flying contraption going to take you in life other than up into the clouds and then back down again?"

Sumayya could hardly imagine that there was anything much to see up there. She pursed her lips disagreeably. 'Well, that's your grandson for you!' she mused – always dreaming, with his head in the clouds.

Uwais shook his head dispiritedly, the light now gone from his eyes.

"But I'm not like the rest of you," said Uwais gently, taking her hand in his. He leaned forward to kiss the back of his grandmother's soft hand.

"I don't have your patience, or your healing touch – and I'm not bookish either, to become a scholar. I have the mind of an engineer – I want to invent things, build things from scratch with my own hands," said Uwais pressing his grandmother's palm warmly now, his eyes holding hers beseechingly.

"*Please* come and watch the flight at *jabal al-arus* – you'll be amazed, I promise you!"

"Well, I suppose I must," she sighed, her expression softening as she gave in to her grandson's plea. Not long after, they both finally stepped outside the house and soon found themselves joining a steady flow of chattering crowds with much the same idea as themselves: to watch 'the birdman' fly. Abbas Ibn Firnas had invited the entire city to witness his maiden flight.

This wasn't the first time Sumayya had watched his 'antics', as she liked to call them. Twenty years ago, Ibn Firnas had leapt off the minaret of the Grand Mosque of Cordoba before a great mesmerised audience – only then he had descended with a huge cloak puffing out into a great big giant ball and floated down to the ground. When he had landed, it was thankfully in one piece and with only a few scrapes and scratches. Sumayya's husband had quickly patched him up with the help of a soothing antiseptic balm she had prepared from her special herbs.

At *jabal al-arus* now, an equally great crowd had turned out and gathered before the hill by the time Sumayya and her grandson arrived. Nearby a familiar face greeted her with an infectious excitement, brought on by the crowd's reaction.

"Peace be on you Sumayya – it's good to see you here," said a small, stooped old man waving a bony wrinkled hand at her. It was Moshe, her Jewish neighbour, standing in the midst with his granddaughter, Hiba, who quickly broke into a dimpled smile beside him upon seeing Sumayya.

"*As-salamu alaikum* aunty Sumayya – isn't it just wonderful!" exclaimed Hiba breathlessly, rubbing her hands together with delight. Hiba was a good girl often seen helping her grandfather. She and her parents were Muslims, unlike her grandfather. In Andalus it wasn't unusual to find lives blended with family members like her grandfather who still practised the faith of their forefathers.

Sumayya greeted the pair warmly, but her eyes soon travelled up the hill in awe. The hill was no *jabal Tariq*, but nonetheless, it was quite a hefty drop from the top of *jabal al-arus* to say the least.

"It would have been a pity to miss Ibn Firnas," continued Old Moshe eagerly, his face beaming with pride. "He's a prodigy this one. I know he'll do it today – I feel it in my bones!"

"I pity *his* bones!" tutted Sumayya shaking her head disapprovingly. Just then, the commanding figure of Abbas Ibn Firnas appeared, silhouetted against the skyline, standing tall on the hilltop. He was wearing a huge pair of wings secured upon his back that seemed to expand out all over the horizon. Sumayya gasped along with the crowds and then suddenly she couldn't help it: a slow smile crept across her face. This was Andalus at its best.

She turned to look at her grandson's face beside her; his broad grin, the twinkle in his eyes and his rapt expression, all melted her heart. This was his calling – and it was what brought so many others like him from far and wide to Andalus. The fountain of fresh knowledge flowed from here, feeding its earth, water and air. It brought the rest of Europe and the world gazing up at them in wonder and awe, eager to knock at their doors with a hunger and thirst for knowledge.

"Go to Ibn Firnas!" ordered Sumayya suddenly. Uwais hesitated for a moment, not wanting to leave her alone, but she smiled wryly with the lift of an eyebrow.

"I'm not senile, just yet. I can very well manage without you," she said reminding her grandson that right now his place was by the inventor's side.

Uwais was relieved. His beaming smile said it all. Planting a grateful kiss on the back of his grandmother's hand he turned and scurried away up the hill, leaving her behind to listen to Ibn Firnas' bold speech to his enthralled audience. Half an hour later, a hushed silence fell over the vast assembly. Sumayya and the spectators watched with bated breath.

Abbas Ibn Firnas' great wings suddenly rose and eclipsed the sun from their eyes. To the delight of a gasping, cheering crowd his feet lifted away from the rock as he leapt. The sight of his ascent took her breath away.

Sumayya smiled, a prayer quietly passing her lips: with faith had her people sailed across the Straits – and with faith may they soar through the sky.

Musa Ibn Nusayr
The Umayyad Governor of the Province of North Africa

Tarif Ibn Malik
An Umayyad General

Tariq Ibn Ziyad
An Umayyad General and the Governor of Tangiers

GLOSSARY OF TERMS

Al-Malik – the King, one of the 99 Names of Allah

'alim – a person of knowledge, an Islamic Scholar

adhan – the call to prayer

AH - after Hijra

akhi / ikhwan – brother/s

akhira – what comes after (death, the next world

alhamdulillah – praise be to Allah

Allahu Akbar – Allah is the Greatest

ameen – so be it *(said at the end of a du'a*

Ansar – the Companions of the Prophet Muhammad who embraced Islam in Madina and who welcomed and looked after the *Muhajirun*

asr salat – the mid-afternoon prayer

as-salamu alaikum – peace be upon you (the Muslim greeting

astaghfirullah – O Allah, forgive me

barakah – blessings

baraka'Allahu feeq – blessings of Allah be upon you

deen – way of life, life transaction, religion

dhikr – remembrance (of Allah

dhuhr salat – the noon prayer

du'a – supplication

Eid – festival; in Islam there are two Eids: at the end of Ramadan and at the climax of the annual pilgrimage to Makkah

fajr salat – the dawn prayer

ghusl – major ritual washing, to be pure for prayer

hafidh – someone who has memorised the Qur'an

hammam – public bath

Hijra – the occasion when the Prophet Muhammad left Makkah to go to Madinah in 622 CE

Ibn – son of

'ilm – knowledge

iman – faith

insha'Allah – if Allah wills

'isha salat – the prayer, after the night is dark

jabal al-arus – Mountain of the Bride, near Cordoba

jadati – grandmother

janaza – funeral prayer

jazaka'Allahu khairan – may Allah reward you with good

jumu'ah – Friday Prayer

Lailat'al-Qadr – The Night of Power (in Ramadan)

Lawh al-Mahfuz – The Preserved Tablet of Forms

maghrib salat – the prayer, almost immediately after sunset

mahr – dowry, paid by a Muslim husband to his wife as part of their contract of marriage

maraqib – a type of boat

masha'Allah – what Allah wants (happens)

majnun – possessed by jinn, mad

miswak – tooth stick

muadhin – the one who makes the call to prayer

Muhajirun – the Companions of the Prophet Muhammad who made Hijra from Makkah to Madina to be with him

nabidh – a sweet drink made from dates

pbuh – peace and blessings be upon him

qibla – the direction which Muslims face in prayer, towards the Ka'aba in Makkah

Ra'is – Captain

Rajab – 7th month of the Islamic lunar calendar

Ramadan – 9th month of the Islamic lunar calendar

ruh – soul, spirit

Sha'ban – 8th month of the Islamic lunar calendar

shahada – declaration of faith in Islam

Shawwal – 10th month of the Islamic lunar calendar

Shaykh - a person of knowledge, an Islamic Scholar

Shaytan – Satan, the devil

subhana'Allah – glory be to Allah

suhur – pre-dawn meal before a fast

sunnah – the way of doing things (words and actions) of the Prophet Muhammad, blessings and peace be upon him

sutra – an object placed in front of someone doing the prayer, so that someone passing in front of them does not break their *qibla*

tahajjud – night prayer

takbir – the saying, 'God is the Greatest'

taraweeh – special prayers, prayed after *'isha* prayers during the month of Ramadan

'ulama – people of knowledge, scholars

wa alaikum as-salam – and upon you be peace

wudhu – minor ritual washing, to be pure for prayer

yawm-al furqan – the day of distinguishing

yawm al-jumu'ah – Friday

Selected Qur'anic Quotations

"Among His Signs is the creation of the heavens and the earth and the variety of your languages and colours. There are certainly Signs in that for every being."
[The Romans, *Ar-Rum* 30:22]

"...With the name of Allah it sails and anchors. Surely my Lord is Most Forgiving, Very Merciful."
[Hud, *Hud* 11:41]

"Yunus too was one of the Messengers. When he ran away to the fully laden ship and cast lots and lost. Then the fish devoured him and he was to blame. Had it not been that he was a man who glorified Allah, he would have remained inside its belly until the Day they are raised again."
[Those Who Set The Ranks, *As-Saffat* 37:139-44]

"Oh fire! Be coolness and peace for Ibrahim."
[The Prophets, *Al-Anbiya* 21:69]

"Oh you who believe! Allah will test you with game animals which come within the reach of your hands and spears, so that Allah will know those who fear Him in the Unseen."
[The Table Spread, *Al-Ma'ida* 5:94]

"Surely Allah commands justice and doing good and giving to relatives. And He forbids indecency and doing wrong and tyranny ..."
[The Bees, *An-Nahl* 16:90]

"We do not have the strength to face Goliath and his troops today.' But those who were sure that they were going to meet Allah said, 'How many a small force has triumphed over a much greater one by Allah's permission! Allah is with the steadfast."
[The Cow, *Al-Baqara* 2:249]

"Oh my Lord, I am truly in need of any good You have in store for me."
[The Stories, *Al-Qasas* 28:24]

"By the clear Book, Indeed, We sent it down on a blessed night (ie the Night of Al-Qadr)...,"
[The Smoke, *al-Dukhaan* 44:2-3]

"The Night of Power is better than a thousand months."
[The Power, Al-Qadr 97:3]

Selected Supplications and Sayings

The Prophet (may blessings and peace be upon him) had said, "Verily you shall conquer Constantinople. What a wonderful leader will her leader be, and what a wonderful army will that army be!"
[Musnad, Ahmad Ibn Hanbal]

"Oh Allah! We seek from You the good of this wind and the good of what it has been commanded with and we seek Your protection from the evil of this wind and the evil of what is in it and the evil of what it has been commanded with."
[Ibn as-Sunni]

The Prophet (may blessings and peace be upon him), was napping in the house of Umm Haraam bint Milhan and then woke up smiling. Umm Haraam asked, "What is making you smile, O Messenger of Allah?" He said, "I dreamt that some people from among my community were sailing on this sea like kings on thrones."
[Bukhari]

The Prophet's prayer (may blessings and peace be upon him): "O Allah make (the months of) Rajab and Sha'ban blessed for us and enable us to reach Ramadan."
[Musnad, Ahmad Ibn Hanbal]

Ibn Abbas reported the Messenger of Allah (may

blessings and peace be upon him) as saying, "The most favoured horses are the sorrel."
[Abu Dawud]

"Oh Allah, I ask for the good in her and the good that You have created in her and I seek Your protection from her evil and the evil You have created in her."
[Abu Dawud]

Abu Huraira reported: The Prophet (may blessings and peace be upon him) said, "Whoever sees me in a dream has truly seen me, for Satan cannot assume my form."
[Muslim]

When someone relates a dream:
"Be it good you receive and be it evil you guard against. May your dream be good for us and bad for our enemies."
[Ibn al-Sunni]

If one sees a fire burning, say takbir: "Allahu Akbar" (Allah is Great). The Prophet (may blessings and peace be upon him) instructed us to do so.
[Ibn as-Sunni]

The Prophet's prayer (may blessings and peace be upon him) for when the new moon is seen: "O Allah, bring it to us with felicity, faith, safety, and submission. My Lord and Your Lord is Allah."
[Tirmidhi]

The Prophet (may blessings and peace be upon him) said, "He is not of us who does not have mercy on young children, nor honour the elderly."
[At-Tirmidhi]

Prayer upon breaking the fast:
"O Allah, for You have I fasted and with Your sustenance I break my fast."
[Abu Dawud]

Anas Ibn Malik reported: The Messenger of Allah (may blessings and peace be upon him) said when the month of Ramadan began, "Verily, this month has presented itself to you. There is a night within it that is better than a thousand months. Whoever is deprived of it has been deprived of all good. None is deprived of its good but that he is truly deprived."
[Ibn Majah]

The Prophet (may blessings and peace be upon him) said, "Ramadan is the chief of all months and Friday is the chief of all days."
[At-Tabarani]

Ibn Abbas said, "When the Prophet Nuh (peace be upon him) left the Ark, the first thing he planted was myrtle." And again from the same source: "Adam (peace be upon him) departed from the Garden, with three things: myrtle – the queen of all sweet smelling shrubs in the world;

compressed dates – which are queen over all dates in the world; and a stalk of corn – which is the queen of all the food in the world."
[Medicine of the Prophet by Jalal Ad-Din As-Suyuti]

Various historians have recorded two circumstances concerning Tariq's passage across the Straits and landing on the coast of Andalus. These are a dream, and an encounter with an Old Woman, as recorded by Ahmad Ibn Muhammed Al-Makkari in his book, The History of The Muhammedan Dynasties in Spain.

Tariq's dream of the Prophet (may blessings and peace be upon him):
"Take courage, Oh Tariq, and go and accomplish what you have been destined to perform."
[Ahmad Ibn Muhammed Al-Makkari – The History of The Muhammedan Dynasties In Spain]

PROPHETS MENTIONED

Adam, Nuh (Noah), Ibrahim (Abraham), Musa (Moses), Dawud (David), Sulayman (Solomon), Yunas (Jonah) and Muhammad (may peace be upon them all)